TRIANGULATION: PARCH

(SECOND EDITION)

The 2014 Edition of PARSEC Ink's Annual Confluence of Speculative Fiction

ISBN: 978-0-9828606-6-3

Cover Art: Susan Urbanek Linville

Layout: Stephen V. Ramey

Assistant Editors: Susan Linville

Fiction Editor: Stephen V. Ramey

PARSEC Ink is a subsidiary of PARSEC, a literary organization. For more information, visit our website at www.parsec-sff.org/

PARSEC Ink
PO Box 3681
Pittsburgh, PA 15230-3681

This second edition includes minor corrections and the Gordon A. Graves Editors' Choice Award Announcement.

Acknowledgements

We gratefully acknowledge substantial financial support from:

Gordon A. Graves, in memory of his father,
Russell D. Graves, 1907-1988

The three *Russell D. Graves Editors' Choice Award* winners ($100 each) are:

Fruma Klass for "The Way We Were"
John M. Shade for "A Prayer at Noon"
Rochelle Potkar for "Dream Warriors: Ramayan Redux"

We also want to acknowledge the buckets of time and talent donated by our Assistant Editor and cover artist, **Sue Linville**. We would not have made it without her.

Thanks to **Diane Turnshek** for having the courage to create this series and **Barb Carlson**, for editing the anthologies in 2004-05, **Pete Butler** for transforming us to an international, semi-pro paying market during his three years as editor, and for establishing a high bar for quality, **Bill Moran** for continuing that tradition in 2010 and **Jamie Lackey** for stepping up in 2011.

Finally, let us remember **Ann Cecil** (1940-2011), whose dedication to this cause was unparalleled and constant. Not only did she handle the financial aspects of the anthology, she also coordinated the Parsec Science Fiction and Fantasy Short Story Contest. We miss her.

Table of Contents

A Prayer at Noon

John M. Shade

Here at Triangulation, we like stories that grab us from the opening scene and take us somewhere interesting from there. It's the same with an anthology, right? You want that first story to reach right through the page, pull you into a new world, and never let go. Case in point, "A Prayer at Noon," by the talented and imaginative John M. Shade. Who could resist a patchwork god thirsting for prayer, a town on the edge of desertification, and a girl... with guns? We certainly couldn't.

It was a day into the third sun when the patchwork man rode into town.

I remember the dust scrabbling at my eyes, and the folk that had gathered on the sidewalks to watch him plod past on a chugging, nearly-spent machine horse. As he came to me, the stitched segments of his face shifted into a new configuration, a hinted smile or frown, and his torso swung around. My breath seized. I'd been around men before, but he was something different. Something more. He was ugly, though, with a wiry frame and a large head set on top, wads of crusted hair sprouting between the seams across his skin. I braced, but he plucked my little sister, Ester, from the crowd instead. The town went silent, but for the shuffle of wind-blown sand.

With his god-strength, the patchwork man tossed Ester into the air like an aerialist, and set her down to swelling applause. The dread was broken. Our prayers had been answered at last.

As the patchwork man continued to the town center, folk whispered between themselves whose prayer had brought him here. For years they had defied the desert, old men and women volunteers moving their brooms back and forth down the sun-stained road, humming the same tunes that had sustained futility for a generation. Those of us with younger eyes knew it'd never be enough. The desert always won, as it had again and again since the time of progress when the factories were touted as our salvation.

There was nothing left to do but pray and hope that whatever answered was what we wanted. You rolled the dice with prayer and sometimes things came up bad, but we thought this'd be different. This'd be pure. This'd be good.

This'd set things right.

Papa's gun shop, where my sister and I scratched a living, was wedged along the border where the market rows used to stand. As the last stop for those traveling into the desert, we attracted treasure hunters, scholars, military men, cartographers, convicts, hucksters, and thrill-seekers drawn by the lure of the dunes and tales of buried factory cities. We were taught never to go into the desert, but some just couldn't listen, or were desperate enough to try.

The gun shop shelves were filled with every type of weapon imaginable: strange, twisted guns with metallic, clattering timers; guns grown from blast gardens, magical jars, and fungal tattoos. There was no make or model unrepresented.

Mixed among these were Ester's inventions: syncwyrms, sawdust dancers, bone tethers, and more. On a shelf behind the counter one particle village still worked, its clockwork apparatus ticking miniaturized machinations through hollow days and dreary nights. A mezzanine of wasted, forgotten dollscapes and carousels crowded other shelves, colors long faded.

Wasted dreams and memories, I thought.

Ester spent most of her time in the backroom workshop Papa had granted her, leaving me to tend the front. Today, she was making something special, a gift for the patchwork man. I heard her giggling as saws bit into metal, as fires pulsed in time. She sounded carefree, as if everything in that room, in the whole world, was made just for her. It irked me that she could be so blind to reality, but also made me jealous. Life ought to be about more than survival.

Before Papa left, he kept a vigil at the town's edge for cobbled gods looking for a bit of prayer to drink up. Some people just couldn't help praying. I remember sitting with him in the blinds when I was old enough, our best guns gleaming on racks behind us.

"We don't need no gods," he'd say, over and over like an incantation.

When a god did come—which was often back then—they always arrived at high noon. Something in them I guess, some mechanism, told them.

Papa'd walk out to the road, blast gun in hand, and a few minutes later he'd return. Most times he came back with another gun to add to the collection. Sometimes gods would be friendly and move on, but usually they wouldn't. It was the way of things.

Papa was faster than all of them. He might have been one of them for all we knew. He wasn't our real Papa, but had found us, gave us water, nurtured us back from our forgotten past, and took care of us from that day forward. Sometimes that mattered more. Sometimes not.

There was always something faster being stitched together he told me once, something more cowardly being manufactured by factories beyond the desert, huge sprawling complexes that covered entire valleys. He told me those factories were made to last, churning out creations long after their creators were dust. Sooner or later he would meet his match if he just waited out here for them to come.

I remember imagining the noises gods made as they crept outside the windowsills of my room at night, the way I lay there, frozen without a sound. I remember the wounds Papa accumulated, the determined way he looked heading out into the desert the night he left us, ambling purposefully toward where I supposed the factories lay.

Later that day of the patchwork man, Ester and I—bearing a box of gifts for our new god—joined a line that stretched from the town center. Everyone had something to give it seemed.

By the time our turn came, the light was red and low and the courtyard wobbled through a dusty film. He sat on the cracked fountain's ledge, guns holstered beneath the flaps of his long coat, face mottled with seams and scars. Stitches curled down his cheek.

"Are you a water god?" Ester said.

"A thousand pardons!" a woman behind us shouted. A quarter of the line dropped to their knees (me included), hands clasped before faces. Soon the whole line was kneeling except Ester, my poor misfit, tinkering sister. I pulled her down from behind, hoping she would have the sense to close her eyes and bow her head.

"It's all right," the patchwork man said. He waved a bored hand over Ester and me. Alien eyes inspected us. "Ester," he said, "Nine years and eight months old; you have a knack for dancing and gymnastics and school, and invention." The patchwork man looked at me. "Sasha. A fair shot and an aptitude for horseback, if there were any real ones left. A waste."

Ester nodded emphatically.

He leaned toward her, "I do have a little water god in me." He tapped at his chest. "Right here, do you see?"

Ester smiled and skipped off toward the gun shop, head in the clouds, no doubt dreaming of inventions.

"Apologies, sir," I said. "My sister doesn't understand. She's not like the rest of us."

"That's what makes her valuable," the patchwork man said. He stood and strolled, spurs clattering, past piles of gifts—baskets and meats and desert salvage (old guns and gizmos) that'd probably never work again—toward the motionless horse. I wondered if it would carry him again, or if it had run out of energy like the rest of us.

The patchwork man took his fill and more. Lines formed each morning for offerings, and the giving didn't end until sundown. At night, he stalked the taverns, and gave more than a few men and women bruises across their faces. He did worse to some and all the while a slow uneasiness crept over the town.

Ester made gift after gift. We fought more than once about it, about *him*. Big, scratchy fights, the sisterly kind. The kind that made you embarrassed after.

One afternoon, I sat at the register giving the particle village its daily tune-up, when the patchwork man pushed the door open. The sun was at his back, coating everything beyond in gold. He walked to the counter, spurs clanging. The air danced between us in the heat.

I found my voice. "H—hello sir."

"Hello, Sasha." He looked at the particle village. "That's an odd little thing. Is it your sister's doing?"

"Yes," I said.

"You use this as a kind of miniature firing range, to test out the effects of a weapon without risk, yes?"

"Very perceptive, sir," I said in my best salesman talk.

"Clever." He smiled. The stitches on his face pulled taut. He scanned the shelves behind the counter and then those around the shop. "I'd like to see your sister. Where is she?"

"She went out," I said loudly. "I'm not sure when she'll be back." She was in the workshop like always, but she would hide.

"Do you think you'll be able to push back the desert?" I said. "It's quite a lot of work, I bet."

"She's very special, your sister."

"Yes," I said. A pause. "Will you begin soon?"

His eyes kept to the shelves. "Do you know how many factories it takes to produce my blood? Do you know how many it takes to keep me going?"

"I've heard stories," I said. I remembered thinking Papa would be the one to end it, to staunch the leeching of the world. I remembered hating him for leaving two girls to fend for themselves. The gods had slowed since he left, but they had not stopped. *Obviously.* I held my gaze firm against the patchwork man's. *Ester is not here*, I told myself. *She is not in the back room, and never has been.*

"As far as you can see," the patchwork man said. "Imagine a world filled with buildings, smoke, an endless assembly line, and you might gain some notion of what it takes to maintain me." His smile dissolved. "Where is she?"

"I'm sorry, sir. Who?"

His arm lashed out, and I was flung against the shelves. Cavalcades and carnivals splashed over me, their crafted denizens—samurai and cowboys and soldiers—staring through horror-filled eyes. I cast my own eyes wildly.

Under the counter lay Papa's favorite pistol, the lightning sieve arcing through its barrel staining the shelf a sickly blue-white. He'd left it for us, a sign, a symbol, maybe a promise of his return.

It might as well have been on the other side of the planet. The patchwork man watched, waiting for me to grab it. I bled on the floor, trying to be still.

"You all started off so well," he said, taking his time stepping over the scattered trinkets. "Sheep, but good sheep."

He crouched beside me, and produced a six-gun from its holster. Nothing fancy. Black metal and a wide trigger. The barrel was scarred, the grip worn, but it still worked when it needed to, I reckoned.

"I think you've mistaken why I came here," he said. Heartbeats pumped beneath his jacket. "You know what your sister is."

"No, si—"

"*Special*," he said. He slammed his palm onto the back of my head and pressed my face into the bits of glass coating the floor. Pain bubbled up. Tears.

"Your sister," he said.

"What—"

More pain. I wanted to scream.

The pressure eased. "Can't let her rot in this backwater town, can we? Can't have the sheep thinking they run the ranch. When we call, you answer, you give, you *sacrifice*. That's the nature of the transaction."

He wrenched my face toward him. Glass clung to my cheek, hot as a bonfire. "Factories need repairs when someone goes and tries to break 'em. I'm here to see they get 'fixed, come hellfire, drought, and desert." Up close,

I saw threads of light leaking from the seams of his face. "You're going to tell me where she is."

"No," I said. "I'm not."

He pushed my head to the floor. His boot pressed my cheek. I watched the spur turn slowly through a film of tears. The pressure increased harder and harder until everything blurred and darkened, and the blood thrumming in my ear was the only thing left to hold. *Hide, Ester. Hide like you have never hidden before.*

Papa found us curled together in a storm drain like mice waiting to die. It was my first full memory, just grown enough for it to stick. I held Ester close as a sandstorm raged all around us. I was praying, rocking back and forth with Ester in my arms, sand starting to fill the drain's open end.

And he came walking through the haze, a silhouette. I remember thinking that was what a god ought to be. Simple as anything.

When I came to, weapons of every kind imaginable lay strewn across the gun shop floor, some dismantled or killed, some bent, and others jammed, detached, siphoned down to a shell. The ceiling was a gaping hole, a wound through which the desert gushed. Sunlight revealed the completeness of the patchwork man's devastation.

Ester's workshop lay in shambles too. She was gone.

I walked along the perimeter of it, not wanting to get close to my sister's work tables, as if proximity would hurt even more. Tools lay scattered on the floor and lines in the dust showed where she had been dragged away.

In the corner, something wheezed. I cleared debris from it and lifted the white sheet my sister always used for her unveilings.

It was larger than most of the things she created, with long, powerful legs, a clicking, breathing chassis with muscle sewn over top. *A machine horse.* Guilt washed through me. Sasha's next invention was meant for me. She must have felt bad about the arguments too.

The chassis was smashed and it lay on its side, trying not to move, trying not to be damaged further, the machine advising the organic. *It must've tried to stop the god from taking Ester.*

Given time, I might have repaired the chassis and helped the organic bits along, at least given it a chance. But there was no time. I reached into the chassis and found the life-release. Locks disengaged. Steam whined—a long, final sigh—as I left the workshop for Papa's blind and the spare guns there.

Into the desert I went, just like in the schoolhouse plays that taught us not to do it. I carried a bag crammed with canteens, bread, salted meats, and the guns from Papa's blind that hadn't soured or packed with sand. People stared, faces pinched by resentment or hopeless rage. They wouldn't stop me; they wouldn't help either. By annoying the patchwork man, I had taken everything. Their prayers had failed, and there was no way left for them to resist the desert.

I set out in the direction Papa had gone. It helped that the patchwork man took his time in everything, especially victory, and that Ester fought him all the way. I followed the signs of her struggle: gouges, plumes of sand in the wind.

I caught sight of them at the end of a winding ravine where the dunes had turned rocky, the ground cracked and brittle. He was dragging Ester with little effort, her feet kicking dust beacons into the afternoon light.

Soon he couldn't ignore me anymore. It was the patchwork man and Ester, and me closing in, Papa's favorite shotgun heavy in my sweating hands.

"You think you're faster," he called over the wind.

"No," I said. I was breathing hard.

"You don't think..." He turned to face me, strange eyes glowing against the haze. "No, that's not it. Why would you want to fight?"

"I don't—"

"Don't you understand what she is," he said, "how important she is?" He sounded smaller than he ought to. It scared me a little, the fear in his voice.

"If I don't bring her to the factories," he said, "then why'd they parch the world? Just to make us for no reason? To let us die? Why put that on us? On me? No, it's something needs correcting. We must survive. You know it, too."

I kept my eyes on Ester, on when he was going to drop her. He'd come then. Concentrating on anything else was a mistake. The world was his hand around her shirt. The world drew down to a moment.

Even so, I was too slow.

The patchwork man jerked quick and odd, folded down onto himself, and appeared beside me. He ripped the shotgun from my hands. The resulting blast tore a hole into the ground. His fist sent me flying, sand bunching at the corners of my mouth. A throbbing ache settled in, as intense and relentless as the sun. He kicked the bag away.

"Sasha!" Ester yelled someplace far away.

The patchwork man took me by the neck and lifted me high.

"You don't have a single notion on how to work those guns," he said.

He tossed me as he had tossed Ester that first day. I tucked my body into a rigid ball and rolled as the canyon struck my back. He was on me in the next second. I drew a pistol from my coat—the aperture spinning up to show the bright, blinding yellow spore inside—and took the shot as best I could.

Close, but sloppy. The spore nicked his neck and sailed into the sky.

"You pray and roll the dice," he whispered. "Nothing to be ashamed of. You're no god, after all. Why do you even call her sister?" His face stretched, light leaking from within. His hands closed around my throat, crushingly focused. His expression wasn't what I expected, not anger, but fear. A frightened boy behind all those seams, all that power.

My vision irised down to a circle. Somewhere, I heard Ester crying. I didn't know what to do, so I prayed. I prayed to Papa. *I'm sorry I couldn't protect everything, the guns, the town, Ester, but you most of all.*

Something came up behind the patchwork man. I glimpsed Papa's lightning pistol. My vision blurred further; the heat-haze wrapped around me. I knew it couldn't be Papa, but let myself believe. It was easy. Ester moved so much like Papa now, a purpose, a power, to every motion.

The hammer went back and the patchwork man noticed the gun behind him. Too slow. Papa/Ester jammed it to the place where the water god lay stitched in, the place the patchwork man had showed Ester all those days ago. The trigger released and light bloomed down his torso, along his arms, first following the stitching, and then on through the skin. Still, he squeezed my neck. I was slipping, almost gone. My peripherals shrank until only his face remained. A sad face, stricken with surprise. As if disbelief were protection.

The blast consumed us, and I sailed back into the still dark beyond.

I woke in a cave the next morning. The early desert air curled in, brushed my cheek, stirring me. The guns lay bundled next to a spent campfire, and Ester's shawl was draped over my shoulder. Ester was nowhere.

And right then I knew she'd gone to the factories.

No matter how loud I yelled, or how far I searched, I couldn't find her. It was what she wanted, what Papa had wanted, not to be found. She wanted me to go back to town, and I could almost see it, the life I would live through the years. Mother to grandmother, and onward in Papa's gun shop, tightening screws, matching grips and ammunition, teaching of the craft to others before I was gone. All of it laid out before me, a bridge to the end. Ester walked a path for gods now, and she wanted me to leave her to it, wanted me to hide like I did with Papa.

So I didn't. I took the other way. I packed up the guns and the canteens and what food was left in the bag and set out after Ester. She had half a day on me, I figured. It wasn't so much.

No more gun shops, no more town, just the all-consuming desert. My sister needs me, and I need her. There's always something faster being made out there, and she can't do it alone. Papa proved that much. We'll find the factories and a way to shut them down. We'll do what Papa couldn't, and make what he did for us count for something.

For the first time, I feel more right with each step, one after the other toward a long horizon, a prayer on my lips, eyes watching for what's next.

John M. Shade *is a fantasy and science fiction writer living in Texas. His work has appeared in Everyday Weirdness and other places, and he is a recent graduate of the Viable Paradise writer's workshop. He is currently at work on his first novel. You can follow him online at twitter.com/dystopiandream*

Koan

By Jacob Edwards

When we first read "Koan" we were dubious that a story with soooo much water could fit the Parch theme. But it was just so darned well done, and, really, how many deserts do we need in one anthology? So, one revision later, here is a story about thirst of a different stripe. Utopia can get a little dry.

Catastrophe struck on day 14,611 of Koan's occupation, a significant number because it equated to day one of his retirement and hence the first morning he'd woken up in legal possession of the flat. It should have been a breakfast of sumptuous liberation. At last he was released from his employment contract, free to peck and scratch about as he wished, stay out late, lie in, wrap his pounding head in a towel. Life beyond indenture promised free run of the building and a small pension. It should have been the best birthday ever.

Instead, the roof caved in and enough water cascaded down to leave Koan wallowing knee-deep and bewildered.

The T-Mat booth fizzed into muffled half-explosion, and only belatedly did Koan think to jump onto his fold-away bed. Dirty liquid frothed all around him, swallowing every piece of low-lying furniture except the cast-iron bathtub—a retirement present—which now had the distinction of having water almost to its brim, but on the outside. A red devil duck sat mocking in its soap holder.

Koan became very aware of his tongue, as dry as one of Judge Salt's closing remarks, and plastered to the roof of his mouth in the sort of gluey morning-after embrace that both parties would long regret. His apartment—his desert island oasis for the past forty years—lay flooded, just as its single, beautiful room had become his to touch. He stared until torrent gave way to trickle and, finally, a steady *drip-drip-drip* from the gaping hole in his ceiling. His bones felt brittle, his arm ghostly weak, as he reached for the ComClip. It popped happily, like a champagne cork.

"Hey, Koan!" Dee's round face beamed from the screen. "How's your first day out? Pig fat and googies, I bet. Sucks to be you, huh?" She brushed a silky bang aside and squinted. "Hey, is something wrong?"

Koan stared for several long seconds, tongue refusing to un-grit itself. Tongue and thoughts both. He was desperately hung-over, post-plastered and drowning. Eventually, he managed a helpless gesture. "My roof collapsed."

"What? Show me."

Dee gasped as Koan angled the screen left and right.

"Holy cow, K.! You're, like, totally flooded."

Obvious, but no less true for the stating.

Koan found himself shrugging, as if that would somehow loosen the enormity. He felt the cracks in his lips—rough; jagged—as he kissed each word on its way. "I thought, you know, maybe the governors could…?"

"Oh, yeah! Of course. Right away, huh? You bet. Only—" Dee's face dimpled into a pucker. "You're, like, retired, K. Pass-key to the pool, remember? When did this deluge thing go down?"

"Just now." *Present moment. Exquisite timing.*

"Oh, well, that might suck, right? 'cause there's, like, no 'u' in *gongfu* anymore, you know? And—okay, okay!" Dee held her hands up. Her fingers looked smooth, almost unreal. "I'll put some calls through, all right? See if there's a period of grace or something. Hang tight, okay?"

Koan nodded as she broke the connection. "Hang tight."

Dee was a good girl, like a granddaughter to him, really, or a great-niece. About the right age, too, although the governors wouldn't have assigned progeny to the same team as Koan's. Come of age; do the business down in MedPreg; move in and start work: no strings of attachment. That's how it was in the building, and sure, halfway through your working life one of your kids could be starting out, but you'd never know it. Who needed that sort of complication?

Koan blinked around him. Yes, Dee would check it out, and if the governors were still liable for the leak they'd have to fix everything.

But they weren't—deep down he knew it—and that was verging on ironic, because they would have been if Koan and his fellow jurors had stayed locked up last night, rather than just finding that guy guilty and rolling out early to celebrate Koan's retirement.

If it even *was* a guy. Koan shook his aching head. It was so hard to tell these days, the way the courts blurred details out. Same with the background, in case you cottoned on to where the alleged crime took place, or when. Chances were it was only a placebo trial anyway, so why not fudge it just this once? Why not, after forty years' due diligence and jurisprudential rigour, simply settle on whatever verdict was closest at hand and head on down to Blue Monday on Eighty-Eight, or Luftballons, or even one of the three-figure clubs? *What harm*, his inner devil duck had squeaked, *could come of it?*

Koan trailed one hand through the water beside his bed—talk about unstoppering a bottle with the genie still under pressure!—then raised a fingertip to his lips. Anathema. His tongue squirmed, preferring its own dried-out rut over this sharply tainted succour. Where had it come from? Broken pipes? Backed-up drains? What about the maintenance crews? Sure, he'd heard scuttlebutt whispers about self-sufficiency turned rank, that the whole building was slowly rotting. *From the ground down*, one of the temps had said (he was an unstable-looking man who'd jittered through one sitting and was gone the next day). *What level are you on? Six, maybe seven? That's near enough a slum, nowadays. Building'll spit you out, friend: up and onto the surface, like a cherry pip.*

The surface! Koan smiled, but with a sickly kind of wonder bobbing up in his stomach. As if there could be life outside the great buildings! The thought beggared belief. And yet—

"K.?" The ComClip huzzahed and its screen cleared to show Dee's face. "Koan?" She frowned. "Koan, you still with me? Hey, there's bad, good and bad news, right?"

Koan's throat tightened, no doubt trying to squeeze one last drop of the good stuff from somewhere. Liquid fire, and all around him, dirty water. "Um…"

"Bad news is the joint's all yours, name and deed. Congrats!" Dee smooched up to the screen and mocked a high-five. She cocked her head when he didn't respond. "Good news, though, is you can claim damages from the bloke living above, right? Name of Charlton, Charleston, something like that."

Koan tilted his head back. An odd sort of light shone down, pale and flickering from the hole in his ceiling. Of Charlton there was no sign—the reek of abandonment was palpable—and for a musty, shrouded second it was hard to imagine the surface being any more desolate than the apartment above. Koan gave a quiet snort.

"And the other bad news?"

"Yeah, well, I *said* bad, good and bad, but it's more like, bad, good, bad, bad and more bad, 'cause this Charlie guy up-level is taking action against the chick above him, right, and *she*'s lodged a claim against—"

"Mmph." Koan tried to picture the stack of units cemented between his and the high-up.

"…and they've all got to go through in order, right, so, ah, yeah." Dee tailed off into a wince. "You're kind of screwed, K."

"Thanks, Dee."

"You can crash at mine if you like, 'til you sort something out. Maybe feed Yoko if I'm locked up or whatever. Bureaucracy, hey?"

Koan shook his head. Across the moat, all acrid smoke and battle sparks, the T-Mat lay sacked. "Can't get there, Dee. My T-Mat's fried."

"Oh. Bum-bag. That's really—well, yeah. So, like, what's the plan, then, K.? You going to grow gills or—? Ah, suck." Her lips twisted. "The new foreman's coming. They picked Ramey, of all people. Can you believe it?" She flashed a crescent smile before the screen blackened. "Hang tight."

"Hang tight," Koan murmured. Judging from the near-silence of the apartments above—the torturous dripping and the absence of neighbourly heads peeking apologetically through the rent between units—hanging tight just wasn't an option. Where had Charlton and the other denizens gone, and how? Their T-Mats were almost surely as frizzled as his.

Koan sighed. Life without a T-Mat. How was that supposed to work? He swung his legs down from the bed and waded gingerly towards the VacFridge. Some of the lower apartments, he'd heard, came with a second T-Mat in a separate room, or perhaps built into the WashCube. (Details were hazy, as with anything to do with the deep-down elite.) Either way, it had never worried Koan. Why should it? Spare T-Mats, apartments with more than one room... fairy tales! The building was kept in pristine condition; and besides, technology was foolproof, the governors said. The chances of anything going wrong were—

Chirp.

The noise came from above, beyond the yawning sinkhole and its pallid revelry of dust mites. It was oddly familiar (though Koan could swear he'd not heard it before), at once lonely and hopeful. So often in his life Koan had marvelled at the unseen depths into which the building continued to grow. Even for someone like Koan who didn't care overmuch, didn't crave, the allure was there. No matter that his own apartment was far-removed from the penthouse depths, everyone aspired to the Down. And yet, now... now he was left high and dry, sloshing thirstily toward a VacFridge half-sunken in swamp. Dirty retribution from the devil ducks above.

Even as he thought this, even as he reached the fridge, there came another *chirp*, bright with yearning. There was nothing for it but to look up.

Up.

Koan blinked and shook his head. He'd need food, tools, clothing, something to carry it in….

Koan floated his familiar plastic chair from the fixed table to the bathtub, and balanced it on the rim. Then, tucking the devil duck into his pocket, he climbed precariously on top and reached for the hole in the ceiling.

Fortunately, he was a slight man, and though never before having had cause to strain against gravity, he found he could lift himself up.

The ComClip went off, an insistent raspberrying noise of a party whistle coming fully unravelled. Koan nearly lost his grip.

Dee's voice came bouncing out. "Hey, Koan! Guess what? It's, like, happy times for foodle fish. I checked the regs, made some more calls, and they can totally get you out of there. Sock me with the sake, right? They'll have to open up one of the maint-shafts and drill through to ventilation, and the guy says you'll need to do most of the assembly yourself, but—"

Her voice caught up with what she was seeing, and went up a notch. Koan could imagine the arch of her eyebrow.

"Is that, like, your nose, K.? Leave me clipped on, why don't you? I'm looking right up your nostrils! What are you *doing* up there?"

"Climbing." Koan managed to thrust one shoulder through the hole and lodge his elbow there. He dangled, lopsided. "Up to the next flat."

"Yeah, sure. Work that paunch, right? But you can come down now, K. We're talking a flat pack T-Mat! You can proxy me for the paperwork, then it's just two, maybe three days for the drilling, and we all shine on."

Koan grunted and tried to look down at the ComClip. A morsel of gunk detached itself from the maw and dropped wetly onto the back of his neck.

"Instant karma, right?" Dee continued. "Well, maybe a bit longer to put it together. But I've got you covered, K. I know you're not, like, savvy with the tech-specs..."

Her words blurred in his ears as Koan shifted his attention back to the sickly tunnel stretching above him. He wondered what had become of Charlton, and the lady on the next level, and all the others who'd had their cosy security washed away. He'd felt so safe in his apartment, put so much trust in the governors. What was left for him now?

"...pull an all-nighter. Heads up for a binge job, right, Koan? K.?" A verbal frown. "K., are you with me? You're not, like, stuck, are you?"

Koan smiled sadly. "No, Dee. And thank you. For everything, but—" He grimaced and shifted his precarious grip. "I can't stay. I have to climb."

“Whoa, K.! Slow down. That’s just the hangover talking. Three days, the guy said, and then—”

“And then what, Dee?” He gave her a moment to think it through. She was a smart girl as well as kind. Once she stopped reacting, trying to help him, she’d work it out. “There’s no room for me. The building, the governors. It’s all—”

He broke off, took a deep breath. The ComClip hissed faintly but Dee remained silent, which had to be a first.

“It’s okay, Dee. Onwards, right?” Koan braced himself as best he could, and then flexed mightily and heaved himself through the rotten skylight. “Upwards!” The ComClip caught on the edge and dislodged from his belt, plopping down to the devil ducks below.

“Koan?” Dee’s voice swam up at him, thick and slow through the murk. “K., are you there?”

And suddenly she was gone, leaving Koan sprawled out and wheezing with exertion. Alone.

The room in which he found himself looked pretty much like his, only without the water and the bathtub. He took a second to wonder who might be living in the apartment below his—how long it would be before they, too, awoke with a dry throat and wet behind the ears—then he cast the notion aside and set his sights on the next climb.

The floor was slimy, its dirt-streaked fissures like veins oozing black blood. There was a plastic chair (just like Koan’s) and some sort of exercise machine, badly rusted. It took some doing, but Koan was eventually able to cajole them into a shaky sort of alignment and clamber his way up to the next level. And so it went—assemble, scale, repeat—onwards and upwards, encountering nobody as he picked out a tottering path towards the surface.

Losing the ComClip had been... confounding. He thought it should probably have filled him with dread—playing to his isolation, his helplessness—but strangely he found the opposite to be true. Cut off from everything he’d ever known, Koan realised just how little that was. The building offered safety, yes, but at what price?

He continued to stack pieces of furniture, piling plastic chairs atop home decor follies. The light seemed brighter now, and there was a sticky heat like nothing he'd experienced.

He felt an ache in his chest, a dull throb that was only partly from exertion. He'd miss Dee, he knew, but at the same time his heart glowed with the first faint kindlings of optimism. Koan was old and set in his ways, and where yesterday he'd known exactly where life was taking him, now a new and uncertain future stretched cavernously above. It was daunting and yet oddly invigorating. But someone like Dee, someone lively and inquisitive and with the knowhow to pull up building specs and dig around in the deep-down... What would she do now? Would she start asking the questions that he'd never thought to?

At long last, having hauled himself through what seemed an endless progression of rifts between ceiling and floor, Koan found himself in the topmost unit. Here stood an upright piano swathed in light from *another* hole in the ceiling. Neck craned in awe, Koan watched as a thousand dust mites spiralled above like tiny angels, and realised that the leak had not sprung from burst pipes at all, but rather from up there in humankind's abandoned past. He swayed, the piano seemingly bouncing off his temples, hammering in and out of focus. Brackish perspiration trickled off his chin and down the outside of his throat. The temperature was stifling this close to the surface.

"Oh, Dee," he whispered. His eyes strained in the gloom and railed weakly against the too-bright glare funneling in from above. Through a hot blur of tears he could see—what? The outside? The *sky*? Whatever it was, he stood swooning at its beauty, a blueness so soft as to wrap him up and gently rock away his fears. *Such sights to behold*. Koan half-closed his eyes and breathed deep. *Such scents!*

The floor seemed drab all of a sudden, lifeless beyond even the rot and decay that had drawn him from his apartment. He pictured himself back there, ensconced in the room he'd worked so hard for. Then he thought of what might lie ahead. The deep-down versus the high-up. The everywhere.

Hang tight, Dee, he thought, and sent a smile down through the earthen mirage. The chirping noise came again, and a scrabbling, scratching sound. Something fluttered overhead, shadows dancing as it came to perch by the edge of the hole. Koan started, blinking. He couldn't quite make out the perpetrator of the chirps, and yet he felt its solitary joy. He could sense it *basking*. And the light... Surely, that was—?

The sun. The corners of his eyes crinkled. He'd lived in the building for sixty years and never seen this object, never even thought about it. Another twenty and he'd have been gone, never knowing.

Heart pounding, Koan climbed onto the piano bench. Its rich mahogany was now rotted and warped, its cushion eaten away and sullied with a paste of off-white splotches. He wanted to say something, anything, even a curse, to mark the occasion, but he couldn't coax the words out.

Gripping his bag, Koan clambered up onto the piano itself, feet making discordant squelches against the stained ivory. The chirper took off with a frenzied flapping. Koan shied back. Only for a moment, though, before he set himself with a deep breath, and gripped the ledge. *Up,* he urged. *Up!*

His arms trembled with exhaustion, but his lungs were somehow full, and he felt the dryness sliding from his throat. Pulse soaring, Koan pulled himself into the world.

Jacob Edwards *majored in post-colonial and feminist bullshit at the University of Queensland, before digging his way clear with a plastic spade and escaping to the Ancient History faculty. He stacks deckchairs nowadays for Andromeda Spaceways (www.andromedaspaceways.com) and edited #45 and #55 of their Inflight Magazine. Jacob lives with his wife and son in Brisbane, Australia, from which sunny vantage point he neither blogs nor tweets (despite having opposable thumbs). When not indulging his nostalgia for 80s synthpop, he writes creative and academic non-fiction, short stories, reviews and poetry, his work appearing in journals, magazines and anthologies in Australia, New Zealand, England, Canada and the US. Jacob may be found online at www.jacobedwards.id.au*

Passages

By Jacques Barbéri

(translated from the French by Michael Shreve)

We like to include a variety of perspectives and voices in our mix, and when I saw a submission from the author/translator pair that brought us the high-octane oddity, "Beast" (Morning After) I was thrilled.

Literature is above all paper being with ink for blood.
—Charles Bignoux

Emptiness

"Observation possible room 5. Holo-projection inside pages Jules Verne Book. First Edition *Twenty Thousand Leagues Under the Sea*," hummed the eardrops. The visitors in their bubble mask outfits bobbed their heads, paying close attention, usually watching the floor, trying not to trip over each other as they followed the holo-arrows. Rooms and aisles and shelves.

Behind the Plexiglas plates the books exhibited their gilding, their leather and their canvas, cardboard exoskeletons that cocooned muscles and paper on which lymphatic ink was permanently clotted.

It was sweaty inside the bubble helmets. Talking, too. Hands raised to the partner's mask, a finger dug obscenely into the ear valve to establish contact.

"Books beautiful, dear... you think, also?"

"Feel weird, answer maybe."

"Maybe... Understand what? Nev... Stupid dear!"

"Direct again dumb whyf and blah and blah."

"That yes, fer sure."

"Blabberator always, pluffy. But where's Jermy?"

☼

The huge rooms with high, darkened ceilings were nothing but silence. Dust pumps slid over the tile; suits brushed against each other; plasti-masks bumped sometimes, but the emptiness absorbed sounds straightaway.

Quasi-invisible ceilings gave everything the weird appearance of an open-air reenactment. On the moon, maybe. A prison-maze where ghostly cosmonauts wandered around. Perpetually.

The man and the woman, their fingers in each other's ears, grumbled as they approached the silhouette.

"Look, dear... Jermy, holo-projection behind."

"Jermy?" the woman asked, sticking her finger in the child's bubble-mask.

He did not say a word.

The man grabbed Jermy's arm and stuck the child's finger in his ear. The child did nothing but mumble, "Indeed... Under the thick foliage of these woods... a whole world of par... rots were flying from branch to branch."

Behind the mask you could see tears running down his cheeks. The mask misted. All of a sudden Jermy shook with spasms and started to suffocate.

☼

In the airlock changing room the woman tried to remove Jermy's suit.

"What happen Jermy?"

The man paced up and down growling, "Son stupid. Shame."

And Jermy was crying.

"Enough!" the man shouted.

Jermy sobbed a last time, and then stood still. "Beautiful," he mumbled.

In the gigantic library-museum, lit only by a few halogen spotlights, the guard made rounds, now and again looking at the books behind their Plexi-plates, keeping a close watch for signs of deterioration. The vacuum pumps never broke down, were serviced daily, loaded with all kinds of security. The guard, reassured, wheeled through the shelves, guiding his dust-pump over the, his red outfit sometimes disappearing behind a row of books.

Outside of this silent cube, winds of sand blew without end...

Dust

Only the top of the building extended above the ochre dune. Desert stretched as far as the eye could see, riddled with the meager technological remains of metal or stone whose roots plunged far, very far into the past.

The man walked along metal beams, sometimes sinking to his knees in pools of sand. He stopped.

He patiently laid out a row of gray marbles around a metal plate, then returned to the foot of the dune. He waited.

A series of explosions sizzled. The metal plate soared up and dropped down. The man was in the control room.

The metal plate had broken two instrument panels, but a steady hum continued. The man headed for the control panel marked *Lighting*. He feverishly pushed all the buttons. A row of neon lights blinked on the walls, and a bluish glow washed over the room.

He blew open another door, descended some metal stairs, and entered the lair. Now he was walking through the shelves stuffed with books, and he was elated. Thirty years after his first visit to the library-museum he was finally going to make his dream come true.

After wandering for hours down long, cold aisles, intoxicated by brilliant vision of bindings with magic titles, he found what he was looking for.

As he thumbed pages, he suddenly felt as if he were making love to the universe. *Twenty Thousand Leagues Under the Sea*, a novel by Jules Verne...

This isn't a simple little holo-projection, Jermy thought, caressing the paper. He read at random. He did not always understand the sequence of phrases, did not really get the meaning of the weird little words that peppered the story, but it did not matter... For, there was music. The music of an endless voyage. Freedom.

After retrieving his provisions of water and food from the barge parked behind the dune, he set himself up in a small, furnished room. Table, chair, desk, cot. Apparently the old guard room. He could hold out for days.

Jermy read. Firstly, all of Jules Verne. Later at random, reading the complete works of an author when his writings were a source of fascination.

The first book started crumbling.

Jermy sat for a long time, stunned, not understanding. Then he realized. Exposed to the elements, the library no longer protected its fragile objects of paper and ink. Corrosive air had started to decompose ink and dissolve paper.

Jermy ran through the rows, searching for the most resistant books. He read as fast as possible, forcing himself to… remember... remember... and the paper dissolved, the books hung from his hands like melting rubber. They trickled down the shelves and puddled on the library floor.

Halfway up the stairs to the control room, Jermy contemplated the ghastly sight below. The shelves were all empty, and a gray sludge covered the floor. Before leaving the building he was careful to turn off all the lights. There was nothing left to see here.

Now I *am what remains of the Library*, he thought. A huge, living book.

And he disappeared behind the dune, jumping onto his barge to go and relate his freedom.

Jacques Barbéri *has been writing his radical visions on the literary edge of France since the 80s. Recently his stories have begun to appear in English. Besides Triangulation: The Morning After, his work has appeared in AE The Canadian Science Fiction Review, Polluto, Liquid Imagination, Voluted Dreams and more. He can be found on the web at www.lewub.com/barberi.*

Michael Shreve *has published dozens of translations from French, both fiction and non-fiction. He is on the web at www.michaelshreve.wordpress.com.*

Noah

By Madhvi Ramani

*It's no secret that I'm a fan of Madhvi Ramani's work. After provocative winners like "Zafir, the Saudi Superhero" (*Last Contact*), and "Lilith" (*Morning After*), I had a suspicion I would like this story, and I was not mistaken. Noah as you've never seen him—unless you've read the Bible.*

The sun pricks my eyes, weaving through the leaves like a needle. Now light, now dark. My throat is as dry as the land. I reach for my wineskin, before remembering that I left it in my tent. I sigh, and reach for the grapes instead. My hand trembles as I pluck them from the vine.

The outer grapes, dusky red, are sweet and plump. The ones on the inside are a little tart. Better to have waited, but there is no time. All of last year's wine is gone, save for that one skin. I curse myself for not having realised earlier.

Cannan squeals with laughter as he runs amid the vines. My youngest, firstborn after the flood, his joy and innocence so pure it hurts.

"Cannan!" The sound of my own voice makes my head pound.

Silence. He appears from behind a vine and creeps toward me, a grin on his face. I continue picking, watching from the corner of my eye. His back is slightly bent, arms folded behind. Where did he get that from? When he is close enough, I strike him. He gasps. His soft brown cheek burns red, his golden eyes grow large and shimmer with tears.

"Get to work," I say. He turns and runs. Fathers can be crueller than that.

The patter of grapes falling atop one another comforts me, the tread of leather moving up and down the vineyard, the sighs of women carrying baskets. My family at work, doing my bidding. Many hands will get the job done quickly.

"It's all right," murmurs a man to a sobbing child.

Which of Cannan's brothers is comforting him? Shem? Ham? Japheth?

By evening, my whole body is shaking. We break bread in silence. I look past the weary faces of my family to the heaps of grapes filling the stone bath. I want to continue. To crush, to see the grape skins rise to the surface, to breathe in their rotting fumes, to press, to siphon, to drink—but it is getting dark. Everyone is tired. Shem and Zedkat tend to their children. Japheth rubs Arathka's feet, which are round and swollen like her stomach. Her body is a landscape of curves, sweet and full, glowing in the sun's final rays. I catch Ne'emah gazing at her too, and we both look away. Ne'emah's eyes drop to the ground while mine travel to her husband. Ham stares darkly into the fire.

"Noah..." Emzara, straight-backed by my side, offers me food. Her eyes are like black stones. Even when she carried our sons, she never became soft and round like Arathka. I'm not hungry, but I take a bite. The cheese is salty. The bread scratches. I wash it down with water, but water cannot quench my thirst.

I stand. Grape mounds form a dark outline in the distance. For a moment, the shape seethes like a creature from the depths. A trick of the light, or the shadows.

"We'll begin the crush at sunrise," I say, and head to my tent.

Inside, I stumble to the wineskin. Just one sip. It is a long sip, and my body craves more as I pull the spout from my mouth. I cap it and stash the skin under the carpet. I must make it last. I lay down. The crush, the ferment, the press… forty days at least. Forty days of drought stretch before me, harsher, it seems, than forty days and nights of rain. I try not to think about that.

Tremors course through my body. Like a vessel, rocked by waves. Seconds, minutes, hours pass. Then, a giggle. Arathka? Chatter drifts my way. Too much time cannot have passed; they are still outside. And they seem to have regained their energy. *Maybe they could start crushing the grapes now*—but it is dark.

Voices fade. People retire to their tents. Creatures scuttle and howl. I toss and turn. My skin burns. Thoughts of animals and wine parade through my mind. All those beasts screeching and hissing, wildness caged, adrift at sea. The crush, the press, the skins. I picture myself lifting the carpet, feeling the leather between my fingertips, taking off the cap. The smell, the taste. In my mind, I reach for the wine over and over again. Then, I sleep.

I wake to the chirping of birds, laughter. The shaking has gone from my extremities, but my insides gently roll. I leave the tent before I am compelled to break discipline and sip from the wineskin to still my rising anxiety.

Outside, the women and children are already in the bath treading grapes. I stand by the olive tree, watching. Zedkat makes a game of it with her children. Emzara is methodical, industrious, Ne'emah, lost in a trance. Arathka lifts one foot and then another in a slow dance while holding hands with Cannan, who jumps about with glee. She looks my way and falls. Arms pull her up and help her from the bath.

"Are you all right?" Emzara asks while Zedkat calms the children.

"It's blood! It's blood!" screams Ne'emah, green eyes ashine as she points at red rivulets trickling down Arathka's body and into the dusty ground. A wave of unease breaks inside me. I turn and leave the women to their business. Ne'emah's shrieks ring like laughter in my ears.

I scrub barrels in the cool, dim cave, washing out insect husks and resin. When the rain came, insects drowned first.

The insides of the barrels are stained red. The wood is dry and shrunken, having not held wine for some time. I douse the wood with water, then move on to the next barrel. I try to concentrate on the job, banishing thoughts of drowned insects and drowned babes. When I reach the end of the row, I return to the first barrel and wet it again. The wood begins to glisten and grow. When the time comes to fill these barrels, there will be no gaps through which wine can seep. I long to be so replenished.

The tremors return; my mind starts to drift. *Is Arathka's babe dead? Why was she treading grapes in her condition? Is it my fault? His work? A warning? Have I offended Him? Maybe it was the way I looked at her...*

Clusters of ants clung to each other in puddles pounded by rain. *I need a drink.*

Perhaps something remains from inside the barrels. I should have thought of that before. I fall to my knees and lean forward. The ground smells bitter, but tastes of what it is: dirty water.

"Noah?" *Emzara.* I look up, slowly. *Noah the Righteous. Noah the Blessed. Noah the Patriarch. Found shaking on his hands and knees, licking dirt.*

Emzara's hard eyes stare down, steadfast as ever.

"Arathka is all right," she says. "The babe too."

"The blood—"

"It was colour from the grapes. She is resting now."

I exhale. The child is all right. Everything is all right. My trembling subsides a little. Emzara says something about work to do. I look at the stores around me, jars of preserves, sacks of grain, glistening barrels, empty bottles—above all, empty bottles. How could I have finished all that wine in less than a year? I am the only one who drinks it.

Emzara walks into the light, leaving me behind in gloom. She has grapes to crush. Valuable time has been lost.

Evening brings nausea. I cannot control the shaking and retire to my tent for the sip I have thirsted for all day, the sip that must sustain me 'til tomorrow.

I lift the carpet, grab the skin, take off the cap, put spout to mouth and... one drop falls onto my tongue. Where is the rest? I shake the skin. I put my eye to the opening and stare into the void. The ground is dry beneath the carpet. There was no leak. Is it possible I did not merely imagine myself drinking wine last night? My gut lurches. The wineskin tumbles from my hand. I keel over and vomit. A sour, rancid odour fills the tent. My eyes sting. I lay back and close them.

Emzara. She will comfort me. It has been so long since I went to her. Nine years, since Cannan was born. Yes, Emzara will help me overcome this terrible thirst. I stand, but at the tent opening, I become aware of voices. My family are outside having supper. I crumple to the ground. I will have to wait.

Time passes. Why are they still awake? What are they talking about? A burst of laughter. Maybe Emzara is recounting how she found me on the cave floor today. No. Emzara is a good wife. Even before the flood, when others ridiculed me, she listened, helped gather the animals. And afterwards, when I was unsure of the ground beneath my feet, she stayed by me as I moved us from place to place according to my whim—but always to higher, drier ground. To here, where the grapes grow sweet and produce good, strong wine, and you can no longer see the sea. That terrible tumultuous being.

Emzara would not mock me. I am the reason she lives, the reason they all live, and they love and respect me for it. Emzara did not even blink when she saw me in the cave today. She probably thought I was praying. Besides, Emzara has not told a funny story since before the flood.

More chatter. Maybe they are in on it together. Maybe they emptied my wineskin as a jest, and now they are laughing about it. I am certain I had only one sip last night. I picture the rows of empty bottles in the cave. I could not have drunk it all. Wine is stored in the same place as the oil, the grain, the preserves—any one of them could have taken it. Shem? Ham? Japheth? Cannan is old enough—he may have developed a taste.

My eyelids flutter down. Row after row of glistening bottles... A shadow rises from the bath. My eyes snap open. Silence. The voices are gone. My heart thumps. I'm drenched in sweat. I force the panic down. We are no longer at sea. Dreadful creatures cannot rise from the depths here.

Night sounds return: scuttling animals, a breeze shushing through leaves. *Emzara.* I crawl outside onto cool ground. I am halfway to her tent when I hear a groan. Arathka having her babe? No, a deep sound, a man in pain. A woman whimpers. The moans swell, my heart races, I cry out—the sounds abruptly stop.

Movement, hushed voices… I realise my mistake and creep back to my tent, hoping that the couple whose love-making I disturbed will not come out and find me like *this*. How can I go to Emzara? I must go to her as a man. As Noah. Not a trembling heap of nerves. If only I had some wine.

By morning, a mass of grape skins and seeds skims the bath's surface. Beneath, grape juice bubbles and whispers as it ferments. For now, all I can do is wait, and push the skins down into liquid whenever they form a cap.

On the edge of the bath, I stand grasping a stick with a plane of wood at one end. I crafted it especially for the purpose. I lay the flat on the skins below me, and push. The spongy layer compresses. I put my weight into it. The rod pierces through, pink foam bubbles to the surface. My head swims. Perhaps this is a job for a younger man, but Shem, Ham and Japheth are in the fields today. I step sideways to push down the next section of skins. I just need to get through this stage. Six, seven days at most. Soon after, I will have my first drink. I prefer wine that has aged, when it is fuller, more complex; bitter. This time, however, I will devour it young.

As I make my way around the edge of the bath, submerging skins, the memory of last night resurfaces like a dream. Whose love-making did I interrupt? Not Japheth. Arathka is heavy with child. Shem and Zedkat? Ham and Ne'emah? They probably thought an animal disturbed them. They would never suspect me, Noah, of shrieking in the darkness.

When I have finished the edges, I climb into the bath to do the middle. Grape skins lick my feet. Black seeds speckle the murky fluid. *Emzara's eyes bore down on me in the cave.* Why was she not surprised to find me on the floor? When was the last time I could read what was in her heart? The churning liquid is making me nauseted again. Sweat beads down my forehead and clings to my lashes. Why didn't Emzara blink? Some truth lurks beneath the surface, impossible to see, slippery to grasp.

The next days are an endless cycle of waiting in my tent and punching down the cap. I sup with my family. My appetite returns. I start noticing things. Japheth and Arathka seem bursting with love and anticipation, Shem moves with a weary gait, Zedkat has dark circles around her eyes. Ham and Ne'emah must have quarrelled—they hardly touch or look at each other. I notice too, that everyone is quiet and respectful when I am around, but after I leave, snatches of conversation float on the breeze. Ever since the deluge, I have spent my evenings drinking in my tent, oblivious to what went on outside. Now, I wonder what they discuss.

Sometimes, when I stand in the bath in the heat of the sun, the wine whispers. *They are talking behind your back, keeping secrets, planning something…* I push these thoughts away as soon as they surface. It was only recently that I mistook love-making for pain and terror. I may even have imagined them altogether. Arathka is with child, Shem and Zedkat seem too exhausted, and Ham and Ne'emah quarrelled, so who could it have been?

I was on my way to Emzara's tent, but such noises could not have come from there. The only other men here are her sons. I must have been disorientated. There was a breeze that night. The sounds could have come from anywhere. I no longer trust my mind.

Every time I approach the bath, I pray the liquid will be still, silent—a sign that it is ready to be pressed—but it continues to murmur…*Maybe Emzara was not surprised to see you on the floor because she knows you are not the man you used to be. Since you stepped off the ark, and she kissed the ground and prayed and was solid in her faith—more solid than before—you have been reeling.*

I am standing in the bath on the fourth or fifth day, when I look up from the potent pulp. The setting sun casts a red glow. Four figures approach from the distance, children, returning from the fields. Ham leads, followed by Shem and Japheth. Cannan lags, tossing a stick into the air and trying to catch it as he walks. Behind him, far away, I glimpse something that turns my blood cold. *The sea.* Fumes from the rotting grapes must be affecting my vision. I was certain I could not see the ocean, but there it is, a mocking grey line on the horizon. Waiting to claim the land once more, to turn everything solid inconstant. A reminder that He can reach us at any time—famine, drought, a plague of locusts, illness, disease, death—with His power, His wrath, His curses and blessings.

I am suddenly submerged in red slop. It fills my nostrils and burns my throat. As I flail and splutter, Ham appears at the edge of the bath. I reach out, but he only stares with dark, unmoving eyes. Why doesn't he help? I recall Arathka's fall, the hands pulling her up, Ne'emah's screams, and in a moment of clarity, realise it was not concern in Ne'emah's excited shrieks, but hope. Ne'emah wanted the babe to die, just as Ham wants me to die. I sink under the weight of that realisation. *Noah survived the deluge, then drowned in a bath of wine.* If I had the breath, I would laugh. Then, I am dragged up, out of the bath. Shem, Ham and Japheth surround me. Wine coughs from my lungs. Cannan runs up the slope. He has dropped his stick.

I sweat and shiver in my tent. The wine must yet be pressed, siphoned... who is going to finish making it while I lie here? I strain to get up, but cannot. I try to recapture the clarity I grasped in the bath before it got away, slippery as a fish. I struggle to follow its course. Ham stood over me while I drowned. He has his mother's eyes. Emzara looked down on me in the cave. She comes and goes now, with her water and wet presses. Sober, I realise that it is not dedication in her eyes, but stoicism. Fear and panic flitted across Arathka's hazel irises before she fell. Tears shimmered in Cannan's eyes. Reality begins to surface. They do not love me. Why? All I did was tend to my vineyard and try to keep control.

I've almost caught it—the reason Ham wants me dead—when memories gush back: spinning islands of dead ants, flailing limbs, the last green tree leaf disappearing underwater, birds clawing and pecking on the ark's roof, the sound of panicked wings. I need wine. I curl up and squeeze my eyes shut, but still the memories come: the white eye of an elephant oozing yellow tears, the salt burn on my lips and in my pores, the cries, the wails. I need wine. A bloated babe floating belly-up. *Wine.*

Someone puts a bottle to my lips. I gulp until wine spills from my mouth and runs down my chin, until the visions and sounds recede, until the spinning stops, and I begin to relax and laugh and dance. Until oblivion.

I stir to the sound of a boy's laughter. The tent is in disarray. An empty wine bottle lies on its side. Ham giggles. Why is he laughing? Why is he still a boy? I look down. I am naked, skin yellow and wrinkled, penis withered. I grab Ham's soft arm and realise it is Cannan. He looks like Ham did when he was small. Now I see the reason Ham wants me dead. It makes sense, the sounds of love-making I heard, Ham and Ne'emah's unhappiness, their lack of children, the way everyone talks and laughs behind my back.

Cannan is Ham's son, not mine. While I was distracted by drink, my family have become wayward. They do not respect me. And now this boy mocks my impotence. Wrath pulses through my body. I pull Cannan to the ground. He yelps and swallows his laughter as I uncover his tender skin, pin his body with mine, and show him, this boy, firstborn after the flood, who has never suffered and does not know respect, that Noah will not be ridiculed. No matter where he goes, he will never escape my curse.

Madhvi *grew up in London where she studied Literature and Creative Writing at university. She writes dark short stories and cute children's books. She lives in Berlin, where she spends her time drinking coffee, making stuff up and speaking terrible German. Follow her on Twitter @madhviramani or find out more at www.madhviramani.com*

Dust Storm

By Chuck Rothman

I was honored to see a story from Chuck Rothman in the slush pile. A thought immediately followed by: Gosh, I hope it's a good fit. Fortunately, it was. In fact it inspired our cover. You can't go wrong with a classic SF tale set in a time and place that is becoming altogether too relevant again.

The wind blew like a judgment from God, propelling dust through cracks in the doorway and walls. The air filled with grit, making it hard to see across the room. Belinda prayed the rattling old house would hold up under the onslaught.

Earl had finally fallen back asleep; he was always a fussy child. Belinda wearily covered him with a blanket. She guessed it was close to daybreak by now, but the black dust made it hard to be sure.

Wind snapped the front door open. Belinda, kerchief pressed to her face, fought it shut. The bolt was broken—another chore that Amos had neglected—so she leaned a wooden chair under the latch to keep it shut.

"The only thing we have to fear is fear itself," President Roosevelt had said. Heartening words, and perhaps even true. But when your farm is blowing away, and dust blocks the sun for days on end, and your husband vanishes for nearly as long, you realize that your fears are as tangible as the grit that stings your eyes and grinds between your teeth. Hope sandblasts into shards.

There was a loud whistling sound, like a bird screech. *Trick of the wind?*

Then came a small explosion, followed by a scream of tortured metal. The storm quickly drowned it out.

"Amos?" Belinda shouted. He should have returned long ago from a trip into town whose purpose was, "none of your damn business." It wasn't the first time he had hopped into the Ford and vanished, but he had never been caught up in a storm like this.

She moved Earl to the farthest corner of the room. The scrawny child sighed and wrinkled his face, but did not wake.

Belinda opened the door. Dust eddied and flowed around her, grains stinging her face like a million bees. The kerchief kept only some of it out. Light diffused from the horizon, the yard a black and white photograph, dust draining the color from everything. A dune heaped where the fence had been, sand bleeding from its edges.

Belinda adjusted the kerchief and brushed at her eyes. Not far from the door, a mass of metal the size of a small shack lay crumpled.

Someone moved beneath it.

Belinda had grown up in Kansas and didn't have to think of what to do. You learn one rule on the prairie: if someone needs help, you help.

She pushed through the wind, pale blue cotton dress whipping around her legs and waist. She couldn't see the occupant beyond a blurred image of face and arm. She just reached down to grab his hand.

It felt strange. "Get up!" she shouted. "You got to get inside!"

The man—she guessed it was, since no girl would go out in this willingly—stirred. Flying sand obscured his features.

"Get into the house!" She tugged at his hand, and he rose unsteadily. She draped his arm over her shoulder and half-guided, half-dragged him to shelter.

Inside, she seated him on the loveseat and braced the door closed. Deciding it was worth the precious kerosene, she lit a lamp. Light flickered in the draft. The visitor raised a hand to shield his face.

No wonder it felt strange, Belinda thought. There were only three fingers on that hand, like Mickey Mouse's, but long and thin, the skin a dull gray.

He was watching her. His brown eyes—slanted like a Chinese she had seen in Wichita when she was a girl—seemed very deep and calm. He wore tight stretchy pants and a shirt of pretty pale blue, like the forgotten sky. Around his neck was a dark red triangular stone set in silver.

"Hello," Belinda said. "Are you all right?"

He didn't seem to understand.

Thirsty, she thought. *He's got to be thirsty.*

She went to the kitchen. The pump screamed as she worked the handle up and down, but it finally brought up a trickle of muddy water. She saved each precious drop in an old pot, then filled a tumbler and took it to the stranger.

He had slumped down in the seat. She lifted him up, surprised at how light he was. She brought the tumbler to his lips, and he drank, slowly at first, then with greater vigor.

"No, you don't." Belinda lifted the glass away. "Don't want you to have too much at once."

The stranger nodded.

"You understand me?"

That only got a blank look. Well, he was certainly a foreigner. What he was doing in these parts was a mystery.

She pointed to herself. "I'm Belinda Miller," she said, slowly and firmly. She had never spoken to a foreigner, but figured that was the way to do it. "Belinda," she said again.

The stranger pointed at himself. "Glory," he said, or something like it. Belinda decided that Glory would do. He touched his chest and winced.

"You hurt? Let me see that." She reached for his shirt. The fabric was thin to the touch, and lacked buttons. A seam in the front opened with a sound like the cloth tearing. She took off the shirt and folded it neatly.

A wound marked his chest. Blood oozed, a duller red than blood should be, but she figured it was the dust. She found a towel and cleaned the area.

"You'll be fine," she said. The cut was ugly, but scabbing over.

Glory seemed to understand. He nodded and gave something like a smile.

A fist pounded on the door, rising above the sound of the wind. "Belinda? Belinda you in there?"

She jumped. And glanced at the door.

"Belinda? You hear me?"

How Amos got here in the storm, she couldn't guess, but he sounded mean, which meant he was drunk. She had to move Glory, hide him so she could explain things to Amos first.

No. That made no sense. She had done nothing wrong, just taken in a hurt stranger. Surely Amos would see that.

Another pounding. The chair holding the door shook, but did not give. "God damn it, woman! What the hell do you think you're doing? Open right now or I'll shoot a goddamn hole right though the goddamn wall."

Glory looked worried. "It's all right," Belinda said. "It's my husband." She stood. "He's a good man, mostly." She raised her voice. "Coming, Amos."

She moved to the door and pulled away the chair. Amos staggered inside. He was a big man—six foot four and strong from working the farm. His brown eyes were bloodshot, and he smelled of alcohol and sex.

"What the hell were you doing?" he said. He propped his old shotgun at his side like a cane.

"Sorry," Belinda said. "I had to use the chair. The lock was broke and—"

"Christ damn it to Hell," Amos burst out. "Can't I even step in the door without you nagging me about chores I ain't done." He peered bleary-eyed across the room. "Who the hell is that?"

"That's Glory. He was in an accident and I took him in."

Amos's eyes narrowed. "Who's he, really? Someone on the side?"

"Amos, you got it wrong. He—"

"I can see his shirt's off!" Amos shoved Belinda to the gritty floor. "Damn you, woman! Can't I leave you alone for a moment?" He raised the shotgun.

Glory watched. There was no fear in his eyes, just deep curiosity.

"Amos, no!"

The shotgun exploded.

Glory jerked back and gave a kittenish yelp. Then he collapsed.

It grew very quiet. Belinda realized the wind had stopped.

Earl began to wail. Amos approached the cradle and paused. For a moment, Belinda thought he was going to strike the child, but his face softened. He gently placed his hand on Earl's chest.

Then Amos's face turned back to weathered stone. He nodded to Glory. "Get that out of here."

"Me?" Belinda asked.

Amos turned to her. "He's *your* boyfriend. *You* bury him." He walked toward the bedroom and stopped just a moment by the baby. "And stop this kid from screaming. Christ, do I got to do *everything* around here?"

☼

It was around ten, as far as Belinda could figure. For the first time in days, the air was still. It was a strange feeling; the calm after the storm seemed so much more forbidding than the calm before.

Belinda wrapped Glory's corpse in an old blanket and dragged it out the back of the house, leaving a furrow in the thick dust. Then she went inside and got Earl; she had keep him nearby in case he got cranky while she worked. She set the makeshift bassinet—made from a picnic basket from the days when Amos still had a a drop of romance in his heart—next to the maple that was supposed to shade Delores's grave. The tree was leafless from the incessant storms. It was a shame.

She cleared dirt from the headstone—just a couple of boards nailed together, with Delores' name and dates painted on—and began to dig.

The work was soothing. After a day huddled inside as dust filled the air and lungs, it was good to be working at something, even something as sad as a funeral.

Amos hadn't always been this mean tempered. When they met, he was almost as awkward and shy as she was, and he treated her like a queen. Delores's death had taken something from him, and the drought and the wind had sucked away the rest. Belinda wished they could leave here and head to California like the Wilsons had done. Just upped and packed their things into their Model T and drove off.

But the farm had been Amos' father's, and his father's father's. She knew better than to bring up the subject.

She glanced at Earl in the basket. He was quiet for the moment, lying with his dark eyes open and dully regarding her.

Belinda was afraid he was about to start wailing again. "I'm coming," she grunted, tossing the shovel aside. She went to the bassinet and found Earl's pacifier shoved down in a fold of the blanket. The rubber was hard and slimy. She shoved it into his mouth and returned to the grave. Earl sucked noisily.

A mother was supposed to love her children, but after Delores was gone, something inside Belinda went, too. Delores had died of the diphtheria a few months before Earl was born, and Belinda had found it hard to warm to the changeling child that replaced her baby.

She had dug down about two feet in the loose soil—a simple enough task, since it was dry, powdery, and lifeless—when a hum seemed to come from all around her. *Storm?* Belinda looked up, expecting to find dark clouds of dust reaching toward the sun.

The sky was banded blue, with concrete-colored clouds stretched to the west. No sign of storm, just a small dot near the sun.

The dot grew larger at an alarming rate. The object resolved into an oval, dark but solid, moving like an aeroplane, but not quite, zigzagging and wobbling from time to time. In a matter of seconds, it was above the farm, hovering as if it did not believe in gravity.

"Glory," Belinda whispered.

The object moved to the front yard and slowly lowered itself toward Earth. Belinda dropped the shovel and ran around the house.

The vehicle landed by the sand-covered wreckage where she had found Glory. The humming stopped. Belinda smelled ozone.

The thing looked like a pair of blue-gray tin plates glued together. The hair on Belinda's neck made her shiver as a door slid open, and a woman emerged. She was much like Glory, gray skin, missing fingers, the same shimmery fabric. A silver pendent with a red triangular jewel hung from her neck.

The strange woman rushed to the wreckage and started pulling sand away with cupped hands. Belinda knew what she was looking for. Hers was the expression of a woman frantically trying to save her loved one.

"He ain't there," Belinda said. The creature stiffened like a prairie dog, startled, as though she hadn't noticed Belinda.

Belinda pointed toward the back of the house. "He's dead. I'm burying him now. I'm Belinda Miller."

The creature made a sound that seemed like "Laurel."

"I can take you to him, if you want." Belinda walked toward the back yard.

Laurel followed. When she saw Glory lying on the dust, she gave off a gasp, then a deep keening sound as she rushed to the corpse.

The sound continued for several minutes. Belinda stood motionless, holding the shovel in her hand.

Laurel noticed the hole, and gazed at Belinda. No tears ran from those slanted eyes, but there was a sheen to them that Belinda understood.

"Amos didn't mean no harm," she said. "He's usually a gentle man. At least, until the damn dust blew everything away." She couldn't tell how much Laurel understood, but there seemed to be something like forgiveness in her posture.

Belinda moved to the grave and dug with exaggerated motions. "I'm just trying to give your man the respect he deserves."

"What the hell was that racket?" Amos poked his head out the back door. He saw Laurel. "Who the hell are you?"

Laurel's robe had slipped down, showing more skin than was decent. She gave Amos a small, sad smile.

Amos saw the smile, but not the sadness. "Well, honey, we don't get many chinks around here." He approached. "You're damn pretty, you know that?"

Laurel glanced to Belinda. Her face didn't move quite like a regular person's, but Belinda sensed confusion.

"Damn it, woman," Amos snapped. "Show some manners. Ain't you gonna introduce us?"

Belinda tensed. She wanted to tell Amos to mind his own manners, but it would be better not to rouse his temper. "Amos, this is Laurel. Laurel, this is Amos, my husband."

"Laurel, huh," said Amos. "That don't sound like a chink name to me."

"I think she's Glory's wife."

"Glory? Who the hell is Glory?"

Belinda nodded at the corpse.

"Oh, him." Amos shrugged. "Terrible accident, weren't it? Such a goddamn shame."

"Accident?" Belinda realized that's what Laurel had thought: Glory had died in the crash.

Laurel said a few words in her own language. She took the shovel from Belinda's hand. Feeling untethered, Belinda stepped out of the grave and moved aside. She rubbed her hands against her dress and went to tend to Earl.

Laurel started digging.

"That's good," Amos said. "I like a girl that pulls her weight. You gals finish up with that and then you can make dinner. He turned and strode inside.

"He don't mean that stuff," Belinda said. "He's just drunk."

The gray-skinned woman continued digging.

Belinda went to find another shovel.

☼

It took most of the morning to dig the grave. The work was hard. Laurel went at it, and Belinda helped where she could, using an old rusted shovel from the barn near Amos's Model T. The barn was dusty too. She'd have to dig that out next, though twin tire tracks marked where Amos had parked the car last night. The dirt couldn't be all that deep.

Finally, Laurel seemed satisfied. She dragged Glory to the hole, and gently lowered him in, wrapped in the old blanket. Belinda regretted losing the blanket—it still had some wear to it—but it was wrong to throw dirt onto Glory's face, so she said nothing.

The filling took less time. They worked together; it was like there was a bond between her and Laurel now. Even Earl seemed to understand the solemnity of the occasion and stayed quiet the whole time.

Finally the job was done. Laurel searched out a big stone, and Belinda helped her roll it to the gravesite.

Laurel unclipped a metallic device from her belt. It looked something like a large lipstick (how long had it been since Belinda could afford lipstick?). Laurel pressed something. There was a slight buzz, and a dot of ruby light appeared. Laurel moved the device slowly, carefully. Symbols appeared, the stone burning white, then orange, then gray again where the light touched.

Wherever she's from, Belinda thought, *they know about tombstones.*

When it was done, Laurel looked over her handiwork. Then, as though it had been pent up in her the entire time, she began to sob, great heaving gasps that shook her body.

Belinda stood dumbly. It was painful to watch. It was plain that Laurel loved Glory deeply. She thought of Delores going into the ground in the tiny pine coffin Amos had made for her. He had worked without emotion, as though the death had wrung it all out of him forever. Belinda had watched, too empty of tears to cry any more.

She wondered what it would be like to love a man so much. Sure, she loved Amos, but she had married him mostly because he asked. She had turned 23, and her prospects were few. He would not have been her first choice, but did treat her kindly. Her parents approved, and he was a good provider before the dust storms. He had too much of an interest in sexual matters, but most men did. In some ways, she was glad he had his tart in town. The sex act was too rough for Belinda. She was glad it usually ended quickly.

"Hey, Belinda!" Amos was at the door. "Where the hell's my dinner?"

Belinda sighed. She shouldn't be thinking like that. She was Amos' wife 'til death they do part, and there was no getting around that.

"Be right in," she said.

She touched Laurel's shoulder. The other woman looked up, eyes gleaming. Like a lost child, Belinda thought.

She took Laurel into her arms and gently rocked the smaller woman. "I'm so sorry," she whispered. "So sorry." She glanced at Earl dozing and sucking at the pacifier as if he would never let the world quiet even when he was asleep.

Eventually, Laurel's crying stopped. She looked into Belinda's eyes and gently touched her cheek. Belinda took that as thanks.

"Damn it, Belinda! Get the hell in here!"

Belinda sighed. Amos had never touched her so tenderly. "Let's go in," she said. "You look like you could use a meal."

As she picked up the baby, a gust of wind caught the basket. Earl snapped awake. A frown squeezed his face, but before the storm of his tears could break, Belinda pushed his pacifier into his lips, rocking him and gently crooning like she had with Delores. He calmed. She looked up to see the impending tempest on his face was mirrored in a furious bank of dark clouds approaching from the west. There was no getting away from the storms.

☼

"Will you hurry up with that?" Amos said from the kitchen table as Belinda beat egg whites. He swigged whiskey from the bottle and turned to Laurel. "I'm sorry about your friend." He shuffled his chair closer to her and draped an arm around her shoulders. "Maybe later we could get in a little comforting. I'm pretty damn good at comforting, if you get my meaning."

Belinda blinked tears from her eyes. It was just the whiskey. There wasn't much she could do about it, anyway. Divorce was for movie stars in fan magazines. Real people never did such a thing. And Amos was a good man, mostly. He didn't beat her. In his own way, he cared about Earl.

Laurel leaned away from Amos. She gave Belinda a glance.

Amos' hand went under the table. "You're goddamn pretty for a chink, you know that? A sight for sore eyes."

"Amos?" Belinda asked. She imagined him grasping Laurel's thigh, working his way higher.

"What the hell do you want?"

"The honey," Belinda said. "Could you please get it for me?"

"Christ, get it yourself. I work hard. I don't have to be your servant."

"If you call drinking working hard," Belinda muttered.

Amos became alert instantly. "What was that?"

"Nothing, Amos. I'll get it." The wind was beginning to rise outside.

"I don't want no back talk," Amos said.

"No, no. I'll get it." Belinda walked to the cupboard. The honey jar was nearly empty, but would be enough for their meal. She picked it up.

Amos was kissing Laurel, his lips pressed to hers. Her eyes were wide.

Something snapped. Belinda threw the jar. It glanced off Amos, but did the job at least.

"Are you crazy, woman? What'd you do that for?" He rubbed his shoulder.

He really doesn't *know.*

"Oh, hell," Amos said. He showed Laurel a smile that Belinda hadn't seen since they were courting. "Why don't you go into the living room, honey? I need to talk to Belinda for a moment."

"Amos…"

He made a shooing gesture to Laurel. "I'll be there shortly. Just give me a minute." He nudged her toward the other room.

Laurel glanced at Belinda, then left the kitchen.

"All right, woman," Amos said when they were alone. "I've had enough of your sass." Belinda was suddenly aware of just how big he was.

"You don't got no call to be making love to her," she said, mustering her defiance. She was terrified, but somehow managed not to flinch. "Not here, not in our home." Outside, the wind continued to intensify, sending tremors through the house.

"Stay out of my business." Amos raised his hand, fingers curling toward a fist.

Belinda held up a kitchen knife. "You stay away from me."

"Think that scares me?" Amos said. "You think—?"

A shriek sounded from the other room, a keening above the wind.

"What the hell?" Amos turned toward the noise.

"Laurel," Belinda gasped. She ran past him, into the living room. The wind screamed. Dust pushed through a labyrinth of holes and cracks Amos never had time to fix.

Belinda came up short. Laurel's eyes were as hard as stone, and she held something in her hand. Belinda recognized Glory's pendant. It must have fallen when she dragged him out.

Laurel detached the metal cylinder.

"That's nice, honey," Amos said. "I like a woman that knows how to make herself pretty."

“That ain’t lipstick, Amos.” Belinda remembered the dot melting stone.

Laurel started shaking, a volcano about to explode. If there was one thing Belinda had learned from ten years with Amos, it was rage.

“She’s mad, Amos. You killed her husband.”

“What are you babbling about?” He gave Laurel a grin and a wink. “If that ain’t lipstick, then I’m a—”

Laurel pointed the tube.

Belinda stepped in front of her husband. “No,” she said.

Laurel gestured with her three-fingered hand, a command to step away.

Belinda stood fast. She didn’t know why, but she couldn’t let Amos die. “He didn’t mean it. He’s a good man.” It sounded stupid even to her.

Amos finally seemed to be getting the point. “Now, look, honey, I swear it was an accident.” He raised his hands defensively. “He tried to hurt my wife.”

“She don’t understand you,” Belinda hissed. “She don’t speak English.”

Laurel gestured more forcefully.

There was a crash as the door gave way. Dust as thick and black as the Devil’s soul poured into the room, obliterating Laurel’s features, turning her into a silhouette against the daylight darkness.

A buzzing sound. “Oh, God,” Belinda shouted. A red line illuminated the darkness. “Look out, Amos!”

Red touched his shirt. He twisted. “Shit, that hurts.”

Belinda frowned. The thing had melted rock. It should have tore right through a man. A burning-sharp smell filled the room.

Dust, Belinda realized. *The beam is light or something.*

“Amos, get outside,” she said. “The dust will shield you.”

Laurel fired again. The beam sliced like a red saber, but barely registered as it grazed Belinda’s arm. No worse than a touching a hot oven. Painful, but not enough to kill anyone. Yet. She felt Amos cowering behind her.

“Get outside!” she roared. “*Now*!”

“But—“

“Listen you murdering bastard! Get the fuck out of my house or I’ll kill you myself!”

She couldn't see Amos's face, but could easily imagine his shock. She had never spoken to him like that. She had never used *words* like that to anyone.

He scrambled for the door. She followed and slammed it shut, wedging the chair into place. The wind bayed like an angry wolf. Earl started crying from across the room.

Belinda turned to Laurel. "He ain't much of a husband, but he's mine." With the wind no longer blowing, the dust was settling already. "I know you're mad, Laurel, but Glory ain't worth killing over. He was just a man. That ain't worth much."

Laurel looked as devastated as the land, sad and angry and hopeless all at once. Belinda had seen a woman's face like that only once before, in a mirror, just after the doctor told her told Delores died.

"My sweet Jesus," Belinda whispered. "He was your boy."

Laurel didn't answer, of course, but Belinda knew she was right. She gently led the other woman to the love seat, and eased her down.

"I didn't know," Belinda said. "Ain't no mama ought to lose a child. When I lost Delores—" She could say no more. Nearly a year and a half and it still hurt worse than ten of those magic beams. "Christ," she said. "I loved that little girl. I kinda felt Earl was trying to take her place..." She glanced at Earl, bawling his baby eyes out in the corner. "Still do, I guess. I hate him for that." She chuckled. "That's a horrible thing for a mama to say, but it's true. In my head, in my heart, he killed my darling Delores." She sniffled. "And took my Amos too." She ought to feel horrible for saying these things, but somehow it was better, maybe because Laurel couldn't understand.

Laurel stared as if she expected Bellinda to go on.

It's horrible, this anger inside me, Belinda thought. She patted Laurel's hand. "Just a minute," she said.

She lifted Earl from his basket. He started at her touch and gave a little shriek. "Hush, hon. Hush. Mama's gonna do right by you for a change."

She carried Earl across the gritty floor. "Here," she said, lowering the bundle into Laurel's arms. "He ain't no replacement, I know, but he deserves a mama who will care for him."

Laurel's eyes went as wide as they were when Amos was groping her, but it was a different kind of wide. Belinda took that strange hand and repositioned it over Earl, curled those three long fingers across her baby's chest. The baby stopped screaming. It wasn't often that he calmed once Belinda roused him.

"He deserves a better life than dust and dirt and toiling on a farm that won't ever pay." She smiled as honest as she could. "And... and I kind of figure you may have things to teach him that I can't." Earl started crying. Laurel pushed the baby toward Belinda, but she would not take him back. Laurel pressed the tip of one finger to the baby's lips, and the crying stopped. Earl sucked contentedly.

"He's yours now," Belinda said. There were tears in her eyes. She never liked the little fellow, but it still hurt to know he was going away. "He's weaned, so he shouldn't be no trouble. Maybe... maybe once he's grown big and strong and knows how to use some of those things you have, he can come back and find me."

Laurel shifted Earl to her shoulder, and touched on Belinda's arm.

"Yes, I'm sure," Belinda said. She understood the question in the gesture.

Laurel understood too. She pressed something into Belinda's hand. *Glory's pendant.*

Belinda nodded. She gave Earl a kiss on the cheek. "Now maybe you best get back to that flying machine. The wind'll die down and you can go."

The storm faded at dusk like a forgotten nightmare. There was a strange calm as the world waited for something new to happen. A little after that, a low-pitched hum started up and gained in pitch and volume until Belinda heard it rise up into the air.

She didn't look. She couldn't bear it.

When the sound faded to nothing, she got up and packed a suitcase. Then she rounded up Amos' shotgun and headed for the barn.

The old Model T was safe. Even at his drunkest, Amos was careful about his car. The dust hadn't piled up too high against the doors. The first swung open easily, only a small grumble from the grit in its hinges. Belinda took that for a sign. The other door opened nearly as easily.

Amos poked his head past the loft's edge. "You see that?" he said.

"No, I did not," Belinda said. She tossed her cardboard suitcase into the back seat.

"The goddamn thing just floated up like something out of a *Buck Rogers* comic. You were right. I think she had one of them ray gun things. She was gonna kill me. Can you imagine it?"

"Yes, I can," Belinda said.

Amos frowned. "What you doing with the car? And that suitcase?"

"Figure it out, Amos." Belinda pulled out the choke and went to the front to crank the engine. It'd been a long time since she had to start the flivver, but she knew how.

"That's crazy, Belinda. You can't leave."

She swung around. Amos hadn't noticed she was carrying the shotgun, but the sound of the pump sure got his attention. "Try to stop me."

Amos gave a grin. "You crazy? Someone'll get hurt with that thing."

"You're right." Belinda pulled the trigger. The blast nearly deafened her, as pellets smashed into the ladder leading down from the loft.

Amos was gone from view. She fired again, and the ladder collapsed.

Quietly, she turned to the task at hand.

The crank turned hard—Amos had been neglecting that, too, probably—but it caught. The motor coughed a few times, then picked up speed.

Belinda ejected the shells and reloaded.

Amos poked his head up. "You come to your senses yet?"

"About an hour ago," Belinda said.

"All right. Fun's fun. I'll admit you gave me a hell of a scare, but I know you ain't gonna really shoot me."

"Amos, you're talking to a woman who gave up her child to go God knows where."

"Gave up Earl?" Amos looked as though a brick had hit him in the gut.

"He's gone with Laurel."

"Gone!" The word was a cry of anguish. There would be no Earl to inherit Amos's worthless legacy.

Belinda nodded. She felt a tinge of loss. *Dolores.* "He'll have a better life than we could give him."

Amos buried his head in his hands. "Bring him back. I promise I'll treat you better. I promise—"

"The time for promises is well past," Belinda said. "As far as I'm concerned, Earl's dead. And if I can do that, you think I'm gonna care what happens to you?" The gun blasted again, the pellets only a few feet from Amos's head.

"Next time," she said. "I don't miss."

It seemed to dawn on Amos that she meant business. "Sugar, look, there ain't no need to get mad. I guess I might've been a bit rough lately. It's the damn dust, you see. But that's over. I promise."

"Yes, Amos. It *is* over." She put the car into gear.

"You goddamn bitch!"

With Amos's parting words vanishing behind her, Belinda drove across the farmyard and onto the road. It looked clear all the way to Fairbury.

And then, to California. Who knew—maybe she would become a movie star.

Vegan

By Diane Turnshek

We love creative interpretations of our theme. Here's a story by the talented Diane Turnshek, that re-interprets not only our "parch" theme, but pretty much every monster movie since Tokyo learned how to film. Grab your popcorn. This one is drive-in quality.

Double dawn caught Ssela with no shelter from the harsh daylight, her newly emerged second set of arms wrapped tightly around her extended egg sac. She braced herself on rocks as she slid ever downward into the valley. For the first time she was grateful for those extra arms whose untimely arrival had embarrassed her yesterday. They had erupted right in the middle of her argument with Mother Latiss, as if her own body disagreed with her.

Her tail twitched and the spikes scored rocks on either side of her. She focused momentarily on restraining it, but why bother? What did it matter if she left markers to her passing? No one from her isolated tribe would follow from their hidden, misty mountain to this valley of desolation. They never traveled. *Why?* Latiss had argued. The Overmother-goddess kept them from hunger and thirst, as long as they stayed close to the sky.

Ssela spat. She abhorred the easy food of her home. Rock hissed as her spittle dissolved it, but Ssela didn't look back. She could rid her mouth of the taste of the easy food, but she could not divest her mind of the echoing mental sorrow projected by the creatures she ate. Latiss never understood. Ssela had tried one last time yesterday as the suns descended into cool, quiet night.

"Our instinct to reproduce where we are spawned is strong," she had argued. "I don't want my children shackled to this mountaintop with nothing to eat or drink but what's here." She rubbed her belly. "My sweet ones will be sensitive to the mental cries of voltars, newlies and, what about spok-lars? You can't tell me you don't wince when you crunch down on them!"

Latiss had shrugged. "Calm your hearts, Ssela. I've done what I can to accommodate your whims—how many times have I killed your meal and dropped it on your burrow step despite my own hunger, despite that deliciousness coaxing my throat to swallow? The simple truth is that we eat this food or we die. You can't afford to be foolish with young ones nearly here."

"There *must* be another way. Food should struggle, not look sadly up at you and whine. Surely my children will feel as I do."

"What will you feed them in the valley? Rocks? Trees?"

"Insects," Ssela said. "Insects do not emote."

Latiss scoffed. "Insects are what prey eat. Do you have any idea how many insects it would require to sustain even one of your brood? No, we need meat, Ssela, prey. Will you risk the lives of your brood? Stay for their sake, Ssela. Once they are weaned, you can go off exploring if you must."

Ssela struggled through a narrow defile. Trees. Rocks. Little else. It was hard to feel connected to this world of glaring light. As the day wore on, she became light-headed and ascribed it to the heat, the lack of water, babies draining her of vital fluids.

She half-dreamed of cool night breezes, the harmonies of mothers singing from haphazard nests, the scents of midnight blooming flowers. It was in that blissful state that she had first understood the truth. Eating the wondrous animal life around her and drinking life-filled water was wrong. Animals had a natural right to live.

Finally coming upon a boulder large enough to protect her from the scorching suns, she settled in the shade and coiled as much of her tail as she could into shadow. Her throat was as dry as the rocks. Her birthing time had come, but if she released her children now, they would surely perish without water and food.

Turn back? She might make it home. She rubbed her hands gently over the sore, stretched skin of her sac, felt the pulse of life within. *They deserve better than that*, she thought. Was she willing to gamble on her ability to find paradise in the valley? *Yes*, she decided. "Young and foolish," Latiss had said. It was time to prove her wrong. She continued down the mountain.

An insistent buzzing sounded. She looked down to find a cloud of insects flying in and out of a hexagonal-walled hive hanging from a near-leafless tree. The trees at this depth in the valley bore little resemblance to the towering ones of her mountaintop. Even the tallest barely reached her lowest arm.

She leaned for a closer look, moving her right eye inches from the structure. *So symmetric*. Dilating her pupil slightly allowed her to see inside the honeycomb to drones feeding the young. She heard no thoughts, felt no sentiment. They were merely bugs. Her stomach churned. How she wished these creatures were large enough to provide a meal.

On a whim, she zapped the hive with her sticky tongue. The structure detached easily, though a few of the insects got away to buzz angrily around her head. Ssela swallowed. Not even a mouthful, but deliciously spicy. She batted attacking insects from her scales, savoring the angry vibration of translucent wings. This was so much better than feeling the sorrow of her prey. Maybe she would find more of these structures in the valley. What a wonderful seasoning they would make.

Ssela plodded on. Pufferbuds burst as her feet hit the ground, pink spores blowing up and out. It reminded her of stomping on pufferbuds at home so she and her birthmates could race the spore-laden wind.

The spicy taste turned bitter and dry. Her mouth felt charged with lightning. She began hissing and spitting, leaving a path of scorched brush. The parched skin of her lips pulled back from her fangs.

The glittering river she came upon surprised her. The moisture detectors on her cheeks must be working poorly in the thick air of the valley not to have picked up such a large body of water earlier. It took a moment for the reality of her situation to sink in.

Water! Her senses opened wide. She swallowed despite the soreness of her throat. Where there was water there would be animals. She instinctively leaned into a predatory stance, acid sloshing in her stomach.

A young voltar crept from a scraggly buttonbush and froze when he saw her. His fur stood on end, creating a purple plume around his face.

Saliva dripped from Ssela's jaws. As her eyes held him in the killing pose, a familiar battle took root in her mind. She felt the animal's fear and his strong desire for life. It set her back teeth chattering. Immobile the voltar might be, but he was whimpering inside. How could she, an intelligent being, kill such a creature? He belonged here—did she? "Unnatural," Latiss had called her.

No. I am one with nature. I refuse to eat the beautiful animals whose innocent lives bring light to my world. Her concentration wavered.

With a joyous hop, the voltar disappeared into the brush. A shock of pain flashed down Ssela's spine. She hunched, clutching her egg sac, and slid into the river. She could *feel* her unborns' hunger, the gnawing jostle as they pushed and shoved for position. They must have felt her prey too, must have anticipated food. Tears dammed in Ssela's eyes, held in by the transparent lids that had closed by reflex against the water.

She tasted her mountain in the cool river. This stream did not brim with helpless life like mountain waters, and soothed her burning throat without the killing price. She gulped, letting the chill numb her aches and worries. Red dust washed from her scales.

Swimming in the river was different from diving deep in mountain pools. Not only did the current move her along, but her tail whipped back and forth, propelling her to greater speeds than she had imagined possible. *Why do freedom and speed hold hands?* It felt so good to be moving that she had to remind herself she was not safe. Her thirst might be slaked, but her hunger and the hunger of her children remained.

She willed the thrashing of her tail to stop. Energy spent only increased her body's need for food. She flipped onto her back and drifted, both sets of arms clutched to her egg sac. The suns set, but only the brightest stars came out; no milky band of gray teased her to follow it across the heavens as it did from her mountain. She missed that about her home above the mists, but hoped this silver path she floated on would bring her to a new home and new wonders for her and her brood.

Pain ended Ssela's dreams. Stings coursed through her sac. Powerful screams rocked her thoughts as the strongest of her brood began eating the weakest. The agony of it broke her form and sent her sputtering beneath the water's surface, She thrashed around and paddled until her head emerged again. Choking, she pleaded to the stars.

"Oh, Overmother-goddess, I beseech you. I'll eat food, any food you want. Just don't let my children die!" The pathetic mewling of voltars was but a whisper against the anguish of her unborn. She should have listened to Mother Latiss. *I was born on the mountain; the mountain is my home.* A wail escaped her, a long, sad keening that reminded her of prey.

A star detached from the heavens. Ssela stared. For the moment, her pains dissolved into silence. This was surely a sign from the Overmother. Forcing herself to focus outward, she tracked the star as it dropped towards the riverbank.

Ssela startled at the drastic change on the shore. Structures had appeared along the shore, squat nests of mud and stone with angled roofs and square glowing eyes. Strange beings walked upright, bony and lean, with tiny heads. Ssela settled lower in the water until only her dark-adapted eyes broke the surface. *How did these creatures balance without tails?* She opened her senses, but felt nothing, no emotion, no intellect, no sense of purpose.

Insects, then, but large ones, nearly a mouthful each. There was a stain of them, as far down the river as she could see. They did not seem to belong here. It was as if the Overmother had heard Ssela's pain and created large insects for her, ungainly meat incapable of tormenting her mind.

Ssela moved toward the bank and stood. She turned her head to the heavens and roared her thanks to the Overmother. All around her, the strange creatures reacted, some running toward their structures, other falling flat onto the ground. That they did not freeze beneath her predatory stare was further evidence of their insect nature. It would make hunting them more difficult, but also more fun.

She grabbed one insect in her claws, and lifted it to her face. Not a mental whimper. She squeezed. Nothing. It was delicious.

For the rest of the night, Ssela foraged, gathering a circle of fresh food, broken into chunks for her young. At some point, the insects swarmed her, but their stingers had no impact beyond a sting or two, and they had a peculiar ticklish light that reflected prettily from her scales. It pleased her that these insects tried to fight back, however ineffectual their attempts. For one thing, it brought more of them within reach.

A grinding sound brought smaller structures into view, with long thin snouts and squat bodies. One spat, then another, projectiles flattening from her scales with dull thuds until the ground around her hazed with impact puffs. She was minded to run with the smoke, but she had business to complete. Next time, she promised herself, her children could run with her.

When the insects had finally dissipated, Ssela released her brood and watched them scavenge among the piles of meat and bone. A sense of spiritual awakening infused her. Her children would never have to know the agony of killing sentient prey. Her journey had been rewarded.

She would teach her young to harvest the insects judiciously. So long as the insects remained, this would be their home. Ssela lifted her face to the sky and roared thanks to the Overmother for providing this bountiful new life.

***Diane Turnshek** is a physics faculty member at Carnegie Mellon University. She publishes short fiction, mostly in Analog, the Magazine of Science Fiction and Fact. For 13 years running, she has organized Alpha, the SF/F/H Workshop for Young Writers. She's always got a new project going: two years ago she went to Mars (MDRS in Utah), last year she started a YA Lecture Series through Parsec and CMU, and this year she's going to convince the whole town to turn off their lights at the same time on April 22, Earth Day so the Milky Way can be seen from Downtown Pittsburgh. Try to keep up. Twitter: @dianeturnshek*

Dream Warriors: Ramayan Redux

By Rochelle Potkar

You will have to work for this one, but trust me: it's worth the effort. A story that nearly did not make the cut for lack of connection to our Parch theme has become, with two revisions, a story of a thirst larger than life, a thirst for justice and purpose and everyday heroes. A story of everything.

He is below the corridors of sleep when he hears words pressing all around. "Lust-crimes will destroy everything," says the one who is camouflaged in light so brilliant it blinds. A trace of a woman breaks through and the dreams bursts.

Kapeesh sat in bed.

In the day, he was a detective. Holstering a Glock 22 (.40) pistol, he set out to work, his physique suiting his job perfectly.

Kapeesh often wondered if any girl would date him, with his hands so thick, his jaws so wide, he so hefty at six feet three, broad-shouldered, square-chested. The women he desired liked genteel, chest-waxed, nimble-fingered, lean, and lanky menfriends.

At his office, a confidential file was slapped on his desk. A case of kidnapping, a woman of 24, missing for six months.

"What's so special about this case?" Kapeesh asked his boss. Women were being treated badly almost every day in the country, the same country that worshipped mother goddesses. Less-than-goddesses were whipped, hacked to pieces, and raped. For a lighter treatment, women might be molested, ogled ingloriously or at the least subjected to lewd comments that trespassed ever so gravely the fine invisible lines of decency and respect.

"The case comes to us from an influential family in Ranchi," the boss said. "An industrialist's wife."

"Ah!" Rich or poor they were mistreated alike.

Kapeesh got out the small suitcase he kept at the foot of his table for just such an urgent assignment. In it was a pair of fresh clothes and necessities.

He set out for Ranchi, taking with him the newspaper of the day. On the flight he pored over a front page that spoke of a fourteen-year-old girl, Rambha Malhotra, molested six years ago in a police station. Her case had now gone to court. Six years later! And only because her family had managed to slap charges against the cop. It had taken them so much time to dodge political clout and wade through a corrupt nexus. During this period, the girl had lost her grandmother, her father his job after suffering a heart attack, and her ten-year-old brother was dragged to the police station and beaten nearly to death under false charges. All this to teach her a lesson. Yet her family had fought on.

Now justice couldn't be delayed, said the newspaper. The hearing was to happen soon.

Supporters of the cop—politicians, ministers and other cops—had rubbished the case in the media. "What is molestation, after all?" they said. "It could have been the girl's imagination. She might be of poor character."

Kapeesh looked at her photo. Now twenty, she was pretty. Fierceness marked her eyes, probably born out of all she had to go through. He froze. Wasn't she the one from his dream last night? Rambha?

The flight landed into Ranchi. Kapeesh frowned. Wasn't it here that Rambha was molested six years ago, that he was now going to for another woman's case?

The rains had followed from Delhi. May gray rains. Grainy moisture bristles turned his spectacles foggy. The windshield of the airport pickup-car went blurry too, pelted with liquid complaints from grudging clouds. It matched the state of his mind in a way. He sensed connection, but the source remained hidden.

After a brief stop at his hotel, Kapeesh headed to the Sharma's residence, where he met his new clients: the tall, elite and bereaved Raghav Sharma and his fine-featured, reserved younger brother, Anuj. Though rich, they were of haggard skin and less willing smiles. Kapeesh was sure they had seen much better and healthier times.

"We miss her," Anuj whispered as they sat down. "We have been very worried. For six years we endured false leads, empty tips, wild goose chases and have been run in circles. Our response was to hire the best sleuths, cops, detectives in the country for the months leading to trial."

Kapeesh took the file the brothers gave him. He knew the details of the case: *A.* Vaidehi was missing since December last; *B.* She was headed to a social do from which she never returned; *C.* Her Mercedes was found near the local police station with its key still in ignition; *D.* There were no phone calls, threats or demands for ransom, no trace of her at all.

Kapeesh considered abduction, murder, business rivalry, personal enmity, family feud, secret lovers, freak accidents, but what did not add up was her abandoned car. It was too near a police station.

"I don't know what else we can tell you," Anuj said. "It's all in the files."

"So it is," Kapeesh said. "I will be in touch." He took the brothers' leave and headed to the police station. Submerged in the din of crime and punishment it looked much smaller than its newspaper photos.

Constable Nathuram was around, and identified Vaidehi's picture when it was flashed. "I have seen this girl," he said, rocking his head. "She had come to report on some eve teasers… around last year, I think. Dashanan sahib went with her to tackle those rascals. Bas! Neither did she return, nor did he. He was transferred the same day to another city."

"Where?"

"Bombay."

"And what about the Rambha case?" Kapeesh said. "Any connection?"

"Oh!! That one? Who can forget it, Sirji?" Nathuram spat red beetle leaf-mulch through a grille. "Rambha had come here to report on some drunk driving and while our sahib spoke to her na, he just touched her… out of sympathy."

"You call it that?"

"I didn't see where he touched her. I am an old man due for retirement. But Dashanan sahib was always very famous with the girls."

"Not every girl, unfortunately," Kapeesh said. "What happened after that?"

"Bas! The girl went home crying, and she brought back her father, grandmother, friends and neighbors. The way they created a ruckus, they stalled our station for hours, tcha! It was a demonstration. Her grandmother even cursed Sahib: 'You look at one more woman with your filthy eyes, touch one more girl with your filthy hands, and your head will burst into flames!' Then the media and women's welfare group came. Sahib cared two paise for such dramabaazi, and that party had to go away empty-handed."

Nathuram dodged his thumb in front of Kapeesh. "I hear the girl faced trouble for opening her mouth too large." His voice dropped. "Her brother beaten up, dad's job gone, electricity and water supply cut, she out of school. Sahib had good connections with her school Trustee, na. So why bother opening your mouth? What does one get, Sir? It was not even a rape or murder."

"A court case?" Kapeesh said. "Now one is filed."

"Arrey! That is nothing. Whom are you telling this to, Sirji? In two days Sahib will be out on bail. He has very high connections." Nathuram chuckled as Kapeesh left the police station without meeting the main inspector.

In the quiet of his room, Kapeesh studied Vaidehi's pictures: fine-arched eyebrows, almond eyes, high cheekbones, a long nose, but it was the otherworldly fierceness in her eyes that was unnatural. The more he looked, the more they seemed revving to life.

Tiredness? Occupational hazards of studying faces for cues? Kapeesh set the photo aside and allowed sleep to excavate his eyes, iron the creases from his forehead, and climb creeper-like over the rigor mortis of his body. *Stage 4, the one before dreams where delta and theta waves simmer at 0.2 to 5 megahertz.*

Rain lashed the window panes. Kapeesh heard it even from deep sleep. The case papers lying around fluttered. He should have bunched them together, he chided himself as his body stiffened into paralysis, and he floated, crisp like a dried leaf, into a dizzying spiral.

When he touched wet earth bottom, he found her: *Rambha. Ethereal, gleaming with femininity.*

Her eyes bear into his. "Come, we've been waiting. Why did you take so long?" She touches his arm, light as a tap, and they are suddenly whizzing past dream highways—interconnecting nodes of fast-moving lanes, surrounded by black cosmos unfurling eternally like a silver-sequined blanket of a zillion stars. They pass vortexes, mazes, swirling corridors, and finally stop before three dim-lit figures. Kapeesh shudders, seeing the blue-skinned tall man, the fine-featured younger man, and—Vaidehi!—the missing woman.

He feels goosefleshy even on his unmoving body above the realms of sleep.

"Sita," Rambha whispers.

And aren't the others Raghav and Anuj Sharma?

"Ram and Lakshaman."

Kapeesh becomes aware of his surroundings. This is no ordinary ground, but a battlefield, karmabhoomi. And he isn't even human. Taller than he could ever dread, broader, bigger, heavier. Giant, brute, and simian.

A bestial rage pulses through him, pacifying itself with only one gaze at the Blue One. They stand in a tight circle around a pool rippling with blood. Dressed in the heaviness of their thoughts, the ornamentation of belief, they chant a war pledge as the ground shakes. Kapeesh realizes he, too, is mouthing the chant in a language so foreign and cryptic that his tongue rolls into gullet.

Kapeesh awoke, coughing. It was early morning. The torrent outside the window made for dripping wet as shafts of lightning daggered through melting gray sky over the dark-leafy tree-horizon. Thunder followed.

Who was he, really? If Raghav was Ram, Anuj, Lakshaman, Vaidehi, Sita, Rambha herself, was he… Hanuman? He recalled the stories his mother told him of Kapeeshwar—Hanuman—the Lord of monkeys from the ancient epic of Ramayan. Wasn't he named after the monkey god because of his appearance alone? Was there more to it?

"You are my little monkey," his mother would say after she had recited enough of the bedtime epic to him. "You will one day grow big enough to rescue Sita from Ravan. You should always help women, okay, Kappi? We are strong, but not against bad men or bad minds."

Kapeesh wondered if Dashanan was Ravan.

He would have to meet Rambha and speak to the Sharma brothers. But would they even entertain dreams? Weren't facts and real leads better than this? He decided to meet Rambha first.

He had to negotiate with her lawyer to get through to her.

"She cannot speak on anything about the case," the lawyer said, "The matter is subjudice and it can affect court proceedings. What is it that you want to talk about?"

Kapeesh wished he knew precisely. He was following something, as nebulous as mist or smoke. "I assure you I will be mindful. But tell her it is Kapeesh." As if his name was going to have impact.

But it did. Like a key to a lock.

The next day, the puzzled lawyer told him Rambha was ready to meet. When Kapeesh arrived in Delhi, she evaded eye-contact.

"What do you want from me?" she said.

He played along. He told her only about Vaidehi, not his dreams.

"You mean he might have abducted her?" Rambha said. "These things happen only to the vulnerable. It was hard for me and my family too. I wonder, sometimes, if I should have kept quiet. But then, what would people like Dashanan learn? That they can do anything if they have clout and impunity, they are bigger than the system, bigger than dogmas of dignity, bigger than human?"

A premonition pressed against Kapeesh's quickening chest. Had Dashanan taken Vaidehi to Bombay? If this was how the epic played out, and Ravan abducted Sita, how much time did he really have to rescue Vaidehi? A shudder of rainy breeze ran down him as he conference-called Raghav and Anuj from Delhi.

"Why don't we go with you to Bombay?" Anuj said.

"First let me find what I can," Kapeesh answered. Six months had passed since the disappearance. What if something had gone terribly wrong? He wanted Raghav to stay away from as much hurt as possible. In spite of having just met him, Kapeesh felt deeply for the man. He couldn't explain why.

In Bombay, he tried contacting Dashanan, now the Commissioner of Police, to no avail. No matter how he tried, he was refused an appointment. An invisible, powerful wall was building before him.

Left with trailing the cop, Kapeesh researched all about him. When he reviewed Dashanan's real estate properties, all in urban settings, Kapeesh learnt of only one located in a far-off village, a farmhouse in Khedagaon purchased seven months ago.

Kapeesh travelled to Khedagaon, lurking on the fringes of that farmhouse. Only a gardener and a caretaker lived there, and he soon closed in on them. Shown the gun and arm-twisted, the two vomited information: "Yes, yes, Vaidehi was here for almost four months. Yes, she was Dashanan's sex slave."

"One night," said the trembling caretaker," she tried to escape. He shot her."

A torrent of rain poured down the late July sky. Lightning teased like a snake's tongue; thunder rolled like bullets firing.

The two servants dug up the burial spot in the courtyard garden while Kapeesh informed his boss, called for forensic lab experts, and summoned the Khedagaon police.

Voice trembling, Kapeesh informed Raghav and Anuj, and sent Rambha a text message. He could feel Raghav's pain. The brothers informed him they would arrive in the countryside and stay in a hotel. They did not have the courage to come closer to the farmhouse.

But when Kapeesh and the servants had dug to the bottom of the grave, they found it empty. No bones, no hair, no skeleton. Kapeesh wiped rain and sweat from his brow. The pit was filling fast with water.

"I swear, Saheb," the gardener said, "she was buried right here after he shot her three times. We don't even come to this side of the house anymore out of fear. And neither has he, and now she is not there. How could she have disappeared so completely? It's impossible."

A silver-sequined scarf swam up from the murky swirls and lodged by Kapeesh's foot. He tugged at the water-sogged fabric. He should call for an evidence bag. Instead, with the servants looking anywhere but at him, he tucked the scarf into his pocket.

Kapeesh and the police officers investigated the farmhouse for fingerprints, hair, and belongings. They found nothing.

"Where are her things?" Kapeesh yelled. "Something! Anything!"

"Everything was burnt down and buried with her," said the gardener.

"The house was completely renovated," the caretaker said.

No one knew of the scarf, the chiffon fabric Kapeesh held. Why wasn't there a larger trace of her in the pit? It was as if the earth had swallowed her whole.

Were the caretaker and gardener lying?

Why would they? It would have been better for them to say she had escaped.

A week later it hit home. This scarf! Wasn't it part of what Vaidehi wore in the corridors of sleep below?

The tunnels are dank and slippery, corridors, thick with information, some classified, some otherwise. Photographs, names, faces fly past as in an iterative ballroom dance. Countenances recycle, morph into frames of familiarity: convicts, bandits, criminals, reporters, journalists, commonplace people. Those he helped, those he nabbed, those he fought, those he saved, whose names are now below the rock-sediment of time.

Kapeesh glides beneath all of it, all that he knows.

He floats through blinding light, and The Four *emerge astride very high horses. Their neighs trample the night sky. He finds himself straddling his own horse, galloping, speeding on vertical roads with capes fluttering outrageously until they reach the battleground.*

They dismount. Vaidehi stands in front. "It is here that we shall fight Dashanan," she says. "Or Ravan. This place of no gravity, no delay. This stage in sleep that lasts for 30 minutes of real time, but feels like years."

Placing a tray of weapons before him, she says, "Choose, Kapeeshwar." He selects a mace, at home with its heavy shaft and glean of eye-stirring length.

The others heft swords, blood axes, spears, bow and arrow.

"Your weapons are with you," Vaidehi says. "Safekeep them in your heart."

Slim light distills onto their way out.

Vaidehi stops at a gate, "Kurukshetra," she says. "It has been fought here every time that history demanded. Not in 18 days but 18 minutes of sleep, every night, for centuries."

Kapeesh gazes at the sprawling ground bedecked with moving clumps of bloodied flesh. Bathed in evening light, these bits of body seem to have some fight left in them.

Vaidehi nods. "There are other planes for other wars—Armageddon—but we are not concerned with them for now."

"But what about you?" Kapeesh asks. "Where are you in the real world? What about the justice you thirst for there?"

Vaidehi turns to Rambha, "She is fighting a case. Let's see how successful that is. Look how time crawls in the reality of the physical world. How slow justice takes in the coming. Sometimes there is only hope. But a day will come when every battle will be fought in the mind, the energy from the subconscious so strong that it will shatter the hardest skull. There will be no need for sword or battleaxe. The fibers of our belief system are not made of tangible matter. The battle between good and evil is an ancient one, and a contemporary one."

"What really happened to you?" Kapeesh says. "We searched everywhere."

"Dashanan abducted me to Bombay. When I tried to escape he killed me. But the earth encroaches and embraces all. She relieves everyone of pain, our Mother. She swallowed me, made me whole again with not a limb cut, not a vein slit, not a wound torn through. She regenerated me. That is the power of the womb, of the earth. She reflowers her children, recycles them by holding them into her warm, mesmeric arms, and even those of you who do not meet their end like me will come to this place. Your restlessness and disbelief with reality, your disillusionments will bring you here."

Head splitting like a thousand detonating bombs, Kapeesh awoke squinting against the dawn. His neck trembled with the effort of holding his heavy skull.

Were the dreams provoking a greatness out of him? Something he had, or perhaps, didn't? Power from judgment, instinct, and experience was one thing, but being a 'chosen one'? Well, that was different. Was he truly the avatar of Hanuman or was he just dreaming big? Today was Rambha's court case hearing, and he hurried to keep his date with justice.

The courtroom in Delhi brimmed with journalists, mediafolk and ordinary people. Dashanan stood in the witness box, gauging the scene with crude eyes. His wife, Mandy, sat on the first bench chewing her *Page Three* fingernails.

A number of people occupied the witness stand, people who witnessed Rambha's molestation in the police station, but denied it under oath. Constable Nathuram was one of those who turned hostile. The two prime witnesses, who had recorded their true confessions in Rambha's FIR, didn't turn up, all attempts to contact them in vain. The media speculated over their absences as Rambha's case teetered on collapse.

That night Kapeesh was again pulled down through the layers of sleep.

The clocks have reversed, the whole cosmos seen through the eye of a gleaming star. Nights upon nights cascade into a century's worth of peace. On the battleground, Kapeesh's view brims with black-hooded men. Enemies. So many enemies, so much evil. He sees Nathuram amongst them and grips the mace more tightly.

He turns and finds an equally large number of white-hooded soldiers, amongst them the neighborhood pizza delivery boy, a TV sports-reporter, a school teacher, an old environmental activist, a neighbor from Kapeesh's childhood home, a long ago best friend, a famous blogger, an actress. The two witnesses who disappeared from Rambha's case are also there. A strange resonance rings from all of them to him.

Vaidehi blows a conch shell.

Next day, in court Rambha was called to the witness box for cross-questioning. Each answer made her seem more whore-like and characterless, each deed by her family was twisted through legalese into ulterior motive.

"Why Dashanan, when there are greater evils?" Kapeesh asks Rambha.

"To each his own Ravan," she answers, striding forth with her sword.

While Dashanan and Anuj clash, Rambha duels with the rest, slashing and slaying many and more. Raghav collides with Dashanan, and the battlefield trembles. Kapeesh can only fathom the hurt and anger Raghav holds within.

Twitches of war-clamor float in fits and starts into Kapeesh's inert sleeping body, above.

On the tenth day, the court verdict came out, declaring Dashanan innocent for lack of compelling evidence. He walked out of the courtroom with his head held high, a smile overgrowing his face.

In dream, the battle rages. Kapeesh, Raghav, Anuj, Vaidehi and Rambha duel hard. Raghav and Dashanan fight with a force Kapeesh would never have imagined possible before now. Movements blur, the Blue one, getting bluer.

"His heads keep regrowing," Raghav complains during a lull. "How do we kill him?"

"Pierce his heart," Vaidehi suggests. "He will lose his spirit too." Vaidehi and Raghav clank spears together, and the two form one long shaft that pushes through the battlefield into Dashanan's heart. Ten heads burst into flame. The battleground quakes molten gray amid shrieks, screams, yells, and cries.

Silence descends. Tears flow from Kapeesh's tired eyes. The battle is over.

The next morning, Kapeesh's head felt as light as a balloon. His office called. He was to start work on another case. A murdered woman had been found in a steel trunk at Churchgate station.

A month passed.

His job as a sleuth now irked him. Things seemed too slow. Yet he refrained from going under the fourth stage of sleep, keen on avoiding its slippery pathways. Was it real? Was he even supposed to access it? Was it right to do so again? He should focus on real life and its purpose, who he really was, and what he wanted to become. Time to take sides, the real, concrete, proof-based one, not some illogical, ephemeral, dream-like state.

But as the season's last rain poured outside the windows and dimmed Kapeesh into a restless daydream, he found himself wondering if it had indeed been one great delusion. Maybe there was no choice to be made at all.

Then, one morning, a newspaper headline: a private plane had caught fire, mid-air, and had crashed into a mountainside. Flames spat ten charred bodies from the wreckage, all of whom were traveling to Hawaii. The list included ministers and politicians famous for their country-looting scams, and one name larger than the rest. Dashanan. Miraculously, the pilot had survived with only minor injuries. Observing the man's photo on TV, Kapeesh was certain he had seen him fighting on the good side in the realms of sleep.

Kapeesh sank into bed that night, chest bursting with inexplicable triumph. It seemed like a joyous festival, like Diwali! He resisted calling Raghav or Anuj or Rambha. Some things need not be mentioned.

As sleep pinned him down, and the edges of his room blurred, he permitted himself one more journey through those corridors. There was so much calm now, beneath closed eyes.

A presence slices through the lull, sharp like a meat knife cleaving cottage cheese. With a jerk he feels himself tearing open. Two roads diverge, moving in different directions and velocity. He is yanked from his inert body that lays recuperating and regenerating cells.

Rambha is with him. Together, they fly, leap, grow as big as their ideas of justice, fairness, equality, as strong as their notions of peace.

"Are we truly incarnates from the Ramayan?" he asks.

Rambha laughs. They embrace in mid-air. "We are the continuation of warrior-selves from unfinished wars of peace, Kapeeshwar. That's why our blood boils when we hear of injustice. Once we battled over other things, but now our war is for the protection of the wronged, the vulnerable. There will always be something to fight for." She touches his face. "A girl was gangraped in Muzzarfarnagar yesterday by zamindars. We need to reach her."

They sped in that direction. North.

It was for them to choose: warrior-on-horse or foot soldier, with weapon or with conviction, but never non-doer, never neutral passive spectator. So many battles had to be won. At stage four—the one before dreams—0.2 to 5 megahertz, where delta and theta brain waves simmer, just so.

Born in small town, Kalyan, **Rochelle Potkar** *craved big city only to realize that Bombay was a small town in a large world. She now waits for the galaxy to become a small town. Her stories have appeared in several Indian and international magazines. She is the author of The Arithmetic of breasts and other stories. Her next book, Dreams of Déjà vu, is a speculative novel. She lives in the pandoramic city of Mumbai and Bombay with people real and imagined.*

www.rochellepotkar.wordpress.com

http://www.facebook.com/AuthorRochelle

Twitter: @rochellepotkar

The Well

By Kenneth B. Chiacchia

I'm always happy to see a story from Ken in the submission queue (e.g. "Course Correction", Morning After). He brings the hard SF slant that we crave, and always seems to find adventure in the everyday. Besides, how could we say no to a story that opens with a hand grenade?

Nothing focuses the mind like a live hand grenade.

The gray cylinder spun on the glasstine table; the little object had become the center of Sergei's universe.

At focus: the bomblet, spiraling outward in gyroscopic precession. Next, two drinks: his, grain alcohol and juice; hers, ersatz beer, brewed for human clientele.

Across the table: Hansa, dark skin, raven hair, massive ponytail. Her sudden appearance, a 12-day local week ago punctuated by her cryptic words: "We each have a well we need to deliver."

A further orbit outward: the cafe. Human clientele and Ehrehnon waiters, tall, fluffy-pated, snaggle-toothed. He wondered if they'd noticed the grenade.

Above, the off-color sun burned intensely.

Hansa reached with an odd calm and tossed the grenade back over the hedge from whence it had come. She pushed Sergei down with a painful thud. Wood, metal, and shattered plastic shrieked overhead, the grenade, reaching nirvana.

"Move," she said. "Now." Her voice was clear in the ear-ringing moment after the blast.

Sergei swallowed an urge to wait for authorities. They would ask questions, and he didn't have good answers. He leaped after Hanasa through the dazed, disordered crowd.

The fact was, Sergei had something to hide.

☼

As Hansa whipped through the cramped, adobe slums of Ssahn's Ratalucon quarter with a local's familiarity, Sergei followed their progress on a map scrolling across his retinal implant. *You'll be okay*, he reminded himself. *The Information Office security guys will be able to track you.* But it didn't really reassure him. He wondered how he'd gotten into this mess, strayed so far from a quiet, even genteel diplomatic life.

The particulars of his fall from grace were hazy to him in this moment of adrenaline overload, but his sins had resulted in banishment to Ssahn—a provincial second city and diplomatic backwater, far from the desert planet Hcnit's capitol—as a mere clerk for a hulking, petty tyrant named Lafontaine.

"I need to get an artifact off-planet," Hansa had said. Despite the legal risk, despite the promise of bloodshed every time another ancient nont'h artifact came to light, despite the voice howling at the back of his head, Sergei had gone all in.

This particular relic, the Well of Ehcalt, dated back maybe 500 Terrestrial years. It had been made during the Hcniton's war of independence against their home civilization on the planet Ehreh. The Well held special religious significance in the aliens' "dream world". Sold to a rich off-planet Ehrehnon or human collector, it was the sort of find that made the sale's facilitator rich. Sergei just wanted enough to buy a damned water well for a damned village he didn't want to care about, but couldn't help himself.

Hansa cut into an open doorway. Sergei followed reluctantly.

In the dim interior, his eyes adjusted slowly. Small windows in the street-side wall gave the only light. It took even longer to adjust to the reality that, without warning, his retinal display had gone blank. Cut off from the net.

With the chill of potential danger seeping in, he looked over his shoulder to see a black box with a blinking light above the doorway. It took serious hardware and software to crack a diplomat off the security net.

Sergei took a deep breath. He wanted to run outside, but he couldn't. Well, he could, but LaFontaine would likely have him translating nursery rhymes for her children if he did. He had to at least extract himself from a very incriminating situation. Wouldn't do to be discovered by Security, he was beginning to realize, without first putting an alibi in place.

A large Ratalucon male cradling a laser rifle glared at him and Hansa. His skin was darker than that of ethnic Hcniton locals, and his downy head-feathers had been braided deep-desert style. His people, the Ratalucon, had colonized this arid planet 10,000 years ago. Some 9,000 years later, the Hcniton, also calling themselves "native," had renamed it after displacing the Ratalucon to the planet's harshest regions.

The male's slit pupils were almost round in the dim light, and his snaggled, shark-like teeth were exposed in a carnivorous smile. A compact, muscular human, hair also braided, sat on a stool near him. He'd missed a couple of shaves and was balancing a knife by its point on one finger. At his feet lay a Spacearm-issue laser rifle.

The human nodded at Hansa. "Figured you'd want the alternate drop."

Hansa scowled. "Thanks for caring, Ash. I'm fine, in case you give a damn."

"Don't be difficult." Ash smiled broadly. "It's not my fault they found you. Got the payment?"

"Nearby. The merchandise?"

"I can take you there." Inclining his head toward Sergei, he added, "Who the hell is this?"

"Sergei," she said. "He's a translator. He works at the *Consulate*." She drew out the last word like a threat. Sergei didn't like Ash's sudden attention: the cold, unapologetic look of a man calculating an act of violence.

"Ash," the man said finally. He offered his right hand, the left holding the dagger—*a perfect metaphor for diplomacy*, Sergei thought. "Special Corps."

Sergei's stomach did flips. *Special Corps?* The dirty-tricks branch of Spacearm, and Sergei's least favorite department of the United Nations Security Council. He shook the hand trying to match, without challenging, Ash's grip.

Ash spun the knife end-over, caught it by its hilt, and slid it into a scabbard on his hip. "Wait here," he said, grabbing the rifle. "Just need to make sure we don't have company."

"We don't," Hansa replied.

"Nonetheless." Ash and The Ratalucon swaggered outside.

"You don't even have the Well yet?" Sergei said once they were gone.

Hansa shrugged. "Things didn't go as planned. I came out to warn you."

That possibility hadn't occurred to him.

He wanted a way out that involved not being caught with her here, now. He said, "I'm going to be overdue at the Consulate soon..."

She pointed at the black box above the doorway. Cutting him from the net would also have deactivated his implant chip. The Information Office might look for him, but the trail would stop here.

"You know, it stings to have those damned things replaced," he said.

Hansa chuckled. "Maybe you shouldn't bother."

"And may—" Sergei shut his mouth as Ash returned, alone.

"Let's get going," Ash said.

He led them through the maze of Ssahn's low-rent districts. Sergei didn't even try to keep oriented. He wished he were the type to raise strenuous objections, ask pointed questions, put his foot down.

He got a bit of reassurance when, with a static flash, his retinal display rebooted. He couldn't get the map back, but red text spooled across the bottom of his field of view: TRACKING FUNCTION INACTIVTED, SEEK MAINTENANCE. *Thanks so much.* He turned the warning off; it was distracting.

Apparently texting was still online, though, because white letters appeared: HAVE YOU CHECKED CENSUS DATA. NOT GOING TO BRING POPULATION STUDIES IN ON THIS. AND WHERE THE HELL ARE YOU.

I'm fine, thanks for asking. He thought it, but no outgoing message appeared. Functionality was clearly limited, and in the wrong direction. He would rather have no access than listen to Lafontaine's nagging.

Technically, his grant request for the artesian well was still in the works. Lafontaine's impending veto was what had pushed him into this hare-brained agreement with Hansa. He tried not to think of the water-starved little ones in the Ratalucon village that needed the well, of them crowding around him with trinkets for sale. More immediate concerns.

DONT INGORE ME DAMMIT SERGEI.

Either Lafontaine had not heard about the bombing yet, or, with her usual geographic incompetence, hadn't connected his tracking movements to the incident—or maybe even noticed his tracking had fallen off the net. *Never mind that hand grenade, Sergei, we've got throughput to think about.* Kind of emblematic, but what really bothered him was the pang of doubt, of self-loathing he felt now. Terrorists had tried to blow him the hell up, and a part of him was still more afraid of his boss.

A few more turns, and they arrived at a metal building with bay doors. Inside it was an all-trac.

Ash drove them into the desert. The baked-yellow-clay plain of Ssahn Valley gave way to cracked, dun foothills, and then the sheer, cinnamon-striped walls of plateau cliffs. Only the sun remained constant, hot and heavy in the sky.

They came to a Ratalucon village. Children ran screaming out to greet them, requisite trinkets in hand. They swarmed over the vehicle—and Ash—with gleeful shrieks, miniature shark teeth flashing. The children were thin, even for nont'h. Sergei relaxed a little. As the third, perennially screwed, member of the nont'h family tree, Ratalucon represented the underdog that Sergei seemed hardwired to root for. He had spent time with them; the village he'd foolishly promised the artesian well to was not far south of here.

Behind the wave of children came a group of adolescents, well armed and menacing. Then a few adults, women and old people mostly, the leavings of war. All looked thin, but somebody had armed the village well.

Sergei shook his head. This village needed far more than a well by the look of it, but what they got was weapons. He regarded Ash with new hatred. Children could not drink laser beams, or eat explosives.

A crone, stooped but still taller than Sergei, embraced Ash. "We wish you [something] and joy, my Son," she said in her language.

"I greet you as well, Mother," Ash said. "And [something] I bring good news. The [something] arrives soon. I ask if it may be that you tell your [something] that they prepare transport."

Sergei's Ratalucon had never been strong. He'd been unapologetic about that; Ratalucon was hardly the language of diplomacy in the Nont'h System. But damn it, he could have used some proficiency right about now.

Ash traded their transport for a larger cargo-truck all-trac. As they lumbered out of the village, Sergei spotted an old, old Ratalucon male wearing the beads and bones of a shaman, peering at them from a dark doorway.

Ash threaded the vehicle up a narrow trail cut into the cliff face. Sergei clenched his jaws, worrying at the steep drop. About halfway up, as they turned into a switchback, Ash stopped the vehicle and got out.

"A little cleft along this foot trail," he said to Hansa, pointing with the knife in his right hand. Sergei saw no trail.

"Your friend stays with me," Ash said. "Remember, my people are watching." Sergei didn't want to stay with Jim Bowie, but the sheer drop of the "trail" was even less inviting. Not that Ash had given him a choice.

"Keep an eye on the vehicle," Hansa told Sergei meaningfully, as if he weren't totally useless. She walked to the cliff face and disappeared into an all-but-invisible gap.

When she was out of sight, Ash said, "Whatever she's told you, don't believe it. The second she gets the chance, she and the Well are gone."

"Pardon?" Sergei said.

"What's she told you?" Ash said. "Intelligence Corps? Information Office? She doesn't work for anybody but herself." He shrugged. "The Well doesn't matter. Your bosses can have it."

"Of course," Sergei said.

"*Don't*, okay?" Ash growled.

Sergei wondered about Hansa. Maybe she really *was* a spook.

Hansa returned from the hidden cleft. She looked vaguely annoyed.

"Sometime on our trip back," Ash whispered. "Be ready."

"For what?" Sergei wondered aloud. Ash frowned.

Sergei had been hoping to escape. Now, though, he was beginning to realize that he was obliged to stay. By agreeing to the plot, he had risked lives. Discovery of these religious artifacts always led to carnage, as various flavors of nont'h extremists battled to control them and their religious meaning. Sergei had seen it before. The original plan was to get the Well off-planet before anybody knew it had been found. If they lost control—and these two clearly already had—innocent people were going to die.

He wished he had the slightest idea how to prevent the inevitable bloodbath.

☼

Hansa directed Ash to continue up. Sergei barely breathed as the all-trac bumped and groaned its way up the ever-narrowing trail. Only when it emerged into pale green scrub atop the plateau did he relax.

Another text scrolled his eyes: IO CALLS YOU PERSON OF INTEREST CAFE BOMBING. WHAT THE HELL ARE YOU UP TO. YOUR ACTIONS REFLECT ON THIS OFFICE.

Sergei just about choked. Hansa, sitting next to him in the back seat, asked if he was all right. Ash looked back and glowered.

At an intersection, Hansa pointed left, and they descended a narrow valley between steep slopes red with iron ore.

"Pre-war stores cache," she said. "Not on any maps. The Rats..."

"No," Ash said with a scowl.

"Sorry," Hansa said. "Ratalucon. Since nobody collected the cache, I'm guessing its owners met with a bad end."

Sergei wondered at Ash's reaction to the racial epithet. Maybe the Ratalucon were *not* just tools to him.

They stopped at the base of a jagged butte and entered a small cave on foot. Ash's light illuminated rows of stacked plastiform boxes, their sides stenciled with Hcniton characters. Hcniton, Sergei could read. These were boxes of military food rations, left over from the war. Useless to humans, with their independently evolved metabolism, but sustaining to the nont'h races.

"As we agreed," Hansa said. "All yours."

In the dim light, Sergei regarded Ash. If the food represented Hansa's payment for the Well, if Ash were making the deal as an extracurricular to his Spacearm duties—which Sergei strongly suspected—the man was risking his career, maybe a jail term, to feed his friends. Sergei found himself starting to like the bastard.

They lugged boxes into the all-trac, Sergei lagging as usual. The boxes weren't so much heavy as they were awkward, sized for long nont'h arms. His arms began to ache with the effort, though he never sweated, the dry Hcniton air robbing his body of moisture before he could feel it. He grew thirsty, but didn't want to ask for water.

Ash pulled out a communications headset. "Tango Alpha, this is Charlie Delta. We're going to need some transport." Then he said it again. And again.

What the hell? Sergei thought. He hadn't thought he could feel more nervous than he already was. He'd been wrong.

"Shoot," Ash said. The mildness of the interjection distracted Sergei from the profound worry in Ash's voice. Had something gone wrong? Sergei looked around nervously, seeing nothing, but feeling something bad was coming.

A spray of powder burst at their feet, showering them with bright orange dust. A dozen figures shimmered into sudden visibility as they turned off adaptive camouflage. They carried Ehrehnon weapons, and their adap smocks bore Ehrehnon military insignia.

"Your escort isn't coming," one of them said with a heavy accent. "Drop the weapons, or the next grenade won't be a practice round."

Grenade? Sergei thought, then realized that the powder must have sprayed from a projectile he hadn't seen. *Practice round* hadn't contained explosive, only powder to mark where it fell. *Real round* would have killed them all, he supposed with a chill.

Ash dropped his rifle, then the knife. Hansa pulled a compact needle pistol from the small of her back, and dropped it. Sergei held his hands out and up, gingerly, trying to look like the noncombatant he was, trying to look as little a threat as he was.

In Ehrehnon, the speaker said, "You search them, you are careful, lads."

Another text: RETURN TO CONSULATE OR RECONSIDER YOUR CAREER. NOT KIDDING, MISTER. Sergei stifled hysterical laughter. *Don't attract attention. Don't surprise anybody.*

As they patted down Sergei and his companions, several waving paddle-shaped units to detect and deactivate tracking chips, a final form materialized, wearing an officer's helmet. He walked to Hansa and held out a hand.

"Cohort Commander," Ash said. "This is a Spacearm operation. Please withdraw." Sergei wondered if Ash recognized him, or just his rank insignia.

The alien gave a toothy smile. Cat-slit yellow irises gleamed with merry evil. "I'm willing to accept that," he said, speaking Standard with an accent but no trace of the alien is-may-be syntax. "Yes, I do believe I can, tentatively at least, believe your assertion."

"My Lord," Ash said, speaking Standard but using the Ehrehnon term of respect, "you have a duty..."

"Duty isn't everything," the officer said. He held up a long, six-digit hand. "There is also *business*."

Sergei guessed what the officer was getting at. The Ehrehnon officer corps in the Ratalucon Province was a repository for the corrupt.

Ash scanned the horizon.

"We have your associates," the Ehrehnon said.

Ash sighed. "So what's it going to cost?"

"It's not so simple as fixing a price," the officer said. He extended his hand to Hansa. "We know what you are carrying."

Hansa and Ash looked at each other.

"An accommodation must be possible," she said.

The officer regarded her blandly. "An accommodation is always possible. We Ehrehnon are the *civilized* nont'h." Smile, broad, jagged-razor teeth.

Hansa could lay it on. Sergei had to give her that much. Even Ash's eyes widened as she spun a tale of a Hcniton military payroll in precious metals buried beneath a desert supply cache that was now an insurgency stronghold. She had the whereabouts, and the Cohort Commander had the troops necessary to push out its present occupants.

It *had* to be a lie. Still, the tale was barely credible.

"The Well may be worth more than your payroll," the Ehrehnon officer said.

"And it may not," she said. "Not every artifact is a weapon, my Lord, not every dream takes reality."

Most nont'h believed passionately in the power of their priests to manipulate dream worlds to visit vengeance upon their enemies. The Well of Ehcalt was one of the artifacts said to increase their power in dream. But not all nont'h were believers. The Ehrehnon officer smiled another ugly smile.

"My air transport lies on the other side of this valley," he said. "Kindly accompany us."

Two of his men drove the all-trac away. Everyone else walked.

The valley widened, into a forest of talus-skirted, tan-and-cinnamon-striated spires. Sergei had never dared going this far into the desert. Here, it was possible to dehydrate and die in a single day, assuming one survived the razorbushes, precipices, and occasional bear-like *s'lens* looking for an easy meal. Humans were indigestible to them, but unfortunately not inedible.

In the war's aftermath, Hcniton terrorist cells vied with a poorly regulated Ratalucon militia for control of the deep desert. The only humans who ventured this far were Special Corps toughs like Ash, carrying out "gray-hat" operations with the Ratalucon.

Lafontaine again: IO SAYS MAYBE YOURE A HOSTAGE. IS THIS TRUE. ANSWER DAMN IT.

Sergei spat, then regretted wasting even that much moisture. This was getting tiresome. For once, he was starting to get angrier at Lafontaine than at himself for putting up with her.

They traversed a furnace of earth tones, Sergei's legs starting to cramp with unfamiliar exercise. His mouth parched. A darkening, cloudless sky hung over striped rock formations. The dusty brown clay of a trail threaded around broad, loose-rock slopes at the feet of the spires, which stood against the sinking sun like dark sentinels.

The first laser-beam shriek took Sergei by surprise. Adrenalin pumped him alert, and he threw himself down. All around him, Ehrehnon shimmered into near-invisibility and fired back. Sergei covered his head with his hands against the flow and splatter of laser beams and impact grenades.

He'd wound up in the middle of a war.

Sergei wondered if he was dreaming, or dead. He recognized the moon—*the* Moon, Earth's companion—in the dark half of a sky split between the night constellations as he remembered them from Earth, and a blue firmament in which burned the too-yellow Hcniton sun.

A figure wavered into focus, a gaunt, old Ratalucon in the hide leggings and beaded shirt of a shaman. The alien's down was white, his eyes gray, and he smiled an awful, toothy nont'h smile.

"Greetings," the Ratalucon said in his own language—though it was, in the way of dreams, also Standard. "I am Kayakutnúl."

"This is nonsense," a voice said in Sergei's skull, as if from a mastoid 'link. But it was his own voice. "That dream business is opiate-of-the-masses stuff."

"When trouble comes," Kayakutnúl said, "you walk uphill. You find the grotto."

"There goes the neighborhood," said the voice in Sergei's head.

Sergei saw his captors and remembered where he was and what had happened. Hansa had made it through the ambush without a scratch. Ash hadn't fared so well. A blood-soaked dressing swathed one leg—sans foot, Sergie noted—and scrapes covered his arms and face. The Hcniton insurgents must have some further use for him, because they'd fixed a human-compatible Spacearm pain-pac, probably captured in a raid, to his calf.

The Ehrehnon commander was less lucky. He lay unconscious on the ground, breathing unevenly as a Hcniton med-tech tended a nasty burn in his chest.

A short—for a nont'h—Hcniton, only about two meters tall, approached. He wore the robes of a petty noble and carried an Earth-made rifle. A tech with flame-red head-down scanned them with a paddle, giving Sergei's chip yet another "off" signal.

"I ask who may have it," the noble said in Standard.

Ash glared. Hansa held her lips in a prim line. Sergei watched her, hoping for some cue of what to do.

"Ah," the noble said. His gaze shifted to Hansa.

Oops.

"It may be that my Lady has it—or knows where it is," the noble said. "You give it to us. This is a nont'h matter. It is not your business."

Hansa, glaring daggers at Sergei, pulled a blue bag from under her shirt.

The noble took it with both hands, holding it reverently as he opened the flap. He held up a broach, an, oval, blue stone set in a rim of silver patterned after oasis plants—*the Well, indeed.* The noble's cat eyes went wide as his lipless mouth gently fell open, revealing a maw of jagged tooth scales. This was no cynic, but a true believer.

An aide proffered a small, ornate chest, and the noble placed the Well inside. The aide closed the box and walked away.

The noble shot a murderous look at the humans. "In the morning we learn whether you may be useful as hostages." The alternative dangled before Sergei's imagination like a noose. Diplomatic corps policy was not to pay for hostages. Certainly, Lafontaine wouldn't go to the mat to make an exception for Sergei.

The noble left a few of his partisans standing at a distance to guard them.

Sergei felt like an idiot, and expected Hansa to say as much, but she said nothing. Ash worried him. The man just sat there holding a bloody stump and chuckling quietly to himself.

"Something wrong with him?" Sergei said.

"Oh, just thought of something funny," Ash said before Hansa could reply. "About your locator chip. And a device I have back in my hooch."

"The deactivator?" Sergei eyed their guards. He'd seen no indications they spoke Standard or understood what they were saying. The guards seemed disinterested, convinced the captives couldn't say anything that could help them, and were probably right. "I knew you turned my chip off."

"What *about* the deactivator?" Hansa whispered, coming closer. She was getting something that eluded Sergei.

"It's no simple chip-burner," Ash said. "I'm Special Corps, remember? I get the good stuff. My device doesn't wipe, it reprograms. A little failsafe. It doesn't just turn a chip off, but also changes the polarity of the 'on' command. That way, any attempts by third parties to inactivate it..."

"You mean the Hcniton just reactivated my chip?"

Ash smiled. "No, I mean the Ehrehnon reactivated your chip about six hours ago. The Hcniton just gave it a redundant 'on' signal."

Sergei frowned. He remembered turning the inactivation warning off. And he hadn't gotten a text from Lafontaine in a while. It made sense that the Information Office would have muzzled her. Clear channel, no unnecessary transmissions that might risk somebody noticing Sergei was back on line.

"So the Consulate knows where I am," Sergei said under his breath. "That's good, right?"

"Only if they don't kill us all trying to rescue you," Hansa said.

The attack came at first light. It was worse than the last one.

Sergei dimly recalled brilliant light and roaring noise, flying earth and wood chips. He remembered crawling across the ground, uphill for some reason, so gripped by cold terror he didn't care why.

He bellied into a shaded rock formation, a shallow grotto he hoped would hide him from fighters wandering up from the valley. Exhausted but too wired to sleep, he tried to think the situation through. The Consulate people would come looking for him. It wouldn't be anybody's choice: standard procedure, even Lafontaine would have no authority to prevent it, as bad a seed as they might think him.

Hell, they'd get him back if only to put him on trial.

It was some time before he realized he was not alone. Sitting next to him was the old Ratalucon shaman. Kayakutnúl, was it? A bag like the one Hansa wore was slung across his hip.

"You again," Sergei said.

"Greetings," Kayakutnúl replied.

"I haven't got the Well," Sergei said. "I don't know where it is."

The Ratalucon laughed a nont'h laugh, a hissing, pulsing thing that always gave Sergei the creeps. He handed Sergei a full canteen.

Sergei said "I thank you," in imperfect Ratalucon, and drank deeply. The luke-warm water energized him. "I've got a chip implant," he said in Standard. "My people will be looking for me."

Kayakutnúl shook his head, a very human gesture. He leaned back against the sandstone wall.

"You know what *does* bother me," Sergei said, looking down. "Ash had a truck-full of food for your village..."

A tap on his shoulder, and he looked at Kayakutnúl. The old man was holding a silver-and-blue-stone broach. *The Well.*

Sergei sat, dumbfounded, for a moment. "Do you think we could find Ash's all-trac? Trade it for the Well?"

Kayakutnúl nodded. "When the fighting dies, it may be safe that we do this."

"Damn," Sergei said. "I just realized; they'll come to pick me up before we can do anything."

Kayakutnúl produced a chip deactivator from his bag.

"That's quite a bag," Sergei said, suspicious now. But he offered his chipped shoulder anyway. "You have to reverse the signal to get it to turn off." He suspected the old Ratalucon already knew.

They'd made it about halfway to the battlefield when Hansa's voice challenged them from a rock formation just above.

"Hands up." She emerged from the rocks holding a military laser pistol. "And just where do you think you're headed?"

Sergei told her.

"No deal," she said. "If you think you can get that food shipment back, you're welcome to try. But you'll be doing it without the Well." She extended her hand, palm up.

"I won't get it off-planet for you," Sergei said.

She seemed unconcerned. "I'll find another way. Hand it over."

"Don't," Sergei said. It surprised him to hear such defiance in his voice. But Kayakutnúl was already giving up the Well. Sergei wanted to lash out, maybe steal the broach in mid-air, but he wasn't feeling *that* brave. Not with a pistol pointed in his direction.

Hansa showed little reaction—just a slight flaring of nostrils—as she snapped up the artifact with her left hand.

"And don't give me that superior look," she said to Sergei, snapping her eyes in his direction as she extended her left hand for the Well. "You're not so far from being me. They tell you you're the best of the best when they ship you here—until they don't need you any more. Then you're on your own. No way to make an honest living. Sure as hell no way to raise enough for the trip home."

Clutching the Well tightly, she waved the pistol with her other hand, backed away, and then disappeared into the underbrush.

Dejected, Sergei sank to the ground. Nobody gave a damn about whether Ratalucon kids ate, not while there were historic baubles to inspire mayhem.

A tap on his shoulder. He turned. Kayakutnúl held out a silver-set, blue oval-shaped gem. Sergei choked. He wasn't sure if he was laughing or retching; but whatever it was, the spasm lasted a good, long time.

And he understood.

Few people chasing the Well believed in its mystic powers—and yet it was even less genuine than they imagined. How many counterfeits had the old shaman had put into circulation, how many spies, traitors, and assorted rogues had the old fraudster flushed out in that process?

The shaman's mouth was widening, widening, into an impossibly broad smile filled with terrifying, jagged tooth-scales. Sergei didn't care whose side Kayakutnúl was on, he just had to give the old guy 10 points out of 10 for style.

He and Kayakutnúl tracked Ash's vehicle to a heavily camouflaged camp. The Heniton partisans were more than willing to trade for the fake Well, and clearly thought they were getting the best of the deal.

Kayakutnúl stayed hidden in the rocks while Sergei worked out the exchange. It was easy. He'd translated lots of negotiations with the Hcniton.

Lafontaine remained suspicious about Sergei's absence, but the official inquiry was mercifully fast and didn't turn up anything incriminating. As far as anybody knew, Sergei had been a terrorist's kidnap victim. Lafontaine had to pretend to let it drop.

For the first couple of days, it looked like business as usual. Then a voice—Ash's voice—intruded into the datafeed of Sergei's mastoid speakers.

"Sergei. It's me."

"How's the new foot?" Sergei said.

"Itches like hell. Don't talk. Only my end is untraceable. You wanted to buy a well for a village. I have an idea for getting one..."

That afternoon, Sergei resolved that things were going to change.

"I wanted to talk to you about that bloc of development grants," he said, walking into Lafontaine's office uninvited, which she hated. "I've put through the paperwork for a census spot-check."

Lafontaine opened her mouth as if to say something. He watched as the twin realizations hit her. First, that he'd already sent the paperwork—a pain in the ass to recall—and second, that he didn't care what she thought and wasn't going to pretend he did.

"All right," she grumbled. "Just let me know next time, okay?"

Sergei smiled, but didn't nod. Maybe he'd take Ash's next offer of assistance—he suspected one would come. But the well? He was going to cram that down Lafontaine's throat, all by himself.

It proved to be a long week. Work had piled up in his absence.

Ken Chiacchia*'s bio reads like a random sampling of events from different people's lives. A defrocked biochemist from a defunct department, he has since been a public relations writer, freelance newspaper reporter, science fiction author, wilderness EMT and search-and-rescue dog handler, firefighter, radio commentator, and hobby farmer. Ken's writing and editing have won multiple platinum Hermes Creative Awards from the Association of Marketing and Communications Professionals. He*

won two Golden Quill Awards from the Press Club of Western Pennsylvania, for Best Writing and Best Commentary, and shared a third for Best Commentary. He also won the 2008 Carnegie Science Center Journalism Award. His speculative fiction credits include Cicada, Paradox, Oceans of the Mind, and Triangulation. He was a nominee for the 2007 Rhysling Award for SF poetry. In an unlikely turn, he's recently rejoined the research community, publishing on the effectors of wilderness search in the peer-reviewed journal Wilderness & Environmental Medicine. Ken lives with his wife, dog trainer and writer Heather Houlahan, and an assorted cloud of canine partners and fosters, barn cats, chickens, turkeys, ducks, and goats, on a 26-acre farm in Harmony, Pa.

Floorboards

By Christopher Nadeau

What is a speculative fiction anthology without a little horror? Enter Christopher Nadeau ("The Party," Last Contact), and this deliciously morbid tale of a man, his house, and an infestation of very thirsty... things.

They were awake again. Scratching, biting, trying to come up through the floor. No sound drowned them out, no amount of mental discipline silenced their thirsty demands. They were too insistent, too ravenous, to be ignored.

It was difficult to remember how long they'd been down there. Benedict often thought it had always been like this; those *things* trapped in the bowels of this great old house while he stood guard, the one and only buffer between their destructive power and humanity.

Humanity.

What choice did he have? Benedict was to blame.

He hardly remembered a time when he'd done anything besides help them drink. The creatures needed someone to bring them their "water" and beneath the floorboards, with their moaning and growling, they formed the word "Drink" as if speaking directly to their god.

Bile stung his throat as he considered that possibility. *Please don't tell me those things worship me!*

He rolled out of bed and barely made it to the bathroom sink, vomiting into it and all over his pajamas. The sound of the constantly running toilet reminded him of better times, good-natured arguments resulting in his wife imploring him to please fix that darn toilet. He reached under the bowl and turned off the water.

For a moment, a brief one, Benedict heard nothing. The silence was wonderful, comforting, and he became lost inside its stillness. Here he could remember those nights with his wife when they simply held each other, when the only sound was the gentle insistence of their unborn child's heartbeat. How he longed for those dimly remembered moments.

Benedict walked gingerly back to his bedroom and opened the dresser drawer for a clean pajama top. Shivering, he headed back to bed and buried his face in his pillow. *I will not allow them to feed again. They will starve. They will wither to dust and their existence will be a painful memory easily drowned by liquor.*

His mind would not be silent as the thoughts continued bombarding him. *They're my responsibility. They have been ever since...*

He refused to finish. It would take him to places stored deep within, dark, horrible realms of memory best not acknowledged. For he had seen them feed.

The following morning, he forced himself to go downstairs and look at the floorboards. They didn't seem different at first glance, but when he stepped on one it bowed beneath his weight and creaked. Benedict stepped on and off a few more times, dreading the looseness underneath.

They're figuring it out.

He rubbed goosefleshed forearms and stared down, wondering if he should just do what the policeman advised so long ago, burn the old place to the ground. But he hadn't been able to go through with it and, in those final moments that test resolve, he'd betrayed the poor officer to the obscenity below.

This old house was all Benedict had left of his former life, the normalcy he once took for granted. Everywhere was a reminder, from the dented wall to the toilet that never seemed to stop running.

This house will be my tomb.

It would also be theirs.

Once the idea took hold, it became an unshakable force with harsh realization as its unwavering companion. He couldn't hold out much longer; the creatures' thirst would not be denied forever.

I wish the policeman was here. I wish I hadn't let them drink him. It wasn't too late to make things right.

Benedict went to the old detached garage and pulled up on the door for the first time in who knew how long. Dust and mold and thick cobwebs greeted him as he entered and searched for the gasoline cans he'd once used for normal things like filling the lawnmower. There were five two-gallon cans. More than enough.

By sundown he had not only bordered the house with gasoline, but slathered the first floor as well. One flick of a match was all it would take to…

"*Drrriiinnnkkk.*"

The scritch-scratching at the floorboards became more desperate. Did they suspect? A floorboard jumped, the creature beneath pounding over and over until the slat flew into the air and landed somewhere outside Benedict's vision. A claw emerged and dug into the floor.

Fumbling for matches, Benedict let out a whimper as another floorboard came loose. He pulled the matches free and dropped them as yet another floorboard went airborne. By the time he'd retrieved the matchbook, three creatures had emerged, claws extended, fangs click-clacking. They crawled towards him.

He recoiled at the sight: orb-like heads resting atop thick necks that seemed incapable of movement, eyes of pure obsidian that somehow displayed expression, and tiny, perfectly round mouths filled with rows and rows of razor-sharp teeth. Their claws dragged along the floorboards, leaving marks as they went, stooped bodies obscuring their true height. They shambled forward as one, as if sharing a single purpose. And of course, they did.

"*Drrriiinnnkkk,*" the one in the middle said.

Don't say it, he thought. *Don't say the other word.*

Hand shaking, he barely struck the match against the flint. The match head flared with blue flame.

"I can't do this anymore," Benedict whispered. "I'm sorry. I'm so very—"

The middle one cocked its head. "Daddy?"

No. Where did it learn that word?

Unwanted memories pour over him. His wife screaming, clutching her belly, dropping to the floor; floorboards creaking beneath the strain; water breaking, Benedict slipping, his head hitting the floor; that woozy vision of the first of them clawing out of her, blood, so much blood; the normal world fading away...

*...awaking to them feeding on her, looking at Benedict as if he were their lord and master. No, not feeding...*drinking*. Suckling his wife's fluids her using mouths, perfect circles rimmed with dozens and dozens of teeth.*

And the sound, the endless, tireless slurping sound, as if all she had been was being sucked through a straw. His dead wife's eyes stared at him. "We did this, Benedict Both of us."

Benedict looks down at her pale, drained body, laid out in the coffin; he remembers what the funeral director said about not needing to remove anything before adding the embalming fluid. His puzzled, disturbed facial expression haunts Benedict even now. How was such a thing possible?

And he thought then as he thinks now, "My children...my thirsty children."

Benedict stood between them, their insatiable thirst, their worship.

"*Driiink, Daddy!*"

He stared into the eyes of the one that spoke, match momentarily forgotten. He cried out as the flame reached his finger. The creatures held his gaze, still imploring, still thirsty.

Knowing the guilt of his next move would follow him to the end of his days, Benedict blew out the match and tossed it to the floor. Daddy would find something—some*one*—to drink.

***Christopher Nadeau** is the author of Dreamers at Infinity's Core through COM Publishing and over two dozen published short stories in such august publications as The Horror Zine, Sci-Fi Short Story Magazine, Ghostlight Magazine and more anthologies than one could take out with a hand grenade. He was interviewed by*

Suspense Radio's up and coming authors program and collaborated on two "machinima" films with UK animator Celestial Elf called The Gift, and The Deerhunter's Tale, both of which can be viewed on YouTube. He received positive mention from Ramsey Campbell for his short story "Always Say Treat," compared to the work of Ray Bradbury and has received positive reviews from SFRevue and zombiecoffeepress. Chris has served as special editor for Voluted Magazine's The Darkness Internal which he created. His novel Kaiju was recently released through Source Point Press and Echoes of Infinity's Core is slated for 2014 release. A former member of the Great Lakes Association of Horror Writers and a current member of the Dark Fiction Writers Guild, Chris Resides in Southeastern Michigan with his wife Lorie and two petulant long-hair Chihuahuas.

A Fine Selection of Wines and Poisons

By John A. Frochio

John's submissions have come close before. He is a man of intriguing ideas and characters, but past stories have not quite come together for us. This one did. Prepare yourself for a fine repast as a crosstime detective very nearly meets his match.

Crosstime Detective Emile Gerdau arrived moments after the poisoning of Sir Talbot Cabot. He handed the widow his card.

"Oh, would you have appeared but three minutes sooner, my husband would not be dead!" wailed the Lady Cassandra.

"You know that could not be, my poor lady," he said. "The irrevocable forces of time and space would not allow it. No time traveler can enter or exit an event of any significance." He raised a hand to his mouth and coughed. His mustache was in desperate need of a trim. "These are the checks and balances that time mandates."

Lady Cassandra sighed. "All that time gobbledygook goes over my head."

"Allow me to worry about such details," Emile said smoothly. He took her fingers into his hand and kissed them. "I am sorry for your loss." Always the gentlemen, he looked quite dapper in his white suit and bright pink tie, top hat and cane. Wisps of gray crept from underneath his hat.

Lady Cassandra squeezed his hand. She was a striking beauty for her age, partly natural, partly the handiwork of skilled doctors. Her hair was full and golden blonde, her features soft and thin. She wore a low-cut gown with a plethora of lace and floral embellishments.

Emile pulled his tablet from a pocket, and glanced through an archway to the dining room, where several guests paced nervously while others remained frozen in their seats. Many chattered into cell phones.

"Have the police been contacted?" he said, returning his attention to Lady Cassandra.

"Yes. Just seconds before you arrived."

Emile nodded. "As you may or may not be aware, I was brought to this event because an anomaly has disturbed the natural order of time and space. My investigation may uncover the murderer, but that is not why I am here." He could say he was there for a greater purpose, but that would be insensitive under the circumstances.

He strode past Lady Cassandra into the dining room. "May I have your attention please? I will need to interview each of you while this unfortunate event is fresh in your minds. Please consider this a separate investigation from the police, as they will also need to interview you." He coughed again. The air was inordinately dry. His gaze fell to the nearly empty glass of dark purple liquid in front of the deceased.

"This was what he was drinking before he died so unexpectedly?" He stepped closer and leaned down to examine the glass.

A well-dressed, middle-aged man several inches taller than the other guests spoke up: "Yes, a Cabernet Sauvignon from his own extensive collection of fine wines. His wine and poison cellar is the envy of many, myself included."

"I told him it was a bad idea, to mix the two," Lady Cassandra said. "I told him it would end badly."

Emile dipped a gloved finger into the liquid, then lifted it to his nose and sniffed. The smell was sweet with a nutty undertone. He touched the glove to a slot in his bulky belt. Lights flashed. A moment later a card popped out. He plucked it and read the analysis.

"As I suspected, a rather rare nano-engineered nerve blocking poison has been introduced into this fine wine. Nanoblock 480. Does this poison happen to be in your late husband's collection?"

Lady Cassandra's eyes glazed over. "I don't know."

The butler, a meticulously groomed man with a mustache, stepped forward. "Sir Talbot has an extensive selection of nerve blockers in his cellar."

"Very good," Emile said. "Shall we begin?" He triaged the guests into groups, and started the interview process.

Sir Donald and Gayle Petri, old friends of Sir Talbot, were visiting from America, a vacation combined with a business trip. Lady Cassandra's sister Miranda and brother Henry lived with their sister, essentially freeloading off Sir Talbot's generosity. Pastor Arnold Dennison was here for a free meal. Doctor Samuel Birch, family physician (the one who had spoken up earlier), was also a highly regarded research biologist and longtime friend of the family. Young, single, ambitious Gaylord Winslow was Sir Talbot's business associate, a normally soft-spoken fellow who valued his privacy and independence. Lamar Wallace, the butler, was a long time employee of Sir Talbot's. Young Chelsea Rosenberg, the maidservant, was somewhat anxious and pre-occupied. Lady Cassandra herself was prim, proper and calm, but her emotions were clearly wearing her down into a state of numb shock.

Chelsea led the police into the dining room as Emile finished his interviews. Emile's old acquaintance, Police Captain Butch Gebhart, led a team of five police officers and a forensic specialist. The officers' faces clearly displayed annoyance when they noticed his presence. They knew Emile by his reputation as well as his ubiquitousness. Captain Gebhart, however, kept his battle-worn face indifferent.

Emile asked if he might be excused with the butler for a few minutes. Captain Gebhart, well aware of Emile's authority and therefore having no real choice, nodded.

"Take me to Sir Talbot's cellar," Emile told the butler.

He followed the servant through a long corridor, a door, and down a double flight of steps. The butler powered up a handheld lantern at the bottom and led him to a large oak door. He unlocked it, and the door pulled grudgingly open. Dampness and a strong musty odor slammed into Emile like the jolt you get when you run up against an important event in time.

The cellar held rows of dusty shelves filled with bottles of all shapes, sizes and colors. There were no labels, which seemed strange to Emile, since wines and poisons were stored in the same location. Furthermore, the two were intermixed. Emile recognized Chardonnay, Belladonna, Pinot Noir, Aconite, Merlot, Cyanide, Beaujolais, Arsenic, Shiraz, and Hemlock.

There were a few blank spaces among the rows of colorful glass. Emile counted three whose pattern of dust and clean shelf indicated recent removal.

"Can you identify the missing bottles?" he said.

The butler shook his head. "Sir Talbot kept a complete inventory, but he allowed no one other than himself to retrieve wines or poisons. I don't know where he kept the inventory list."

"I will have to search his private belongings. Does he have a safe or safety deposit box?"

"A safe in his bedroom," the butler said. "That's all that I'm aware of."

As they returned to the cellar entrance, Emile spotted an orange marker pointing to the top of an old wooden cupboard. Only he could see the marker, since it required special iris enhancement contact lenses.

"Could you get me a stepstool or small ladder?" he asked the butler.

An orange marker indicated a clue of moderate value planted by a crosstime detective—most likely himself. He could not assume that it was him, since any of his colleagues might have taken over the case at any point in time for any reason.

The butler returned with a three-legged stool. After positioning the stool next to the cupboard, Emile stepped up and peeked over the top of the cupboard.

"Dust," he said, "nothing but dust." He saw a small baggie, and picked it up. It looked to be filled with... dust.

"Fascinating," he grumbled.

He hated spoon-fed clues, but time was a harsh dictator. Intrusions into its natural course were strictly prohibited. Only the subtlest disturbances were tolerated. In the *Crosstime Traveler's Handbook* it was called the Traumatic Exclusion Principle. Those who attempted to intrude too aggressively were temporally pushed past the critical event, sometimes a few hours or days, sometimes into a future so far that the crosstime traveler was never seen again. When leaving clues, it was better to err on the side of caution.

"Dust," he said again as they mounted the stairs. He managed to suppress a tickle in his throat. "Curious. I wonder why the air is so dry in this house."

"Sir Talbot was a germophobe," the butler said. "An AntiBacterium Ionization System constantly cleans the air of particles and bacteria, which causes it to become dry. To compensate, a state of the art humidifier system was installed to keep the house humidified with bacteria-free water vapor. I change the filter once a month." He sniffed. "However, you are right. It's very dry, yet I changed the filter only two days ago."

"Could you show me these systems?" Emile said.

"Certainly, sir."

☼

The ionization and humidifier system filled most of a small basement room, leaving little walking space between cabinets and tanks. The butler disconnected a breaker and popped open a cover.

A cloud of dust burst from the opening. Choking and covering their faces, they backed quickly away. When the cloud dissipated, the butler stepped forward and yanked out the filter. More dirt poured onto the floor.

"I don't understand how it could have gotten so dirty," he said.

"Exactly! Someone must have swapped the new filter with a dirty filter, and it appears they added even more dirt."

"Why would they do that?"

"To create a dry, dusty climate. Does Sir Talbot have respiratory issues, perchance? Asthma? Emphysema? COPD?"

"Sir Talbot suffered from severe asthma."

"This was well known?"

"Yes."

"And he took medicine, an inhaler?"

"Yes." The butler held the dirty filter away from his pants. "Do you need this, sir?"

"Lean it against the wall," Emile said. It was possible there would be fingerprints other than the butler's, but he doubted it. The murderer would have worn gloves.

"If you'll pardon me," the butler said, "I'll get a new filter. Unless, of course, you're finished here."

Emile shook his head. "Let me look around a bit."

"Of course." The butler left him alone.

Emile methodically inspected the room and found another orange marker. Another moderate level clue. Following its lead, he squeezed behind a hot water tank and found a clean filter. A smattering of garbage indicated it had been pulled out of a trash can or dumpster. He shook off the loose garbage, and held it out as the butler returned, still unwrapping a new filter from its packaging.

"I'll need this for evidence," Emile said.

"Of course, sir." He replaced the dirty filter with the one he had brought, and they returned to the dining room.

Emile handed the discovered filter to police captain Gebhart. "You may want to fingerprint this, though I suspect you won't find anything. And there's another in the basement, in case your man gets bored. Do you have a suspect?"

"No standouts," Captain Gebhart said. "Everyone had a motive, just like in an Agatha Christie novel. The Petri's lost a fortune in business dealings with Sir Talbot. He treated Miranda and Henry with open disdain. He belittled and mocked the Pastor. Sir Talbot nixed many of Gaylord's investment ideas. Doctor Birch was called to his home constantly. His widow no longer slept with him." He slipped his phone into a pocket. "Do you have leads on your time anomaly?"

"Nothing yet," Emile said. "I have one more place to check out and then we can put our heads together."

"Thank you."

Emile long ago discovered his job became less stressful and more productive when he worked *with* the local authorities rather than against them.

He said to the butler, "Take me to Sir Talbot's safe."

"This way, sir."

In Sir Talbot's bedroom, Emile discovered another orange marker on the binding of a particular book in his bookshelf, a collector's edition of Homer's *Odyssey*. He found a series of numbers on the last page, went to the wall safe, and punched them in. The safe popped open.

It held important personal and business papers, passports and a folded document in a sterling silver case. Emile removed the document from its case and unfolded it carefully. The page depicted a rectangular room like the wine and poison cellar. And indeed, there was a top-down grid with callouts to vertical shelving units in the margins. Shelves were notated with the names of wines and poisons written by hand in black marker. This could be the key he was looking for. He captured an image to his tablet, and returned the original to the safe.

"Back to the cellar," he said.

"Yes, sir."

Emile compared the map to recently removed bottle locations: two bottles of Cabernet Sauvignon and one of Nanoblock 480.

"Lamar?"

"Sir?"

"You've worked for Sir Talbot a long time. You must be a loyal servant."

"Yes, sir. He was generous and kind toward his servants, but he did demand much in return."

"What can you tell me that is not common knowledge?"

The butler hesitated. "Well, I guess it won't matter now. This was bound to come out. Sir Talbot and Doctor Birch have been involved in a great scientific experiment. The doctor has been injecting nano-implant enhancements into Sir Talbot's body for many years. Over time his body was converted into a poison antidote factory, with the antidotes easily extracted from blood samples."

Emile gaped. "That is astonishing."

The butler shrugged. "In addition to synthesizing remedies, Sir Talbot could absorb poisons and neutralize their effect. Over time, he and the doctor effectively made him immune to most."

"Apparently not all," Emile said.

"He was immune to the poison in his drink."

Emile nodded. "I suspected you were holding something back. Is there a definitive list of the poisons to which he was immune?"

"Yes," the butler said. "I was the only one he felt he could confide in. Not even Lady Cassandra knew. She never took much interest in his life, never questioned the doctor's frequent visits."

"An autopsy will find the true cause of his death," Emile said.

"They will find many poisons, sir, but the actual cause may never be certain." The butler hung his head.

"Is there more you have not told me, Lamar?"

The butler sighed. "Yes, sir. It was common for him to test his poison antidotes on guests."

"What?" Genuine surprise was something Emile seldom experienced, but he felt it now. This was an incredible and despicable revelation.

"He introduced small doses of poisons in drinks," the butler said. "Only enough to make them sick. Then he gave them the antidote in whatever medicine he offered. Many have unknowingly contributed to his research."

"Could someone have discovered this and decided to put an end to him?"

"I wouldn't know, sir."

"I'm merely speculating. Was he testing antidotes this evening?"

"I don't know," the butler said, "but it wouldn't surprise me."

They returned to the dining room. The guests were even more agitated now. Most were in various stages of pacing, grumbling and complaining.

"You must tell the police everything you know," he said. The butler nodded and approached Captain Gebhart.

Emile went to a corner of the room to ponder his accumulated information: First, what, where and when was the time anomaly? Did it have anything to do with Sir Talbot's murder? *Was* it a murder or had his unscrupulous experimentation finally backfired on him? Second, which clues came from his past persona and which from now? How did they fit? Did he miss one? More?

Something did not add up.

As far as the murder went, there were several individuals with motives, but who would know what could actually kill Sir Talbot? Probably only the doctor and butler, and *they* didn't have an obvious motive.

Plus, if the butler was correct about Sir Talbot's immunities, it was unlikely the poisoned wine had killed him. Where else could he have ingested a deadly toxin? The choking manner of death suggested foul play.

The asthma inhaler! The murderer had orchestrated a dry climate, which would encourage guests to drink, but Sir Talbot would also need his inhaler.

Emile approached a young officer who held an evidence bag. He said, "May I ask if you have an asthma inhaler among your items of interest?"

The officer frowned and hesitated. Emile was about to quote the pertinent rule regarding jurisdiction of crosstime detectives when the officer reached into the bag and handed him the instrument.

Emile sprayed a sample into the slot in his belt. Moments later an analysis came back. Flashing red: "Unknown substance."

He sprayed a second sample and ordered a spectroscopic elemental analysis. The elements were similar in concentration to a fast-acting gaseous poison that caused the trachea to close up. Perhaps it worked faster than Sir Talbot's body could produce an antidote.

Emile synthesized the information. It was a new poison administered by someone who must have known it would take a new poison to kill Sir Talbot, preferably one that affected his breathing and acted quickly. It seemed clear that whoever had done this must be well versed in biochemistry.

The esteemed Doctor Birch! Emile glanced at the doctor sitting quietly at end of the table, aloof to the mayhem around him. According to the butler, Doctor Birch had been vital to Sir Talbot's poison antidote experiments. Perhaps Sir Talbot was preventing the doctor from unveiling his research to the scientific community and reaping the many rewards it might bring. That was a viable motive, making Doctor Birch a viable murder suspect.

All fine and good, but what about the real reason for his presence? What time anomaly had occurred? What went amiss in time and space? How? Why? And how might he correct it?

He coughed. And again. And again.

What's this? His mouth felt dry. How long had the humidifier been working with the new filter? Shouldn't the dryness be easing? He had found the dirty filter, but hadn't really checked the humidifier. What if the dirt hadn't been used to just filthy the filter, but to clog the humidifier as well?

Others were coughing too. Several reached for their drinks. Emile scanned the room. The maid was gathering up silverware and plates, but the butler was nowhere to be found. He frowned. A faint acrid smell burned his nostrils. His belt beeped. *Airborne toxin.* Something was very wrong. He looked around frantically for answers, clues, anything.

There! A red marker, a clue of high value, posted beside a cabinet across the room. Why hadn't he noticed it before? He hurried to the cabinet and peeked inside. *Gas masks?* He whipped the door open.

"Quick, everyone grab a mask!"

He grabbed one and stepped out of the way. He quickly put it in place, and then took another, ran to Captain Gebhart, and handed it to him.

"Gas in the ventilation system," he said. "We must find the butler."

Captain Gebhart, to his credit, reacted immediately. With a wave he directed two officers in one direction and joined Emile in the other.

"Cellar," Emile said. His voice was muffled. He hurried down the stairs to the cellar, trusting the good captain to follow.

The sound of smashing glass greeted them as they exited the stairway. Emile ripped off his mask. His belt was no longer flashing. Captain Gebhard followed his example.

Captain Gebhart drew his weapon and stretched his arm in front of Emile to hold him back. They approached warily. Emile pressed his back to the wall beside the cellar door. Captain Gebhart took position opposite him. Inside, the sound of smashing glass intensified.

Captain Gebhart peered around the doorway.

"What's he doing?" Emile said.

"Smashing bottles." Captain Gebhart frowned. "Tell me your theory, Emile. The sound bite version. I want to know what we're getting into."

Emile nodded. "Forgive me the cliché, but the butler did it. He told me half truths. Sir Talbot was experimenting with a poison antidote factory, but it's the butler who has the nano implant." Being fearful of germs, Sir Talbot would never have used his own body, nor would he have disposed of the filter with his own hands. "Doctor Birth designed the implant, but was sworn to secrecy. He was in it for the glory of the research."

"I think I follow you," Captain Gebhart said. "The good doctor and Sir Talbot were in cahoots and this butler fellow...?" Another bottle smashed. The butler laughed maniacally.

"The butler had no choice but become Sir Talbot's human guinea pig," Emile said. "Until he had enough, that is. He poisoned Sir Talbot first and fast, and then he planned to poison the doctor and every other witness in the room afterwards."

"What was his plan once everyone was dead?"

"I don't know for certain," Emile said, "but I suspect the power of his enhancement went to his head. He hid it well, but I should have seen the clues. His schemes were clearly grandiose. I suspect the butler's rise to power initiated the time anomaly. I am not certain about that part yet."

"There," Captain Gebhart said. "What's he doing?"

Emile risked a glimpse. The butler had come into view between two shelving units and was drinking great gulps from each bottle he grabbed, before throwing it to the cement floor.

"Expanding his immunity, I should think," Emile said. He watched with fascination as the butler quickly identified and picked out specific bottles. "He knows the location of every bottle he wants to consume."

"What do we do?" Captain Gebhart said.

"Stop him?" Emile said. There was a mad gleam in the butler's eyes, but he did not seem particularly violent, beyond smashing bottles. When he smashed the bottles, it was with the vigor of a celebratory victory.

"Stop me?" the butler said. "Stop me? I doubt that. I'm unstoppable." He raised his arms and dropped to his knees, heedless of the glass shards blanketing the floor. Liquid soaked into his pants.

Captain Gebhart holstered his gun, leapt into the room, and tackled the butler in one fluid motion. They wrestled briefly, but it was really no contest. The butler was not a physically formidable man. Footsteps sounded on the stairs, and two officers arrived, guns in hand.

The butler laughed as he was handcuffed. "I am invincible!" he screamed. He continued to laugh as Captain Gebhart's men led him away. Once they were gone, Emile pulled out his tablet and took inventory of the butler's damage.

He had consumed every poison in the cellar. There were only wines left.

☼

Later, Emile sat with Captain Gebhart in the dining room, now cleared out. Emile enjoyed the peace and quiet.

"So, Emile, this case appears to have caused you more consternation than usual. Have you figured it all out?"

"Mostly," Emile said. "Perhaps I'm getting too old for this stress and should retire. Let the young ones take over."

"I think about that myself sometimes," Captain Gebhart said.

Emile sighed. "I believe it boils down to the butler's mad aspirations for world domination. Something snapped in his brain, probably triggered by that poison antidote factory in his body. It changed him. Doctor Birch developed the biotechnology. Sir Talbot funded him and provided the test subjects. He apparently harbored no ethical concerns about what he was doing to the butler's physiology and mental state."

"Not all men are capable of sympathy," Captain Gebhart said. Emile nodded, having seen ample evidence of that assertion.

"The butler came to hate his master," Emile said. "He came to hate the doctor. Eventually, his hatred grew to encompass everyone in Sir Talbot's circle, his wife, his business associates, his friends. This ultimately led to his mad plot to kill them all."

"And us with them," Captain Gebhart muttered.

"Sir Talbot was killed first from the poisonous gas in the inhaler. The doctor had to die too because he knew about their great experiment. From there it escalated. The butler wanted no witnesses." Emile scratched his chin. "I'm still not certain about the time anomaly, however. What was it exactly? When did it occur: in the past, present, or future? Did I correct it by identifying Sir Talbot's murderer? Did keeping one of the guests alive do the trick? Or have I not corrected the anomaly at all?"

"But you will know when it has been corrected?"

"Yes, at some point, I will know."

The Captain offered his hand. "Well, Emile, I'd better get going. It's been a long day."

"Yes." Emile accepted the captain's handshake. "It's funny how I was able to save everyone except Sir Talbot. Perhaps time understands justice after all."

"I would like to believe that," Captain Gebhart said. He let himself out.

Emile stood, still uneasy about the anomaly. A sudden twinge of a headache came and went. He leaned against the table. Maybe he had moved too quickly.

Lady Cassandra entered the room.

Emile bowed. "Again, my condolences for your loss, dear lady."

"Thank you," she said. "Fortunately, my husband left me a sizeable estate. I'll not be destitute."

"He did amass quite a fortune," Emile said. "As well as an excellent and well-stocked wine and poison cellar."

Lady Cassandra's brows pulled together. "Wine and poison? Who would keep poisons with their wines? What a ludicrous idea."

"Of course," Emile said. "I don't know why I said that. Poison on the brain I guess. Well, I must be going." He kissed Lady Cassandra's fingers and left.

Although the murder case was solved, he still needed to resolve the question of whether or not the time anomaly had been corrected. He would probably find the answer in the past. And then he would fix it. Or maybe he already fixed it. Or maybe he would fix it some other time. *Whatever.*

Regardless, he had plenty of work yet to do. He had to get those clues planted in the past while they were still fresh in his mind. How many markers were there again?

***John Frochio** is a curious study in juxtapositions: a clean-cut Christian country boy from Western Pennsylvania injected with a healthy dose of nerdlike quirkiness. His favorite things include sf&f, rock music, travel, and bizarre humor. For a living he develops and installs computer automation systems for steel mills. A member of Pittsburgh Worldwrights, he has stories in Triangulation 2003, Interstellar Fiction, and Kraxon Magazine, as well as general fiction novel Roots of a Priest (with Ken Bowers, 2007) and sf&f collection Large and Small Wonders (2012). His wife Connie, retired nurse, and his daughter Toni, flight attendant, have bravely put up with his strange ways for many years.*

The Straw-Mother

By Jamie Lackey

Jamie ("Protection from the Darkness," Morning After) brings a unique perspective to her work, and this story is no exception. Prepare to be wowed.

When it rains, she walks with face bare into the wet wind. Her straw stuffing soaks and plumps and her burlap skin smoothes and knits. The resentment in her dusty heart unspools and floats away like clumps of dandelion seeds in the river.

She leaves pans sticky in the sink, laundry piled on the floor (she doesn't know why it is so hard to toss it in the hamper), cups scattered throughout the house—glass unpolished, shelves undusted, floors scuffed and sullied—and she walks in the rain. When the drops slow, she stretches out in a meadow filled with tiny white flowers that only bloom in the moments after a shower. She breathes their scent as the last gray clouds scuttle toward the horizon.

She goes back to her work refreshed. She smiles at the family's hungry faces and whips potatoes and carves the roast and juliennes thin strips of carrots and bakes the fluffiest of cakes.

Spring falls into muddy memory, and diamond-bright summer days string together, each dryer than the last. Not even wispy white clouds touch the hard blue sky or filter the golden-hot sun. She cooks and cleans and tidies. Counters gleam and glasses glisten. She puts fresh flowers in crystal vases that paint false rainbows on the walls. She makes sandwiches and wraps them in waxed paper, then later finds the papers crumbled in a corner, crumbs ground into the rug, a pair of ants creeping along the wall. She has asked them a million times not to leave crumbs, to put garbage in the bin, to put dishes in the sink. She finds another ant in the bottom of a coffee mug, swimming in thick black sludge.

Her limbs crackle when she hauls the rug out to beat it with her broom. Her fingertips fray as she scrubs down walls, her straw slips out and floats with the ant in gray dishwater.

While the family is away she soaks in the copper washing tub—just climbs in with the linens and they swirl around her like ghosts. The water soaks in, but doesn't soothe the ache. She drags herself out, heavy and disappointed. Worry edges out resentment in her sun-baked heart. What will happen if it doesn't rain?

She pulls bread from the oven, and sparks settle along her arms, smoking spots. Flame soon licks her wrists. She runs to the sink to douse them. The water hisses.

She takes to wearing long sleeves. The scent of smoke trails her.

No one notices.

Her joints ache and lock and her limbs snap and creak as she moves. Dust bunnies gather in the corners. Ants creep in at the baseboards.

The father frowns and shakes his head sadly. He leaves his coffee cup on his nightstand, and she leaves it there as well. Soon, the surface is crowded.

Three course meals shrink to salads and fruit. Touching the oven dial fills her with dread. She makes toast and spreads butter and jam in thick layers. The family grimace and pull bits of snapped-off straw from of their teeth.

The boys smear jam on the wall, and the ants rejoice. The father knocks a coffee cup over. It cracks against the dirty floor. He yells and threatens, and she cowers. But he seems far away. It is hard to focus through dusty eyes. She spends the night in the rocking chair, banned from her bed.

The sun rises, bright and clear in a cloudless sky. She stands, and her straw snaps with every movement. Burlap unravels as her feet scrape the ground.

She finds the meadow dry and brown and hot, almost unrecognizable. She falls in the dust, then rolls onto her crinkling back. Ants crawl inside her collar, carry away bits of broken straw.

The straw mother stares up at the sky and waits for rain.

Jamie Lackey *lives in Pittsburgh with her husband and cat. Her fiction has appeared in Daily Science Fiction, Beneath Ceaseless Skies, and the Stoker Award-winning After Death. She's a member of the Science Fiction and Fantasy Writers of America. Her short story collection, One Revolution, is available on Amazon.com. Find her online at www.jamielackey.com. She's currently waging a war against the ants in her new apartment, and she's very pleased with how her story in this issue of Triangulation turned out. She hopes that you enjoyed it. She also hopes that you pick up after yourselves, for heaven's sake.*

Smitten

By Tinatsu Wallace

Tinatsu Wallace ("A Womb of My Own," End of the Rainbow) writes ambitious explorations of gender and relationship. I read this story and knew immediately we had to have it for the anthology.

The slap of Bing's hand on the alarm woke Simone from her dream. The bed shifted as he rolled out, but Simone kept the starched sheet pulled tight to her chin and let the muffled tinkle of his morning piss in the toilet lull her back to sleep. In her dream she heard the crashing of ocean waves, and she smiled as she searched for where the miles of sand turned to shoreline. Then the bed rocked and Bing's hand, now cold, grabbed her inner thigh. Simone pressed the smile back into place, just a shade more upturned than a frown, while her brain scrambled out of sleep to think.

Was it Wednesday? The day Bing started work an hour later? She knew the routine by now. Days and weeks went by, all the same, which made it easier to notice the progressing symptoms of her illness.

Symptom one: nausea.

The butterflies in her stomach, that pleasant tingling she remembered from when they first married, had turned to roiling acid wasps. She kept her mouth closed tight against the bitter surge in her throat, while Bing nuzzled the curve of her neck. He felt like an unwelcome stranger, squirming there on top of her, not the husband she'd clung to when they married.

The nausea reminded her of her first love, Tariq. "Come with me to the moon," he'd said, but she'd stayed, love and regret wasting her body until Dr. Abula had wired her memories to feelings of seasickness, so that the very thought of Tariq made her sick.

Simone wondered if those neural wires had gotten crossed somehow, to make her new love this stomach-churning thing.

Symptom two: lack of desire.

He pushed against her, impatient and oblivious to the fakery in her whimpers and moans. No acting could hide her painful dryness.

Eyes squeezed shut, she conjured memories of the first time they met, of their wedding day. She'd been pumped full of dopamine, oxytocin, adrenaline—all timed to release at the sight of him, wide-eyed and pale in his tuxedo. Seeing Bing then, her very veins had almost burst with love. She'd fainted into his arms before she even reached the altar.

"We'll dial down the release dosages," Dr. Abula had said when she awoke, but Simone refused. Though the throbbing in her head and chest felt like pain, she knew it was only the coursing of a fierce love.

Now her body felt dried out, drained. A sure failure of sub-cortical *somethings*, synaptic others. Her memories played without tickling a sympathetic sighing of her heart. Even clicking through images of their honeymoon failed to yield a single drop of desire.

Symptom three: loss of memory.

Bing rolled off her, fitting himself against her side. He traced the outline of her face. "Happy anniversary, babe." A kiss on the tip of her nose, and then he disappeared towards the shower.

"Anniversary?" she blurted and stopped herself, because it was. Bad enough not to remember Wednesday, but to forget that a year ago she'd been transformed, transported with ecstatic love, when every detail of that day was etched in hypermnemonic cells? Simone could not understand the lapse.

While Bing's shower ran, she dialed Dr. Abula's office. "Please, I need an appointment," she said. "Today."

The reception system chimed as it guided her through its menus. Comforting, familiar melodies that she'd come to associate with hope. Hearing them, Simone discovered with relief that her body had not shriveled completely dry. Tears were leaking from her eyes.

Bing returned, and pulled a clean shirt and trousers from the closet. He dressed on his side of the room, after a glance to note her sitting naked on the edge of the bed, phone in hand. "Who were you calling?"

She kept her face turned away, scooping away tears with a fingernail. "Doctor's appointment."

"What's wrong?" He finished buttoning his shirt, and then checked to make sure his socks matched, as if she was untrustworthy of that task, as if one day she'd decide that happily mated socks should have complimentary differences: short and long, ribbed and smooth, navy and cream.

"Nothing," she said. "Just a check-up."

For a moment, he didn't speak. Then Bing strode across the room and pulled her up by the arms. His narrowed eyes sought to pin hers.

"Don't tell me 'nothing,' Simone. What are you hiding?" The belt in his hand dented her skin.

She shrugged away. "Female problems. Probably hormonal. I didn't think it worth worrying you about."

"We're married," he said. "I worry." He looped the belt around his waistband, already headed for the bathroom to comb and tousle his hair.

They said nothing else until he called out before leaving, "Tell me what the doctor says."

When the door clicked shut, Simone curled back into bed. "Happy anniversary," she said.

Her voice came muffled and hoarse, just audible in the closed exam room. Far easier to admit to a lump in her breast, a dark spot in her vision, or a compulsion to pull out her hair strand by strand.

"I don't think I love my husband anymore."

Simone tucked the paper blanket another inch under her bare legs, while the doctor leaned against the counter and tapped his handheld's screen. Every visit she changed into a flimsy backwards robe and covered her legs with an oversized napkin, and yet it had been years since Dr. Abula conducted an actual physical exam. All the information he needed ran from her arm-jack through a thin cable to his tablet.

"No chemical spikes, neuro-transmitters functioning well." He unplugged his end of the cable. "Everything looks good." Uncoupled, the red wire dangling from her arm reminded her of an exposed vein.

"That can't be," she said. The blanket crinkled into precise folds between her fiddling fingertips. "When we're together now, I feel different. No light-headedness, no tightening around my heart, no warmth in my stomach. All gone, for the past few months at least."

"Completely normal." Dr. Abula tapped his screen as he talked, heavy eyebrows knitted with concentration. She wondered if he was keying notes about her case or playing a game, maybe updating his grocery list.

He glanced up. "The body is not meant to sustain the strong emotions you associate with love. Those initial bursts are for bringing you together, then we taper the dosages after a few months. And naturally, the stresses of negotiating a life together will dampen them further. Feelings lessen, allowing you to respond to other stimuli, other concerns."

Simone folded one cold, bare foot over the other. She waited for him to say something more, but he kept his head bent over his screen, tapped a few more times, and then slipped the handheld into his jacket pocket.

"Was there anything else?" He pushed away from the counter.

Simone crumpled the edge of the paper gown. Her body felt dead inside, and her doctor was going to declare that normal and walk away. She cleared her throat. "A lessening of emotion would be one thing, but I don't feel anything for him at all. Nothing."

"A rough patch," the doctor said. "What I can do is give you an extra boost to get you through for now." He pulled an ampoule of amber liquid from a wall dispenser and fitted it into a hypodermic needle. "You'll need to wait a few hours before seeing…" His eyes flicked up to retrieve the name. "Bing. Allow time for the entire system to reprogram. Okay?"

Simone nodded without thinking and gazed thirstily at the needle. Her sigh when it slid into her skin was almost a moan.

Simone's tea had grown cold and her salad warm by the time she dialed Iris' phone. In the hour since leaving Dr. Abula's, the only change she felt was the familiar nausea growing stronger as she debated whether to call Bing. Outside the café window, the sky darkened toward night, the moon a bright wedge in one corner of the glass. She called her sister instead.

"I don't want to talk," Iris said. Her eyes were puffed and red. Tear stains glistened beneath her lashes

"Oh, honey." Simone lifted a hand to stroke Iris' cheek, but the phone screen intruded between them. Her fingers settled against her own cheek instead. "Again?"

"Been a great ride, but not ready to make a commitment." Iris snuffled and wiped a blanket across her nose. "Except to his wife apparently."

Simone grimaced at the oft-heard tale. "I'm sorry." She knew better than to say more. She sat for a few moments, twirling a fork on the table, while Iris wiped her face clean. "I'll call you later."

"No," Iris said. "What do you want?" The screen wavered as she disappeared and then returned with a tissue in hand.

"Nothing," Simone said. "I just won't be home tonight, and I wanted you to tell Bing."

Iris peered over the edge of her tissue. "You're leaving him?"

"No, no." Simone tried to laugh, but the sound caught in her chest and turned into a cough. "I got another shot, and it's like the time before my wedding. You remember."

"Yeah, yeah, you can't see him until the love juice is ready to fire." Anger tightened Iris's voice. She shook her head. "You can't keep drugging yourself, Sis. The heart wants what the heart wants."

Simone bit down on the inside of her lip. "Just tell him for me please."

By the time she hung up, the moon had slipped past the window's edge. Only the headlights of passing cars lit the darkness. She'd need a hotel room. The expanse of a whole evening alone stretched before her, but for a moment, she simply sat and stared at the woman reflected in glass, head tilted, faint smile pulling at her lips. When was the last time she'd seen herself smile? She noticed a tingling in her arms too, a lightness in her chest. The injection was working faster than before.

Whatever Iris thought, Simone thanked God for Dr. Abula.

She was awakened by the pain that squeezed her heart. A glorious, longed-for pain. She stretched her toes to the end of the hotel bed, spread her arms wide across the sheets. Sunlight edged the curtains and shone in bright bands along the carpet and walls.

All the way home Simone kept a hand to her chest, to feel her heart's fluttered beating. The world spun dizzily whenever she turned her head, but she couldn't help staring at the colors that popped from every surface. Even as she stood swaying in the subway car, she felt a thrumming of energy through her body, its wild surges sizzling her skin. She could have run home easily, or flown.

The front door was unlocked. "Hello?" She could have sworn her voice trilled. Two empty wine glasses sat on the coffee table, but before she could think what that meant, Simone heard footsteps stumbling down the stairs behind her. She braced herself for the bursting of her heart as she turned.

But it wasn't Bing.

Iris stood with rumpled hair in the hallway. A bra trailed from her handbag. She gripped the newel post, seeming to waver for a moment on her feet.

"Iris?" Between the thundering of her blood and the dizziness in her head, Simone could not make sense of her sister being here.

But then Iris was stomping to the front door, fists at her sides. "You told me to call him last night. I did. He needs real love, not…" She spun and flicked her hands at Simone. "Not your drug-addled bullshit."

Simone laughed. "What kind of prank... This is crazy." What did Iris mean "real love"? Her whole body was coursing with love. The look of scorn Iris shot her pricked her even through those surging waves. Her smile faltered.

"The heart wants what it wants," Iris said, turning away. The slamming door rattled the glasses on the coffee table. Simone stepped toward the closed door, love compelling her after her sister.

A hand closed around her upper arm. "I was worried sick about you."

The fluttering of her heart started anew. Simone savored the sensation even as Bing's fingertips dug into her arm, hurt grounding her before she fainted away.

"I was at the doctor's," she said. "I'm fixed now. Everything will be wonderful."

Bing whirled her around, his face pressing close to hers. "Worried sick."

At the sight of his face, a pattern of recognition ignited across her synapses. Nanocapsules released their hormonal flood. A searing, sensual ache arced through Simone's body. Serotonin burst through her brain until she wanted to sing out, "I love this man!"

His palm struck her cheek. The slap rocked her head. She stumbled backward, Bing slipping from sight. Euphoria ebbed, exposing shards of anger, shoals of self-loathing. Her mouth felt dry, her skin scoured raw. She raised a hand to her stinging cheek and thought of Iris' warning. For one sickening moment, Simone wondered if this was what her heart wanted. Her eyes sought Bing's face, familiar even with his eyes narrowed and lips twisted into a scowl.

Then waves of love crashed back over her, causing her heart to race, her skin to tingle. Call it biochemistry, call it neuropharmacology. Drowning in sensation, Simone knew it only as love.

She rained kisses on Bing until she'd washed away his anger and they both overflowed with desire. Afterward, as they drifted in the swirls of their bed sheets, a smile curled Simone's lips, and she slipped into dream, too love-drunk to feel the bruise yellowing her cheek.

Parched in Purnululu (A Phantasmagorical Piece in Three Emergences and Six Resonances)

By Jetse de Vries

When I think of Jetse de Vrie, I think of hard science fiction that is ambitious, intelligent, and just a touch weird. You may share my opinion after reading this impressive feat of fabulist life history docudrama.

Zoom in: Terra, a fragile stronghold of life.

Zoom in: Australia, the far-off continent.

Zoom in: Purnululu, one of nature's weathered masterpieces.

Shift from: the striped sandstone domes through a maze of well-worn canyons into a narrow chasm with a fresh-filled stream.

Natural light, single camera, surreal action!

Emergence (III): Helter-Skelter

It's near the end of the wet season. At the peak of its growth cycle, life is rejoicing. The landscape is repainted with explosive regrowths of vibrant green, rapid currents fill once barren riverbeds now teeming with plankton, algae, and patches of moss. The air is abuzz with insects, the rivers virtually overflow with fish and the undergrowth bristles with such a great number of mammals that the predators have become opportunistic to the point of near standstill.

Yet, in the art of *joie de vivre* nobody outdoes the young frogs. Barely metamorphosed into adulthood, they retain the spunky restlessness of the tadpole. Partying like there's no tomorrow with the persistence of the pollywog, young frogs jump and dive, swim and play in the gorge stream, contentedly bask in the sun.

One group does not partake in this exultation of life. They are headed by a big old frog that urges them to redirect their youthful energy at planning for the future. Not all the young ones in the group are happy about it though.

"Why can't we join them for a little while, Sally?" asks a young frog bursting with energy.

"I told you, Philip, we must finish this task first." The old, leathery frog remains adamant.

"Planting seeds? Making food stocks while it's everywhere, more than anybody can eat?"

"Especially now, while we still can. It is necessary for our survival."

"But why? Having fun can't be such a bad thing, can it?"

"No, and after we've finished this cache you can play all you want. Let me explain why we must do this."

Emergence (I): Diaspora

It was a season wetter and wilder than this. The torrential rains that fell from the sky seemed never-ending. Streams soon built up to mighty rivers overflowing. Large tracts of land were flooded. The currents were sometimes so powerful that trees were torn from their roots, big stones swept from their age-old withering spots, water cutting through rock layers too hard for the strongest of our burrowing cousins to scratch.

No living thing could fight these irresistible streams. Once captured there was no way you could swim against it, only go with the flow and hope to survive. It was one of those crazy currents that upset the gorge where I had hatched. My brothers and sisters and I were young tadpoles, hardly halfway through our transformation. Water swept us away like dry leaves in the storms that precede the wet.

Although I was too young to fully realise the dangers, the exhilaration of the wild ride soon evaporated as I found myself in a strange territory, far from my hatching place. The only family still with me was my brother,

Jacinto. All the others were gone: alive, dead, or lost, it was impossible to say.

After we overcame our shock, Jacinto and I set out to search for our siblings. The others—not a single group but a varied crowd mostly unfamiliar with each other—followed us, apparently because we were the oldest.

Our motley crew travelled far without finding any of our family. Eventually we settled in this gorgeous pool, wedged within a rock rift that beautifully captured sunlight in the middle of the day. We'd be gloriously basking at noon, but mercifully shadowed before the daytime heat became too much.

Emergence (I): Hemimetabolous

Little did we know that this thunderous, excessive wet would be so short. In retrospect, I think the chaotic weather somehow compensated for the violent downpour by shortening its period. Anyway, we were caught unaware when the waters retreated, leaving us trapped in this cul-de-sac cunningly crafted by nature.

In the beginning we did not see the trap for what it was, as the walls of our prison were disguised as gates to paradise. There were no predators, food was in profusion, and a nicer surrounding was hardly imaginable. We had entered the gates of Xanadu; we were kings of the world. But this Last Supper was merely a prelude to Purgatory.

Naïveté prevented us from seeing the signs. Nobody's transition to fully developed frog was complete. Even Jacinto and I—the oldest ones—had barely changed. In any normal wet, the metamorphosis is carried through before the rains stop. The very asynchronicity of the hatchings indicated that something fundamental was wrong. Still, we were too young to conceive that such an explosive wet would be followed by such a towering, terrible dry...

Morphological Resonance: A Metamorphism

The dry lasted for a long time, longer than we'd been taught. As I could no longer stand to be near Jacinto I wandered at times off into the rocky surroundings of our gorge.

The intense heat, slow dehydration, and my evolving thoughts gradually changed the way I viewed reality, like working the Ptholo forge. I don't know exactly how it happened; my normally persistent memory was disintegrating. At a certain point the stones seemed to speak to me.

The way you young ones perceive change is blunted by your ultra-fast metabolism. What you see around you seems stable. On geological timescales it certainly is not. Look at the rocks. They seem at a perfect standstill, but they have travelled great distances, through enormous depths and vast periods. These journeys have changed their deepest inner structure.

See these two rocks lying next to each other, brought there by the enigmatic processes of chance. To the untrained eye they look alike. Even the younger rock is ancient, burst from deep strata where it was compressed into being from grains of sand. However, it is but an earlier, unformed version of the other one.

The other rock has completed a longer voyage down a subductive tectonic plate into the liquid heat below the crust. It underwent a metamorphism, became harder and more crystalline. It is more durable than its neighbour.

Emergence (I): Desiccation

The rivers dried out much too soon, disconnecting our gorge from the rest. We didn't care. We bathed ourselves in lavishness even as the pool slowly became ever more shallow. Then, like the cliff's shadows at sunset, crisis fell.

Jacinto and I were not dependent on the algae and plankton of the lowering waters since we could feed on insects that remained plentiful. The first fights could be calmed by intervention by one of us, but as the situation became grimmer, food clashes escalated into desperate battles.

Dawning realisation of doom turned the once idyllic lake into a tiny pool of despondency. Famine and despair blunted the edge of the fighting's ferocity. And then the inexorable hand of fate closed on its first victim.

This dreadful event was soon overshadowed by Jacinto's shocking next act.

Morphological Resonance: An Allomorph

Differences are not limited to those between rocks. Strange variations occur even in a single stone. Minerals, metals and compounds consisting of the same chemical formula can diverge in their crystalline structure.

Graphite might be compressed into diamonds, and silvery white tin may decay into amorphous grey powder.

These allotropic forms are only rarely captured within the same stone. Still, the principle is clear: although chemically identical, not only their outward appearance, but also their inner being is essentially different. The same basic ingredients can be used for different expressions.

Emergence (I): Mucus Mutilation

Jacinto devoured the dead body. Cannibalism was not unheard of in prehistoric times. Today, however, it is an intense taboo. Circumstances were not nearly desperate enough to justify this behaviour. Although the number of available insects was declining, Jacinto and I were not yet near the edge of starvation, even if we could sense its boundaries closing in on us.

I was too bewildered to even think of fighting him. However, I was disgusted to share our pool with him so I stayed out in the dry. My skin developed strange blotches and my mind became haunted by vague recollections of surrealistic visions.

When Jacinto ate the second famine victim my outrage was immediate. Furiously, I attacked him, but my condition had worsened so much that he thrashed me within an inch of my life.

Nothing can excuse my next act. When the third of our group fell victim to malnourishment, my fear of dying overcame my deepest cultural restraints. I became the second cannibal. However sorry and ashamed I feel now I cannot guarantee that—under similar circumstances—the wish for a dignified death will not succumb to the will to live.

Needless to say, it was not my last act of cannibalism. As the sound of the last insect dwindled to a vague buzz in my memory, gnawing hunger pangs pulsed ever more insistent. I tried to suppress it, but ultimately failed, again and again. While Jacinto showed no outward signs of a struggling conscience, at least we waited until somebody died before committing our next unspeakable act. If this was of any solace to those remaining, I do not know...

Morphological Resonance: A Relict

Maybe you are getting the impression that the only constant is change, however gradual. Superficially this may be true, but there remain things that are extremely resistant to change. They retain structure and integrity as long as possible, even under extremes of pressure, temperature, and duress.

Take that rock there. Erosion has decreased his size, but not his identity. That old blockhead has the same crystalline structure and minerals as when it formed, and he is almost as ancient as this planet. Plate tectonics, convection streams, volcanic action, and weather patterns have brought him over and through large parts of this world. Still, this monumental odyssey has left his quintessential being intact. A true relict.

Nonetheless, the one principle affecting all of us remains entropy: corruption and decay. Some resist, others try to escape by embracing change. Who is right? Only time will tell...

Emergence (II): Ecdysonal Ecstasy

Through it all I could not escape the feeling that something other than the ongoing drought, heat and hunger, and mental distress was causing my feverish fugues. I ate as little as I could without actually dying and still my body fat tissue grew. Did it not realise I needed the energy for sustenance?

Although my dwindling companions barely noticed the embarrassing bulge near my genital glands, it added a dimension to my guilt.

Then Dominique died. One of the few females remaining, she was the closest friend I had. The contradictory effects of a famished body fervently trying to finish metamorphosis were too much for her. She fought till the end and managed to keep a positive attitude throughout.

The prospect of eating Dominique cut deeper wounds in my soul than I thought possible, but the idea of her ending up as a meal for the immoral Jacinto was even more unbearable. Visions of suicide surfaced. The brightening of the fires in Hell made me realise that the preceding Purgatory was just a warm-up.

Doubt and guilt and penance *avant la lettre* made me procrastinate until the rot in her body had begun to set in. Still, the innate persistence to live triumphed again. After I had digested her I couldn't sleep for days. Feverish slumber became the only rest for my raging mind and convulsing body. Strange sensations surged through my hormonal system, feelings not dissimilar from the pulsing pains of metamorphosis.

Morphological Resonance: An Allotropic Juxtaposition

Over time, as red dust covers the materials of life, different forms emerge. Burnt, blackened bush gradually layered over might become graphite, the soft black stuff that artists employ for their rock paintings.

Even the hardest rocks have crevices, bursts and cracks. Water creeps in. As it dries, minerals fill the rocks with quartz, the hard white stuff meandering through old stone. These veins and nodules are more beautiful and durable than graffiti powder.

There are circumstances, however, that can force a more distinct change. Under extreme heat and pressure, applied over a long time, graphite can be transformed into diamond, the hardest and most beautiful gemstone.

☼

Emergence (II): Gender Bender

At this point, my psyche was so paralysed by permanent waves of guilt that I failed to register the fatty tissue near my genital glands being consumed. Fever and fatigue overcame my angst-ridden mind, and I fell into a near-comatose sleep.

I awoke to find the fever gone, and a vague realisation of something missing. At the same time there was this fishy feeling of an odd extra. I felt better physically, healthier than before, but also *different*.

My voice was creaky, but that surely stemmed from fever and aridness. I was more aware of hormones surging through my body, but that must be an after-effect of inflammation. A queer combination of a fresh fragrance and an essence lost, compensating but not quite adding up.

It eluded me until I had to pee. I was a woman!

Morphological Resonance: A Spiracle

Some changes are not gradual. Pressure can build up in a closed system, and force its way out explosively, like a volcanic eruption.

The build-up is mostly initiated by the introduction of strange matter through subduction. In contact with lava this matter transforms into magma and noxious gases. If enough is transformed, and if the build-up takes place near a fault in the crust, a new volcano is violently born.

The event is rare; otherwise the planet would be a flaming inferno. Thankfully the natural timely occurrence of spiracles vents this pressure in the asthenosphere. These structures are like pores in the planet's skin allowing fresh air to circulate through its body, in a sense keeping it alive.

Emergence (II): Axillary Amplexus

I changed my name to Sally. At first I tried to keep my sexuality hidden from Jacinto, but to no avail. Men! In the beginning he kept his distance. Later he made advances. His two remaining brain cells must have figured that after a course of cannibalism, a little incest was in order.

I wouldn't have it. My mind repelled at the thought. Why wasn't hunger suppressing his sick desire? This dual suffering of soul and flesh continued, and I failed to notice the change in the air. A fresh breeze, almost imperceptible. The wind grew stronger and soon a storm was building. Thunder shook the ground, and huge bolts of lightning cracked the big sky, heralding the coming of the wet. It was like the first recital of a poem to a soul starved of beauty:

Crackling tension clouds the sky
And swallows the sharp sunlight,
Casting shadows on lands so dry
They soak up the promise of night;
Great rumbling heads of thunder
In a dark and ominous mood
Throw lightning flashes asunder
In a bright, brilliant prelude.

Torrential rains splatter my body camouflage my tears of relief and shame. The exhausted land soaks up heaven's gift like an innocent child baptised by holy water. Life rejoices. Our pool slowly fills. I prepare to escape as soon as the riverbed floods. In the meantime my strength slowly returns. The natural food supply replenishes.

Then, with Jacinto's amorous overtures becoming ever more aggressive, I am betrayed by my body's evolutionary clockwork. Hormones run rampant, and a mating instinct as old as time takes over. Intellect is reduced to a feeble spectator. The urge to reproduce is irresistible, and the only male is Jacinto.

I offer no resistance as he mounts me. A small, sane part of my mind watches helplessly as we mate like mad metabolisms programmed by nature's cycles. Riding the crest of hormonal waves, we achieve sexual synchronisation; your hatching is inevitable.

Morphological Resonance: A Hidden Inflexion

At a certain point, optimisation is reached. Content with achievement, a satisfactory slumber is a reward for results. Ages of stasis follow in which the optimal steady state reigns supreme.

For all the world this optimisation appears to be the master of the game, but its refusal to change carries the seed of its own downfall. In the far away, hidden nooks and niches, less-optimised beings go through changes the hard way. Many end up in evolutionary blind alleys. Many evolve only minimally, and their small improvements are neglected by the *status quo*.

A very few, however, go through a shape-shifting transition and survive. These attain an edge that pierces like a needle through a tautly filled balloon, exposing the lazy equilibrium for the folly it has become.

Emergence (III): No Sleep for the Wicked

"So now you know why I want you to prepare for the dry," croaks Sally, a leathery old frog who has seen and experienced too much.

"But such an exceptional long dry will surely not come again?" Philip says. He wants to play and party.

"Young tadpole, I ate my friends, fucked my brother, and saw through to the other end of madness and despair. The only thing that kept me alive was an oath that this would never happen to *my* offspring."

Sally gathers her breath. "So, yes, you *will* plant these weeds down under in that deep pool and be prepared. While the others gorge on present abundance, this gorge will be your salvation in your time of need."

> *I do not paint a portrait to look like the subject, rather does the person grow to look like his portrait.*
>
> —*Salvador Dalí*

Jetse de Vries—*@shineanthology—is a technical specialist for a propulsion company by day, and a science fiction reader, editor and writer by night. He's also an avid bicyclist, total solar eclipse chaser, beer/wine/single malt aficionado, metalhead and intelligent optimist. Publications include Clarkesworld Magazine, Rudy Rucker's Flurb and Michael Moorcock's New Worlds.*

Bitter Water

By Julia August

I have a fondness for fantasy that grounds itself in some aspect of our history and takes time to develop its world. This story by Julia August hits that sweet spot for me. I hope it will for you as well. It certainly fits the Parch theme.

There was a butterfly. It was gray in the pale dawn light. There was a crow, the kind the Tekel said never drank water. It eyed a lizard beadily, as if calculating which would be quicker to reach the next man to die. There were ants, a great many of them. Also beetles. The blood seemed to attract them.

Cursing, Arion kicked sand over the clotted mess. Master Kallon was badly wounded. They had lost three men in the ambush. There was no food. There were no roads. There was only sand, great burnished hills of it, curved crests slicing up into the iron sky.

"How's he doing?" he threw over his shoulder. "Any better?" He could hear young Master Kallon's laboured breathing.

Talos, on his knees, himself white-faced, shook his head. "Worse."

Arion grimaced. They had to find shelter before the sun rose much higher. Shelter, water and food. He was sweating already.

"We could follow the bastards," he said. "They must know where they're going. The camels will leave a trail, but—"

"The Tekel might find us," Mikkos said. "They'll kill us all!"

"This is kel Hàhlé country," Arion said. "The barbarians here are supposed to be peaceful." He shook his head before anyone could point out the obvious problem with that logic. It was hard to sound calm. "But they've got water. They can go as far as they want. We don't."

Gelo, who had been dragging the third body to rest beside its fellows, sat abruptly in the churned-up sand. "We're going to die." He was only sixteen, his eyes unfocused and his hair still matted where he had taken a blow to the head. He stared up at Arion. "We're going to die. We're all going to—"

"Shut up," Mikkos said. "Stop saying that."

"The birds will pick—"

"Shut *up*," Arion said. "I'm going to climb that dune and see if I can see anything." Most of the slope was still in shadow. It was receding fast, though.

Arion hit the sun when he was no more than halfway up. Sand shifted under his feet, making progress slow. His throat was full of dust. He forced himself to keep climbing. The back of his neck was starting to burn.

He crawled the last few yards. From the crest, it was possible to see the froth and wind-swept spume of the sand-sea rising and falling for miles and burning miles in all directions.

"Anything?" Mikkos yelled.

Arion cupped his hand above his eyes. The wind was picking up, which made it hard to make out much. He couldn't see the end of the sand-sea or the broken hills of black volcanic slag beyond it. On the farthest horizon, mountains formed a smudge of a mirage. Closer, though, in the shallows of the sand, his eyes fell on something that just might be a date palm.

Sun, he said without sound, *if I live to see home again, great Sun, I'll raise an altar to you. If I get back safely, it won't be a calf I sacrifice, but a bull.*

He cleared his throat. "Maybe. It could be worth a try."

By the time he returned, the others were arguing again. Mikkos, who had bandaged his arm with a strip of patterned cloth torn from his chiton, wanted to set off at once.

Talos stood unsteadily. "Master Kallon's in a bad way. I think he'll die if we try to carry him."

Mikkos spat in the sand. "Leave him," he said. "No one will know. We can tell his father the barbarians killed him."

"We're not leaving him," Arion said. Master Kallon's father liked to recall how he had made a fortune from trading with the kel Memar at Taramsett when he was young and no one else would dare. His reaction if they made it home with neither goods nor his eldest son was not to be imagined. "Talos, you stay with Gelo. Mikkos and I will see if what I saw is real."

Gelo peered through bloodshot eyes. "What if you don't come back?"

"We will," Arion said. A deflated waterskin lay like a flatfish in the sand. He picked it up and shook off the sand.

"But what if—"

Talos let out a startled cry. "Look!"

Arion spun around. At the end of the dune, out of the sand, as it seemed, had sprung up riders.

There were too many to count. *Where did they come from?* Sunlight glinted on the elaborate metalwork bridles and harnesses of the sleek riding camels. Had the bandits returned with reinforcements? It was impossible to make out faces muffled in blue-black cloth. This deep in the desert, they probably didn't speak much Dorikan, if any. And he didn't understand their language at all.

Gelo moaned under his breath. Arion wanted to yell obscenities. How could anyone deal with barbarians who insisted on masking themselves?

They seemed to be just watching. Maybe they were waiting for something. Maybe they were merely interested.

Arion was suddenly furious. He had possessed, for a handful of moments at least, a sliver of hope. To have it snatched away like this was worse than never having hoped at all.

He hurled the waterskin at them. It flapped at the feet of the foremost camel, whose rider glanced down at it, then up at Arion.

"Take it!" Arion said, voice cracking. "Can't your Great King keep the peace in his own country? We don't have anything left to steal!"

The Tekel lifted the skin with the tip of a spear, then let it fall.

"He does try," she replied in what was unmistakably a woman's voice. "My dear, I think it may be an excellent thing for you that I came this way."

The parched date palm Arion had spotted from the dune was one of several clustered around a single-roomed house beside a well of slightly bitter water. It was the finest liquid Arion had ever tasted. He sat beneath the oldest tree with the Tekel woman, who squatted on her haunches and let him tell her about the treacherous camel drivers Kallon son of Sinon had hired at

Taramsett, the kel Memar town where they had found a glut of grain and olives and someone had told Master Kallon there was a shortage of both at Teleleiyya.

She seemed sympathetic. "It's a trick from the bad old days. You get paid to carry the goods in the first place, then again when your riders swoop in to carry them off. Well, I say 'you'… I don't know these names you tell me. Do you remember the brand on the camels?"

Arion spread his hands. He had no idea.

"Huh," she said. "Well, I believe it's true that there's a shortage of olives at Teleleiyya. Maybe we'll find them there."

Her Dorikan was impeccable. Arion said as much and regretted it at once, but she seemed only amused. "Most of us in the southern desert have at least a little Dorikan. Some of us have family in the Six Cities. Where did you say you were from?"

"Dorkytia." He had told her his name and Master Kallon's. She had not told him hers, which was a piece of typical Tekel rudeness Master Kallon's father had complained about, but Arion would have known she was an aristocrat even without her manner. She wore enough silver rings and wrist-cuffs to buy half a dozen caravans and her veil was full of sapphire charms.

"A day's ride south of Pallatinë, no?" she said. "My brother has guest-friends there. I remember the crack in the acropolis where the Sun-god's chariot fell to earth. And the fountains. Very fine." She hauled herself up with her spear before Arion could express surprise.

"It's a pity you don't recall that brand," she said, moving a few restless steps towards the well. Her riders had replaced the wooden lid. She leaned on it, winced, and pressed her shining hand to her side. "You came rather far out of your way. And I would say your bandits were heading back to the mountains, so they might as well have ambushed you on the northern caravan road. Didn't it occur to your Master Kallon that something was wrong when you left it?"

Arion shook his head. "He thought it was an adventure. His father never went farther than Taramsett."

"Let's hope it's the sort of adventure he returns from. It's a curious thing, I think, that you were brought all the way here to be robbed. This well is rather special to us."

The midday heat was making it hard to think. "It is?"

"All wells are sacred places. This one is..." She traced the Tekel letters burnt into the wooden well-lid. "This is Mossral's Well. It was discovered by the Great King when he was only another drum-lord. Ambushing a caravan at the Great King's well sends a message the Great King won't like to hear. Nor do I."

The only thing Arion could think of was that maybe the bandits had needed water. He managed not to say it. After a moment, the lady straightened, wrapping her brown hands around her spear. She was a rangy woman, as shapeless as a man in her robes, although the smoky eyes above the veil were fine.

"Well, we shall see," she said. "Meanwhile, my dear, I know someone at Teleleiyya who will be grateful for the thought, even if you didn't manage to get the olives all the way there. Your Master Kallon will be lucky to get that far, I think. I suggest you rest."

It took two weeks to reach the kel Hàhlé town, because Master Kallon had to be carried every step of the way. By the time they emerged from the sand-sea onto a cracked clay plain and saw the wild groves swaying in the shadow of the mountains, it seemed possible Master Kallon might live. He still was alive, in any case, although too feverish to recognise anyone.

They walked through unkempt stands of date palms and lote trees toward the massive walls. Arion stumbled alongside Tairyel kel Hàhlé, the Tekel woman, who used her spear as a walking stick and whistled cheerfully behind her veil.

A limewashed gateway arch inscribed with unintelligible Tekel writing admitted them into a square occupied by a number of grave elders and a few others. It looked as if some public business was being conducted; then everyone started to rise and it became clear who they were waiting for.

Mistress Tairyel had slowed her long stride to a stately amble and probably meant to accept her welcome graciously. As she passed under the arch, though, a couple of bright-eyed Tekel brats hurled themselves at her, knocking the breath from her with a startled *whoof.* Laughing, they danced in circles as she picked herself up, rubbing her side in a pained way, and brushed dust from her robes.

Whatever she said to the children failed to bring them to heel, although it seemed to calm them. The boy hung on her arm, while the girl proffered the spear with both hands and the widest smile Arion had ever seen.

Mistress Tairyel shook her head and slung her arms around the two, absently straightening the boy's disordered braids. Her tone was all indulgence. *Hush now*, she must have said, *let the grownups speak.*

The elders escorted her through a maze of shady gardens. Arion was swept up in their midst; all he could do was to break through his exhaustion and push after the bright, bobbing head of the lady's spear. He was struggling to find Mikkos and Gelo in the crowd, and to see whether Talos was sticking close to Master Kallon's litter, when he burst into the midday sun.

An avenue of well-watered mulberry trees stretched before him. *Ornamental*, was his first thought. He had a sense of order, of organisation, of thought-out paths and manicured streams. The fountains would have drawn praise in the marketplace back home.

At his shoulder, Mikkos whistled. "Think that's the Great King's house?"

Arion followed his gaze to a huge white house at the nexus of the mulberry avenues. It was bigger than any public building in Dorkytia, five storeys tall, at least, and the sun sparked off its limewashed walls.

"It certainly fits the bill," Arion said. Gelo appeared in the human stream. Arion grabbed the youth's arm to keep him from wandering off.

He nodded at the structure. "If this is the Great King's home, we're going to tell him what happened. We're going to ask him to do something." He was trying to convince himself, mostly. He thought he could stand up and complain on Master Kallon's behalf, especially when he remembered everyone who would not be coming home, but it might be harder in the Great King's presence.

They followed the flow to the building, then elbowed their way forwards. A narrow inner courtyard was visible through wrought iron gates, which currently stood open. The crowds were sparser here, with Mistress Tairyel and the children at their head.

A man in indigo robes came out of the house. His bare head was too sun-bleached to be Tekel, and his smile was slightly abstracted as he approached the gathering.

Mistress Tairyel took her hands from the children's shoulders and held them out to him. "Hospitality, darling?" she said in Dorikan, while the children bounced expectantly.

He pressed her hands to his forehead. "Sure. Of course."

Family in the Six Cities! Arion thought. This man's Dorikan was so natural it had to be his mother tongue. At Arion's side, Mikkos rubbed his hands together. "A countryman! He'll put in a word for us, right?"

"Can't hurt to ask." Arion watched Mistress Tairyel flick the man's cheek.

"Mama's hurt," the little boy announced. "She's cracked her ribs."

His sister balanced on her toes. "She fell off Fakru." When her mother swung round, the girl darted between the open gates, dragging the spear behind her. She peeped back gleefully. "And then Fakru sat on her."

Mistress Tairyel burst out laughing. "You wicked little monsters! I told you not to tell your father that! I had a much better story for him."

"Really?" the man said. "What?"

"Oh, I forget. Believe me, it was very heroic."

"She *was* fighting," the boy said anxiously. "It was when—"

His mother swatted him. "Hush, you. I told you not to tell him that too. Really, darling, what have you been teaching these terrible children, if not to do as they're told?"

"To tell me the truth," the man said. "I guess."

He glanced around the mulberry garden. Arion tried to catch his gaze, failed, realised it probably didn't matter since he was obviously not the Great King. The man spoke a few words in the Tekel language, then added to Mistress Tairyel in Dorikan, "Come and take tea."

☼

Mikkos maintained that no good would come of making a fuss. They should wait and see if Master Kallon survived and let him decide what to do. All Gelo wanted was to collapse in the mulberry-scented shade. Talos, who had gone with the Tekel to see Master Kallon safely settled, shrugged and said he didn't know what to do. "He's Mistress Tairyel's husband," he reported. "He lives here with the children. It's a library. The Great King's out in the desert somewhere."

Arion rubbed his eyes. The sun was blinding. If they ever got out of this godforsaken country, he was going to have to take incense to Askleos on the Sacred Way to make his eyes stop running. "Well, I say we find someone to complain to. The Great King's meant to stop things like what happened to us."

"Let Master Kallon complain," Mikkos said. "I've had enough of these barbarians."

"Master Kallon can't complain," Arion said. "Not like he is now. We ought to complain for him. Anyway, we need somewhere to stay."

Mikkos snorted. "Fine. You do it."

"All right. I will."

He waited. They watched expectantly.

"Go on, then," Mikkos said, sitting beside Gelo. He pulled a sticky handful of dates out of his chiton, presumably gleaned from one of the Tekel girls who had been wandering around the garden with trays of dainties and tiny teacups. "Aren't you going to complain?"

"Screw you!" Arion said. "Get off your backside, you lazy son of an ass. We're in this together."

They were still quarrelling when someone tugged Arion's chiton. He looked around and found Mistress Tairyel's little girl smiling up. She was a lithe brown child of nine or ten, with dusty feet and a quantity of braided black hair.

"Hello," she said. "Are you Master Arion?" He nodded. "My father sent me to ask if you'd come up to take tea with him."

Arion straightened his chiton.

"I shall be very glad to," he said. "Thank you, young mistress." He shot a glare at Mikkos. *And that is how it is done*, he thought.

The child danced off towards the limewashed library. Arion limped after her, wondering whether it might help to take off his sandals, and if it might be taken as an insult to wash dust off in one of the fountains, when something snagged his attention. He stopped unthinkingly.

A gaggle of girls gossiped by a fountain while children tossed knucklebones into the dust. A great many veiled Tekel riders lounged in the shade or strolled the garden. Because they were barbarians, they carried swords and spears openly even within the city walls. There might not even be any laws against it here.

Arion backed into a tree. He couldn't work out what had struck him as so important, until he heard a familiar voice coming from a tall man talking to someone almost within arm's length.

"Hey!" Arion said. "Hey, I remember you." He jerked forward and caught at a blue sleeve. "Weren't you with those camel drivers at Taramsett?"

The man stared down his nose. The veil rendered him anonymous, but there was a lingering familiarity about his fine black eyes. He said something to one of the riders, who spat out a piece of gum.

"Master Malekal says to tell you he doesn't speak Dorikan. He has better things to do than waste time with Dorikan caravans."

"Just ask him," Arion said. "Please. If he knows the camel brands—"

The rider glanced at Master Malekal, who adjusted his veil and shook his head. The next thing Arion knew, a shove sent him flying. He hit the ground hard and pushed himself up painfully. He tasted blood and dust. Nearby people stared, but Master Malekal strolled off, followed by most of the riders.

"Hey!" Arion said. He almost chased after them, then thought better and hobbled to the nearest fountain. His temples throbbed, either from exhaustion or heat. He ducked his head into the spray and caught sight of Mistress Tairyel's Dorikan husband gazing down from the library roof.

The courtyard was a geometric puzzle of cedar stairs and crisscrossing galleries. Arion was breathless by the time he reached the roof, where Mistress Tairyel sat on a white antelope skin with her two children and an older girl.

Her husband straightened from the wall where he had been leaning. "Some problem?"

Arion sucked in a searing breath. "He didn't need to be like that. I only asked about the brands on the camels Master Kallon hired at Taramsett. He was there with the drivers. Who is he? Master Malekal, I mean. Is he very important?"

"Malek kel Hàhlé?" Mistress Tairyel said after what even Arion could tell was a rather long pause. "He's a cousin of the Great King through his mother, which is a bloodline that matters to us. But leave that aside for now. Come and meet the master of the library, Tomas, who has offered his hospitality to you and your companions for as long as you need it." She smiled over her veil at the older girl. "Amestrin, will you pour for Master Arion?"

☼

Malek kel Hàhlé was staying with guest-friends in the town. Arion learned this from Master Tomas, who divided a dish of stuffed olives between them and remarked that these would be the last until the autumn harvest. "Unless you recover your goods, I guess." He added a splash of musty milk to his tea. "Or another caravan comes in."

They were all sitting in the courtyard a little after dawn. Mikkos jostled Gelo to get at the olives. He was sick to his back teeth, he had been saying, of choking down dates.

"Speaking of that," Arion said, "could you point us to the magistrates in charge of hearing bandit complaints? Master Kal—"

"These aren't half bad," Mikkos said to Master Tomas. "What d'you call 'em?" Arion sat back in disgust. Mikkos was still talking about olives when a conversation between two familiar voices became audible in the gardens outside.

He jumped up. Mistress Tairyel and Master Malekal were strolling up one of the mulberry avenues, all but indistinguishable in their enveloping Tekel clothes.

They had been talking in the Tekel language, but Mistress Tairyel switched to Dorikan to accept her husband's invitation to take tea. She sat beside him, selecting a fat black olive with particular care. Master Malekal leaned against a pillar and said something incomprehensible.

"Malek, my dear," Mistress Tairyel said. "Won't you speak Dorikan for my husband's guests?"

Arion opened his mouth, then closed it again. The Tekel prince's eyes passed over him indifferently. He sat down hard.

If anything consequential was said, he didn't hear it. The two Tekel did most of the talking. Mistress Tairyel repeated what she had said at Mossral's Well about the attack being a message. "Though some people might say it was a dangerous message to send, no?" she added. "The laws against robbing the caravans are quite stringently enforced these days."

Master Malekal seemed mostly bored. When Mistress Tairyel talked about the difficulty of disposing of the cargo, he twitched his veil higher and said the cargo should be the least interesting thing. "If it really is a message, as you seem to believe."

"The cargo is not uninteresting for Master Arion and his master," Mistress Tairyel said. "They do deserve some recompense for their trouble. And my husband feels it would be a sad thing for all those olives to go to waste."

"I daresay the robbers hid everything in the mountains," Master Malekal said. "Impossible to find. You know those caves."

Mistress Tairyel closed her kohl-rimmed eyes. "Do you think?"

No one mentioned the camel brands. Master Malekal took his leave shortly afterwards and Mistress Tairyel said solicitously she would accompany him to the end of the mulberry garden. Mikkos gave Arion a glance that said: *well, go on, then, complain.*

Arion shot back a dirty look. "You and Talos go see how Master Kallon's doing," he said, "You too, Gelo."

"Did you want to speak to the magistrates?" said Mistress Tairyel's husband, who had said very little so far. "I can take you there."

The magistrates inhabited an airy complex of buildings surrounded by completely covered streets. They treated Master Tomas with overt respect, but Arion got the impression they considered *his* business trivial, or at best a matter for public record rather than anything they could do something about. Their politeness flustered him so much he ended up getting angry, then had to apologise, hot-faced, under Master Tomas's faintly surprised gaze. He wasn't used to dealing with magistrates, let alone Tekel ones. Master Kallon would have done it better. Once the ordeal was over, he sat by a fountain with Master Tomas and vented his feelings to everyone within earshot.

"It's not Master Kallon's fault," he said. "Gods! How was he to know? We thought the Great King was keeping the peace. It's meant to be safe to travel the desert. I don't know how we can go home unless we recover something back for his father. I mean, if he does live." He threw a pebble at the turquoise water. "His father'll kill him. And the rest of us, for letting it happen. But it's not his fault."

"You're very loyal."

"Yeah, well," Arion said. "He's my half-brother. We were brought up together." He looked up and found Master Tomas regarding him with what seemed to be slight speculation. "Our father freed me before we left," he added. "On condition I see Master Kallon home safely. He would've freed my mother too if she'd lived long enough. He says these towns are full of runaways. Is it true the Tekel really don't keep slaves?"

"The kel Hàhlé don't," Master Tomas said, smiling a little.

He was a tall man, but so quiet he seemed to fade into the background, although some particular quality of his quietness compelled Arion to fill the silence now they were alone.

"Our physician thinks your brother should survive," Master Tomas said. There was ink on his hands; it seemed ingrained. "You can stay as long as it takes to nurse him back to health. As for your property, leave it to my wife. She'll get it back, if anyone can."

"What about justice for Master Kallon? Did she ask Master Malekal about the brands?"

"What brands?" Master Tomas said gently.

Arion stared. "Never mind."

He got down from the wall. He couldn't make out more than detached interest in Master Tomas's face, but he got the impression that was the man's default expression anyway. Arion's stomach was knotting up. "Is Master Malekal staying here?"

"We're going to do *what*?" Mikkos shouted.

"We just have to ask him about those brands, is all."

"Hell, no!" Mikkos said. "If some Tekel prince is involved, count me out. I'm not crossing any Tekel prince. Especially if Mistress Tairyel won't!"

"Well, you stay here, then," Arion said, exasperated. "I'm going to find out what he knows."

No one kept him from leaving the library's quiet, sun-washed gardens for the crowded streets. He passed a great many people buying and selling and drinking tea in shops and shady passageways, speaking half a dozen languages and wearing as many styles of clothing. Here and there, sunlight flashed into open squares and danced in the streams that carried water throughout the city.

At Taramsett, people spoke of Teleleiyya with admiration and jealousy. It was a great kel Hàhlé jewel, they said, but any town would be that had so much wealth pouring into it. Master Kallon had thought it would be worth the journey to see it. *Some prices are too high*, Arion thought. Even if Master Kallon did survive, only bringing back a profit would satisfy his father.

It was easier to find Master Malekal than Arion had feared, or perhaps, deep down, hoped. He only had to ask two people before he got directions to a bright courtyard full of spears and veiled men.

Arion planted himself in the archway. His stomach twisted.

"I want to talk to Master Malekal," he said. "Now."

Up the stairs they went, then up again, and through an ornate doorway. The prince was sitting with his host, who removed himself tactfully upon Arion's entrance. It was impossible to tell what Master Malekal's expression might be behind his veil. He gestured to the vacated cushion. "Sit."

It felt as if he was measuring Arion up. Arion sat jerkily. It was on the tip of his tongue to call Master Malekal a liar, as he had wanted to do since listening to the prince talking to Mistress Tairyel over olives, but he had already lost his temper once today and offending the Great King's cousin might be more dangerous than shouting at the magistrates. He couldn't resist a jibe, though. "So you *do* speak Dorikan."

Master Malekal adjusted his veil. "I speak Dorikan. I don't waste my time on Dorikan slaves."

"I'm not a—look, I just want to know about those men who attacked our caravan, that's all." He saw from the glint in Master Malekal's eye that the prince had meant to provoke him. He forced himself to calm down. "You were there at Taramsett, when Master Kallon hired the guides who led us to Mossral's Well. I heard you speak to them." He rubbed his sweating palms against his thighs. "Please, master, if you know anything..."

Silence stretched. Then the prince said coldly, "Not their names."

"The camel brands, then? Will you tell Mistress Tairyel that much?"

"No," Master Malekal said. "Do you want your goods back?"

Arion jerked back. "*Can* you?"

"Half a day's ride on the northern caravan road is a place called Aghrèm n-Ălžăynăn. I think your robbers will be hiding in the caves nearby. They may be willing to bargain." He held out a small pouch of red leather stamped with Tekel letters. "You may want this. Go alone."

This time, Arion spared himself the trouble of telling Mikkos anything. He struggled back to the library, trying not to think of several hundred reasons why going to Aghrèm n-Ălžăynăn alone was a terrible idea. If bandits didn't kill him, the desert might. His own scattered bones flashed sickeningly before his eyes.

He was too preoccupied to pay much attention to where he was going, with the result that he fell over Mistress Tairyel's little boy on the grass by the waterwheel that filled the garden's streams.

"Hey," Arion said. "What are you doing out here?"

"Watching the wheel. It's fine, isn't it?"

Arion gave a cursory glance. It was a great creaking thing hung with swinging clay pots. An exceedingly bored mule trudged in circles nearby. Water flashed in the evening sun. "Yeah, whatever," he said. "Shouldn't you be in lessons?"

"Papa's looking up the laws," the boy said. "Everyone else went home. Are there wheels like this where you live? Mama says there's a thing like a snail that screws water out of the river in Pallatinë. She's going to take us there when we're bigger."

"To see the water-screw?"

The boy grinned. "No, silly! To meet Papa's mother. But I want to see the water-screw too. Are you from Pallatinë?"

"No," Arion said. "A town nearby. Hey, can you keep a secret?" He crouched beside the child, who nodded solemnly. "What do you know about a place called Aghrèm n-Ălžăynăn?"

"Lots," the boy said. "It's where the kel-èsuf gather to share news and make decisions. It's where they keep their treasure. No one goes there."

"Who are the kel-èsuf?"

"The ălžăynăn. They're like the daimones you have in the Six Cities, Papa says. They live in the wilderness. If you aren't careful, they possess you. They hang around old campsites and play tricks on travellers. They can look just like real people, but you know it's an ălžăyn, because they can't greet you properly and they don't have thumbs." His eyes rounded. "We call them the People of Loneliness. That's what kel-èsuf means."

Arion hadn't thought his stomach could twist any more. "That doesn't sound much like a daimon to me."

"Doesn't it? What is a daimon like?"

"Different," Arion said. "Look, never mind about daimones. How do you keep these kel-èsuf off?"

The boy shrugged. "I've got an amulet." He pulled a red leather pouch, not very big, from within his shirt. "Don't you?"

Arion ran his thumb over the pouch Master Malekal had given him. "Yeah, I think so. Can I get a horse in the market?" He rubbed his forehead and tried to work out how much money he had. "What shrines are there around here? Any altars to the Sun? What about that one in the library with the bowl of water?"

"That's for El. Papa has an altar to Luck over by the peach tree."

"El will do," Arion said. "I left my luck in Dorkytia."

☼

Arion got up well before dawn. It was pleasantly cool, the moon was just setting on the west-northwestern horizon, and the wind had not yet risen. All the world slept as Arion crept down to the courtyard, fumbling for a handful of almonds to lay by the bowl on the Tekel altar. It was plainer than any Dorikan altar would have been, a block of blueish marble inscribed with a line of Tekel writing. He didn't know Tekel prayers, so he whispered a Dorikan one instead.

After a time, he squared his shoulders, taking the deepest breath he could, and pushed from the altar. He had to buy a horse before he could leave the city.

He reined in hard when the black spires of Aghrèm n-Ălžăynăn reared over the windswept foothills. The whole mountain must be a haunt for spirits: there were towers everywhere, and stumps of towers, and what looked like fortifications carved into the basalt. He fumbled for Master Malekal's amulet pouch, which hung reassuringly around his neck. From the caravan road, less a road and more a trampled ribbon of camel tracks running at a respectful distance from the foothills, it was not possible to make out caves.

He turned his new mare reluctantly. She didn't seem any keener than he was.

The Tekel appeared when Arion was halfway across the parched waste of slag and gravel. He caught movement in the corner of his eye and saw veiled men between the boulders. He dismounted and waited for them to come to him.

They were on foot, so it took longer than it might otherwise have done. "I don't have any money with me," he announced. "I just want to talk about getting Master Kallon's property back."

There were three of them, tall and lean and nearly identical behind their blue veils and dusty robes. The foremost motioned for Arion to follow, and he did, into the lee of Aghrèm n-Ălžăynăn, and up a steep, slippery path.

It was close to midday, and the air was burning when they came to a cave. Arion felt relieved to duck inside, where a handful of men sat around a clay lamp. Arion wanted to melt to the ground with them, but braced himself against the wall, flapping his hat for a fan. The cave was not large. An opening towards the back must lead deeper into the mountain.

One of the guides crouched and said something to the closest man, who replied curtly. “He says to tell you he doesn’t know anything about any Master Kallon,” the first said. “A quantity of goods has fallen into his hands. Do you wish to discuss business?”

Arion gritted his teeth. He had known extortion was the order of the day, but that didn’t make it palatable. “Yeah. Business. Sure. How much does he want?”

They suggested a number. “Are you mad?” Arion said, then bit his tongue. He tried to sound reasonable, like Master Kallon’s father when facing a difficult trading partner. “We don’t have that much. We brought goods to sell to buy goods to take back to Dorkytia. Now we don’t have any goods to sell, so we don’t have any money. I can’t give you more than an obol a bushel.”

This was relayed to the men with the lamp. “You’ll make six times that when you sell the olives in Teleleiyya,” the interpreter translated. “Four obols. It’s a fraction of the market price.”

Arion rubbed his forehead. “What I might get doesn’t change what I’ve got now. Nor does the market price. One obol is all I can pay.”

“There’s nothing to stop us selling the goods. Why sell so cheaply to you?”

“You’d have to travel to Elavrir, or beyond. You can’t sell in Teleleiyya, because the magistrates are watching for Dorkytian olives. There’s no point in selling at Taramsett; there’s a glut there. It’s me or nothing.”

The men conferred. One stood, brushed his robes with slow, exaggerated strokes, and picked up the lamp. He nodded to the interpreter, who did likewise.

“Come and see the goods,” the interpreter said. “Remember, you pay to carry everything to Teleleiyya.”

They entered the narrow passage at the back of the cave. The air was cool and dry, and reinvigorated Arion’s tired body. As they walked, he calculated how high he could go. *Not much higher.* Even if he and the others sold everything they had with them, it would not be enough. He was trying to work out whether he could go as high as three obols when he realised there was daylight ahead.

He frowned. “Is this the right—”

Someone shoved him into the blazing sunlight. He stumbled, caught himself, turned slowly. The spires of Aghrèm n-Ălžăynăn towered over him. He couldn’t see a way back to the road.

The interpreter barred the cave mouth with his spear. “Four obols,” he said. “Don’t come back empty-handed. If your master doesn’t have the money, try begging the kel-èsuf for alms.”

“Screw you!” Arion said. “If I meet them, I will!”

He plunged down the hillside towards what looked like a path, wishing he could have thought of a better retort. It was impossibly hot and the slope was steep. Pebbles and shards of marl rattled around his feet. He fell again and again, but did not stop his momentum, sliding and stumbling to the bottom as fast as he could. On either side, the black shoulders of the kel-èsuf castle stooped over the spreading valley.

He should rest until it was cool enough to travel. There was no shelter, though, so he pulled his hat tight over his ears and ignored the sensation of the top of his head floating gently away. He licked his cracked lips and got his bearings. What had these towers looked like from where he had left the horse?

Nodding, he chose a narrow ravine that led in the direction he thought he needed to go. There wasn’t so much as a magpie to be seen. Would the horse still be there? Had the Tekel stolen her and his water too?

The ravine levelled, and emptied onto hardpan. A hot wind swept sand from the wilderness, a great deal of the stuff. It threw what seemed to be half the desert at Arion as he got to level ground. He buried his face in the crook of his arm and struggled forward. He could barely see anything. His throat clogged with dust.

Phantasms sprang up, illusions of movement. Arion wiped at his gummed eyes, but his vision would not clear. How would he ever find his way? He steeled himself against the sandstorm and pushed on. He would not let those bastards defeat him. And he *was* making progress. When he craned his neck, he could almost make out the tops of the towers.

He slammed into something, put out his hands, felt bone. His arm slipped through a hole. Feeling his way round it, stretching up, he felt teeth. Through a momentary lull, Arion made out the upper half of a grin that could have swallowed a camel without chewing. A monstrous ribcage jutted from the sand.

Arion scrabbled backwards, slipping and skidding, helplessly repelled. The bones shifted, spilling sand. With a yelp, Arion jumped back and tripped over a half-submerged boulder. He slammed onto his back, clutching the amulet pouch Master Malekal had given him.

Somewhere, drums were beating. His hat lay several yards away. Sand crept over him, but he hurt too much to care.

A spear plunged into the sand. He stared up into bronze-flecked eyes. Robes billowed in the wind. He couldn't move. The ălžăyn was veiled, like a Tekel, but its exposed skin gleamed like sand-scoured bronze.

The creature bent over him curiously. Arion thrust the pouch into its face. "Go away!" he burst out. "I've got an amulet!"

The ălžăyn took the pouch from Arion's trembling grasp and held it up with a thumbless hand. Its fingers teased at the pouch's drawstrings. Arion couldn't hear anything over the blood pounding in his ears.

The ălžăyn gave a rumble of laughter and tossed the pouch onto Arion's chest. It pulled the spear from the ground, the bronze tip sliding past Arion's cheek. He rolled instinctively, but the ălžăyn only raised the spear as if in salute. Arion caught a galaxy of spear-points glittering in the swirling sand. There was nowhere to run. Everywhere he turned, the kel-èsuf blocked his way.

It hadn't worked, he realised with growing horror. Master Malekal must have given him a defective amulet. Of all the stupid things Arion had done lately, trusting that smooth bastard an inch had to be the worst. Now he was going to die in this barbarian country, and no one back home would know or care he'd been trying to recover Master Kallon's goods. He knelt, breathing hard, and squeezed his eyes shut as the wind rose up with a mocking roar.

Nothing. His heart gradually slowed. Had the amulet worked after all?

When the wind died, and he could see again, the kel-èsuf were gone. Only that huge skeletal grin remained, sinking deeper into the sand.

Arion got unsteadily to his feet. The air was clearing; already it was possible to see the way back to the desert. He half-stumbled, half-ran towards it.

The mare was nowhere to be seen. But that was not the most pressing issue.

On the plain below Aghrèm n-Ălžăynăn, two bands of Tekel riders faced off. One band must be the men from the caves. The other, larger band, which had spread out into a loose crescent across the road, was impossible to identify.

Arion slowed until he was hardly moving. He felt as if he was dreaming. Then he heard voices and realised one of the speakers was Tairyel kel Hàhlé. A burst of unexpected energy carried him the rest of the way.

"Ah, Master Arion," Mistress Tairyel said. "I am glad to see you. My husband would be cross if I let his guest come to harm." She sat with a spear at ease across her knees. A man from the caves made a scornful-sounding remark.

"Speak in Dorikan, if you please, cousin," Mistress Tairyel said. "As a courtesy to my husband's guest."

Arion stood swaying. "*Cousin*?"

"You see no harm came to your lost lamb through us," the man from the caves said. "You can shepherd him back to Teleleiyya now. Neither of you has any more business with us."

Mistress Tairyel hummed. "But you forget, Kăroza. There's also the small matter of a caravan attacked at Mossral's Well some days ago."

"None of us has any business robbing caravans. Your father prohibits it."

"So he does," Mistress Tairyel said pleasantly. "Believe me, I am *sure* you can swear to me that you and your brothers had nothing to do with the attack. I have no doubt whatsoever that your brother Malekal can swear the same. But trafficking in stolen goods is against the law too, no? However you came by them. I shall be sorry to tell my husband he's wasted his time looking up the charges. But I should be even sorrier to have to lay a complaint against you before my father. You know how he dislikes these little quarrels."

Kăroza leaned forwards to soothe his camel, which seemed skittish. After a moment, Mistress Tairyel nodded.

"So you will turn Master Arion's property over to me," she said. "I hope you won't argue. My husband will certainly scold me if I get into another fight before my ribs heal. And when we return to Teleleiyya, your brother and I shall discuss compensation for the men who died at Mossral's Well. That's fair, no?" She might have been smiling. "Call it a message for anyone else who wants to challenge my father's peace."

The journey back to Teleleiyya was mostly a blur. Arion remembered collapsing at Mistress Tairyel's feet and emptying a waterskin someone passed him down his throat. His head felt so light he thought he was floating. "My dear, my children don't keep *my* secrets from their father," the Great King's daughter said through the buzzing in his ears. "What made you think they'd keep yours?" Her men were bringing jars out of the caves. She looked on with satisfaction.

"Your courage is commendable," she added, "even if you could do with a little more common sense." She said something else about Arion looking as if he'd been pulled out of a foxhole, but he didn't really hear. He managed to stay on his horse all the way to the library, where it was fine to fall over, so he did.

"Why *did* the Great King's cousins attack us?" he asked her husband the following morning, after the master of the library had accepted ten jars of olives as a gift from Master Kallon, who was in no state to be giving gifts, but was not going to argue.

Master Tomas looked momentarily more opaque than usual. "Mischief. Boredom. Old family feuds. Ask my wife, it's her family. How was Aghrèm n-Ălžăynăn?"

Arion told him. He was even more indignant about being thrown into the kel-èsuf castle now he had returned safely. "Thank the gods I had Master Malekal's amulet," he said with a laugh that sounded a little desperate even to his ears.

"May I see it?" Master Tomas asked.

Arion pulled the pouch from under his chiton. Master Tomas turned it over on his palm. "I shouldn't really do this," he said. He loosened the drawstring and fished a strip of papyrus from the pouch. "But it's interesting. Oh."

"It's a magic spell?"

"No," Master Tomas said. "Tekel aristocrats like to think of themselves as great jokers. So do the kel-èsuf, I suspect." He seemed to disapprove. "It's a receipt for two hundred jars of olives and a hundred of oil."

Julia August *lives in a particularly green patch of the UK and prefers dates to olives. Her short fiction has appeared in Lackington's, SQ Mag and Cabinet des Fées. She is @JAugust7 on Twitter and j-august on tumblr.*

Mask of Sleep

By Rosemary Bensko

This story reminds us that epic-ness is not measured in word count.

The man inside the mask can no longer see through the eye-holes as the mask's eyes droop into the last increment in the horrible progression of a month toward closure. It sleeps its wood, paint peeling off the edges of the visible world. He hates the darkness encroaching day by day. He hates the movement toward nothingness, the mask-blindness that makes him think continually about what he did to his tribe. He should never have released the strange perpetually thirsty animal from the wooden pen and let it fly. Once in the air, the creature widened, became soft and white, and turned into a cloud that grew larger and larger and ate all the other clouds in the sky. No rain fell for months.

Elders died of thirst and starvation. Children would never grow up because of him. The new leader had turned to him after the previous leader died from thirst, and she bound the stiff, dark magic face to his. The mask is the worst punishment his village can implement. He should have never questioned authority. He would never question anything again.

He must find a way into the mask's dream world in order to escape the pain of hunger and thirst. His lips are crunchy, his tongue like sand. He scrapes his eyelashes against the edges of the wood. He sticks out his lower lip and angles his breath upward into the mask's eye sockets, first left, then right. He hums with fierce intensity, vibrating the evasive dreams invitingly, and stuffs moss into his ears to become deaf.

The green of the mask, invisible to him inside its darkness, becomes real in other ways. He caresses its pointed chin and wishes his own square jaw were as elegant. Everything about him has become inferior during these weeks. He has no right to live. He remembers the oldest woman in his tribe, how she reached for him with tenderness before she starved, before he was enmasked. His ill conceived action stopped the children's laughter. He remembers their faces. The sound of their voices haunts him. He wishes he could drink these memories. He wishes he could make new ones instead of being haunted by shame.

Breathing feels like death, so little oxygen gets in with the eyes sealed. He sticks out his tongue to lick puckered lips of wood, as dry as his own. He cannot breathe, can barely breathe.

Dizziness overcomes him. He falls mask-forward onto soft emerald moss. His head strikes wood. His brain dissolves and his mind becomes a hairy vine probing the magnificent tree's root system, on and on, until he has reached the bottom tip of its taproot. Nothing makes sense anymore. He tries to sip dry water through tendrils. There is no air.

The mask was carved from a branch of this tree. He shakes leaves. He wants birds. Their voices open stomata underneath the leaves so they can breathe. He must breathe or he will turn to dirt. In this state, he cannot be certain whether he is human, a tree, a mask, or an evil. He only knows that he is parched.

He seeps into the dreams of the mask, dreams that have nothing to do with words. They are sunshine and bacteria interacting. They are animals burrowing in holes, loam and bark becoming each other.

The dreams appreciate him being inside them; they whistle to the birds, which land on songshine. Birds groom twigs into nests of hair and future. They plant symmetry. They perch on faith, on death to invaders. A flock launches to better illustrate that concept with the cloud-like shape of bodies in synchronicity. The mask remembers being the tree so well. It can hear the sound of the flock's configuration. They form the shape of the bird-god of death.

As one, birds land. The tree trembles. The mask lifts its eyelids toward them, listening intently, wanting to take action. Its love awakens. It is not alone. It wants to share more with the man. It doesn't want him to die and disappear.

Dreams spill from the mask's eyes, goaded by the man gulping air. He rolls, spits out greenery, and bursts rank breath through the eye holes as they watch the birds. He sees the world around him now, something besides the awful pictures of his wrongdoings. He stands unsteadily and lurches off to search for water.

But his brain will never be the same. He has found the way inside the mask-dreams. He will forever after go back into the mask throughout all times, past and present. He has become a hero.

Tantra Bensko *teaches Interstitial Fiction Genres, those styles she finds endlessly fascinating that lie between Literary Realism and traditional Speculative tropes–like the story in this anthology. Some of the dreamlike characteristics could be explained by lack of oxygen in the man's brain. I like to trace the fallible subjective, biological origin of experiences that we take to be faithful representations of objective reality. The tribe used the regret arising after he caused a disaster, amplified by his time alone with his feelings inside the mask, as his punishment, combined with the dementia's ability to connect him with the world around him by becoming something other than human. Humans are not what I consider the best thing to be. I'd prefer to be a tree or a vine, at least as my body decays after death. http://onlinewritingacademy.weebly.com/*

The Hope of a Thirsty Planet

By Kaitlin McCloughan

It's nice to see a theme used to comment on a pressing social issue. This story by Kaitlin McCloughan joins a long tradition of such stories. I will not soon forget the world and characters she creates.

The ship launch is delayed to search for signs of aliens.

Although the anonymous call about an extraterrestrial saboteur was light on details and reliability, protocol insists on a thorough equipment inspection. I wait in the astronaut crew quarters, wringing my hands although I know the security team won't find anything.

They don't know it's me they're looking for.

The other astronauts are more bored than concerned. Boyu's eyes are glassy saucers as he reads a mystery novel on his visual implant and Maria sips coffee, pouting prettily over the cup at the video feed of her boyfriend back in Brasilia. Rajan slides his chair close to mine until our shoulders touch.

"Lin's first trip to Mars!" He says, punching me playfully. "Don't be so tense, you'll do great. Maria will show you the ropes."

I grant him an uneasy smile. "I guess I'm a little nervous. You know, first time going so far from Earth."

It's a lie. I was born light years from here, on a ship traversing deep space.

☼

My cradle was a reappropriated drawer from the ship's supply pantry. My mother played lullabies over the sound system in Mandarin and English and Arabic so I would learn those languages with the accents of Earth, and the other refugees crowded around to place sweet drops of their own water ration onto my lips. *You are part of a new generation*, they said. *You are the future of the Rogovan people.*

☼

When mission control detects no tampering, I take my place in the copilot's chair next to Maria. I touch my boot, my water bottle, and my sleeve. *Boot, water, sleeve.*

Maria raises her eyebrows. "You look really freaked, Lin. You know you basically don't have to do anything. Dropping supplies at Mars Base One is the most simple, boring mission we do." I nod. *Boot, water, sleeve.*

Basic supply runs don't warrant first-class vehicles, so the trip takes almost four hours. I pull my uniform away from my body where it has stuck to me in sticky pools of sweat. Fifteen minutes before we enter Mars's atmosphere I excuse myself to the bathroom.

The first part of the bomb is hidden in my boot.

I slide out the dark metal contraption, fifteen centimeters across, with a timer and an attached canister. Sneaking it aboard proved easy—United Earth Alliance trusts its astronauts.

I unclip the water bottle from my belt. Mother has insisted I carry water with me my entire life, *just in case*, but today it isn't filled with the nectar of life but a highly explosive compound. I pour it into the canister on the first piece.

The last part is the detonator. As soon as I lock this into place the timer will begin counting down two hours. I've been told that if I try to take the bomb apart after this, or if it is handled too roughly, it will discharge prematurely. My hands shake as I complete the assembly. The bomb almost slides out of my sweaty grip, but I catch it with a shuddering breath, and tuck it carefully into the uniform's waistband. When I return to my chair, I hold my hand over the bulge as if my stomach aches. My coworkers are chatting about the anonymous call.

"... alien threat seems old fashioned, doesn't it?" Boyu is saying. "I don't think many of them are coming over anymore. Maybe things are getting better in the colonies, or they just figured out they're better off staying home."

"I get that Bennetton is a real horror story with all the cyclones," Maria says, "but Rogov actually has a beautiful natural landscape. Have you seen those colorful mountains? I would love to go there."

I grip the lump under my shirt and stare at the floor.

"Rogov has a severe water shortage," Rajan says. "It affects food production, sanitation, everything. It's not so beautiful to actually live there."

I knew I liked Rajan.

"But still," he says, "I don't understand how people can be so crazy to spend six years traveling to Earth knowing perfectly well that there's a good chance they'll be killed the minute they arrive."

I answer before I can stop myself. "The six year survival rate on Rogov is even worse."

Everyone is silent for a moment, and then it's time to start landing procedures. Rajan taps my back and points to the monitor.

Mars glows from the screen, and I am awestruck in spite of myself. My mother was right—the Martian oceans are even more spectacular than Earth's.

To her, these oceans are humanity's greatest curse. It was only the successful terraforming of Mars that led deep space colonists to arrogantly believe they could tame planets like mine.

The survival rate of the ship I arrived on was fifty percent. Seven refugees died on impact when we soared through Earth's atmosphere with tail ablaze from United Earth Alliance's missiles. Three more, including my father, were shot by the ground patrol as we fled the ship for which he had spent his life saving. My mother took my hand in hers, and we ran into the desert. Our first Earth night was spent shivering in a rocky crevasse. The next day we found her cousin Olivia's house in Flagstaff.

They cried together about my father. Then Olivia stopped, went into the kitchen, and returned with a sparkling glass of cool water for me. I will never forget the heavenly taste as it slid down my throat.

"Yaeko, cousin," she said with her hand on my mother's shoulder. "Your daughter will never be thirsty." Then they cried again, but with smiles.

My name was Nadya. I was one of many young Rogovans named for our founder, the first brave and deluded soul to colonize the planets beyond

Earth's solar system. My mother took that name away and gave me one more common on Earth, and now I am Lin.

☼

As a teenager I turned up the volume on my second-hand holoplayer to eclipse the raucous sound of my mother and her Rogovan friends gossiping in the kitchen. I was tall like a spoiled Earthling and didn't tell my classmates I had a mother at home with tattoos down her back in the popular fashion of another world. She and I ignored each other more each day until around ten years ago, when the kitchen conversations suddenly grew hushed and intense. News had reached Earth of a new Rogovan plan.

After years of small groups making haphazard escape runs, a number of the top engineers on Rogov had organized a large-scale emigration. A fleet of six ships would come to Earth, each carrying a few thousand Rogovans.

Meanwhile, the United Earth Alliance's stance on alien landings had become increasingly hardline. They discovered decades before my birth that the desperate offspring of the first colonists were happy to fill Earth jails where life was safe and water plentiful. This, of course, at great expense to native taxpayers. Soldiers began shooting refugees on sight, citing the need to protect Earth from historic problems like overcrowding and resource depletion. If the Rogovan fleet was detected by Earth, as most approaching ships were, the loss of life would be devastating. Rather than abort, mission leaders on Rogov found a solution. If the deep space surveillance system on Mars Base One were disabled, the fleet would have a small window to slip through undetected. This would require destroying most of the base's East Tower. Certainly there would be some casualties, but how could you compare those few to thousands?

By the time the fleet was en route from Rogov I was training for the astronaut corps, in the perfect position to request simple assignments to Mars Base One. I joined the astronaut corps for the reasons everyone does: to explore, to serve the progress of humanity, to make a good salary. I wasn't pushed into it.

I'm almost sure of that.

☼

Mars Base One looks more like a grove of office buildings than a military complex. A single guard lounges by the gate. I'm relieved that security is relaxed, yet also oddly annoyed that the United Earth Alliance is so confident in its galactic dominance. The guard stands straighter as we approach.

"We've got the monthly shipment out of Fort Alba," Maria calls.

"Great," the guard says. "You coming inside?" We nod.

"Okay," the guard says. "I know it's not standard, but given the anonymous threat, I'm supposed to search you guys." I blanch and grip my waistband, but release it quickly.

"Sure thing," Maria says, agreeably raising her arms. The guard does a cursory pat-down, then moves on to Boyu, and Rajan. My chest tightens. When the guard reaches for me I hop aside.

"What's wrong?" Maria says. She stares so sharply I have to close my eyes.

"What's the issue? I'm military, I have C8 clearance, I'm allowed to be here, and I'm not comfortable with this man touching me." It seems I wait forever for a reply, but eventually the guard shrugs.

"Fine," he says. "I wasn't trying to cop a feel, but don't worry about it."

We enter the base. Maria and Boyu keep glancing at me, but Rajan retains his trademark relaxed smile. I breathe easier when I catch his eye.

It was that smile that interrupted my studious routine when I was a trainee, drawing me into friendship after other peers had written me off as too serious. Last week, unwinding over a microbrew after work, Rajan surprised me with a quick kiss and the suggestion of an actual dinner date. My only previous boyfriend was an illegal alien from New Palu I met in college. Unlike me, he was born on his home colony and wore his hair long to cover the welts toxic air had carved into his skin. When I admitted I found the scars sexy, he complained I was as shallow as Earth women. Thankfully Rajan is more easygoing.

☼

"Let's check out the recreation area," Rajan says with a grin. "Fifty soldiers stationed here, and it's practically a luxury resort. These guys live the good life."

I follow him down the hall, mortified at the tears pressing behind my eyes. I can't do this. I'm not a killer, just a human being who worked hard and became an astronaut, the same as Rajan and Maria and Boyu.

The bomb is timed to go off shortly after we leave Mars. My mother's friends didn't tell me how to defuse it, but it's not too late. I'll take it with me when we leave and find a way to eject it from the ship. No one will ever know.

I have settled happily into this decision when Rajan opens the gate to an indoor paradise of palm trees and singing birds and I see it: a swimming pool.

The decadence makes me furious. I think of my father, who gave everything to quench my thirst. I think of the hopeful refugees on the Rogovan fleet, people whose ancestors were Earthlings, but who are now unwelcome in utopia.

Later, with Maria and Boyu splashing in the pool and Rajan asleep in a deck chair, I slip away.

I raise my eyes to the metallic glint of East Tower. Mother and her friends went over the plan so many times that I feel as if I have been here before. Still, I pause in the shadow of the building, hand clutching the bulge at my waist. Then I clench my jaw and push open the heavy door.

A corridor gleams with sterile white light. Each movement I make is illuminated as if by stage lights; every step echoes sharply. I straighten my uniform and try to walk with purpose.

Operation Room One. The door is closed, but behind it I hear a low hum of serious voices and tapping keys. The men and women who man the Operation Rooms monitor for illegal extraterrestrials. These are the people who will perish in my attack.

I slow near *Operation Room Two*, delaying what will come next. As I pass, the door swings open and a tall young soldier steps out. I jump, my mind rushing ahead to find an excuse for being in the hallway, but the soldier just gives me a friendly smile and walks away. My legs go weak.

The next door is labeled *Personnel Office*, but it's a ruse. It's really an unoccupied room housing essential equipment for the surveillance program. This is my destination.

A lock with a keypad and fingerprint scanner protects the door. I glance both ways, take a metal card from my belt—Rogovan technology unrecognized on Earth— and press it against the keypad. The lock clicks and beeps once.

I pull the door open. There's no one inside. I let out a breath I forgot I was holding.

I ease the door closed. The room is dimly lit and I slide my hand along the walls to either side of the door, but there are no light switches. Squinting, I slip the bomb from under my shirt.

A row of metal panels marks the opposite wall. According to my mother's friends, the third panel is the best option for the device to ensure total destruction of the surveillance system. I lift the sheet of metal aside, exposing a tangle of colored wires.

The bomb fits snugly. For a moment I can't let go; my hand lingers on the device. It looks innocent, a toy abandoned in a dusty corner. I run a finger beside the detonator, and back away.

My hand is on the doorknob when I hear voices.

"... missed you last time," a man says. "I took time off to be with the kids after Binah left."

"I was so sorry to hear about that. You two were great together." The second voice is unmistakably Maria's. Their steps come closer.

I release the knob and wait, but they stop right outside.

"No way," Maria says. "Is that really Chloe? I thought she was still a baby." She laughs boisterously. Her voice is loud through the door. I want to move away, but my legs are frozen. I look over my shoulder at the bomb. The panel gapes open, baring the device to anyone who enters. I should hide it.

The door thunks. I stifle a gasp. Heavy breathing sounds and something slides against the wall.

"Mark, I can't," Maria says. "I have a boyfriend now."

"You had fun with me, you know you did." The heavy breathing morphs into sloppy kisses. A rapping on the door startles me and I jump, barely catching my balance against a narrow shelf.

"You know, this is a totally empty room," Mark says. "I have the access code. We have time, right? How long before you have to head back?"

My stomach lurches. I feel as if my chest will burst at any moment. Taking a deep breath, I turn the knob and burst out of the room.

Maria and Mark stumble backwards. Mark is the baby-faced Operation Room soldier I saw in the hallway earlier. Maria brushes her uniform straight, while Mark wipes lipstick from his face.

"Lin?" Maria says. "What are you doing here?"

I push the door closed behind me. "I got lost. This door was open, so I gave it a try." Maria and Mark stare down at me. They're taller than I remember.

"Lin," Maria says in a softer voice. "You've been acting pretty strange today. Is there something going on you want to talk about?" She nods at the door. "Is Rajan in there?"

"No, of course not!" My cheeks go hot. "He's at the pool."

Maria frowns, but there's only concern in her gaze, not suspicion. For an instant I'm tempted to let my confession spill out, but I pull my eyes away and focus on the blood-red United Earth Alliance insignia on Mark's uniform.

"Everything's fine," I say. "I got confused. See you on the ship in twenty."

As soon as I'm on board, a wave of exuberance washes over me. It's done. I picture six unharmed ships landing gently in the desert. Rogovans spill out to marvel at their new world. Refugees like my mother hand them all the water they can drink.

I will be a hero.

☼

I'm already in the copilot's chair when Maria and Boyu arrive. I look behind them nervously.

"Where's Rajan?"

"He's staying," Boyu says. "They wanted some engineering help, and we're overstaffed for this trip anyway. We'll pick him up next run."

The ship seems to spin. "He can't stay," I say too softly for them to hear.

Maria takes her chair, and Boyu sits by his console.

"Well?" Maria says. "Do we have confirmation?" It dawns on me that this is my job and I fumble for the controls. Mark's face appears on the monitor against a backdrop of Operation Room workers. Rajan is working on a computer with one of the doomed soldiers.

My tongue goes thick in my mouth. I can't seem to say our mission number. Maria steps in and confirms the launch.

"Let's go home," she says. "Initiating launch mode." Boyu taps a key and the doors seal with a deep sucking sound.

I eye the controls by my left hand. An inch from my fingertips is the emergency override.

"Ready engines for launch," Maria says. Boyu flips a switch. The ship roars to life, humming beneath my feet. I verify our launch activation, and the ship's computerized voice begins a countdown.

"10 seconds... 9 seconds..."

"See you next time, astronauts," Mark says on the monitor. He gives Maria a subtle wink.

I hit the emergency override. The engines go quiet.

Maria gapes. "What are you doing?"

"I forgot something," I say, "I have to go back." I start to tap a code to open the doors, but Maria grabs my hand.

"What did you leave behind? You didn't bring anything with you."

I shake her off. "Just let me out. Please trust me." I start toward the door.

Maria blocks me, expression hardening into suspicion. "What's going on, Lin?"

For five excruciating seconds I hold my silence before the words break out of my mouth. "There's a bomb." I hear my heartbeat in the pause. "I put it there."

"Why would you do that?" Maria looks genuinely confused. Boyu, however, is quick to act. He presses the code for the door, grabs my arm, and drags me down the gangplank before it has fully deployed. We jump the final step, and the three of us race back to the base.

"Where?" Boyu demands.

"Personnel Office," Maria and I say together. Boyu frowns, but does not slow. We careen past the guard into East Tower.

"Wait," he says, but we're already past.

Rajan is in the corridor. "What's happening?" He matches our sprint.

"Lin planted a bomb," Boyu says in a voice like ice. Rajan's expression changes quickly from calm curiosity to an anger that stabs me in the gut. I want to collapse in shame, but Boyu won't let go. We reach the Personnel Office, and I disarm the lock. The timer on the bomb shows ten minutes remaining. I pull it out of the wires.

Boyu grabs the device from me. "How do we disarm this?"

"I can figure it out," I promise frantically. "I'll fix it." Boyu sets the bomb in front of me and backs away. Maria puts her hand over her mouth. Rajan won't meet my eyes. I gawk at the detonator and ticking clock, but it only makes my head feel faint.

A soldier pushes me roughly aside. He handles the device with a cautious touch as one of his colleagues locks a muscled arm around my waist. The first soldier peers at the bomb for a few seconds, then cuts a wire on the detonator. The digital display blanks.

"That should do it." He leaves the room, carrying the bomb in cupped hands.

It's over, nothing but *that should do it* to signal the moment my life, and the hope of thousands of Rogovan refugees, unravels.

Silence roars in my skull. I fabricate excuses: *I only wanted to disable the surveillance systems and didn't think anyone would get hurt; I was forced to plant the bomb.*

I look at the stony faces of my crewmates, and the lies catch in my throat. "I'm sorry," I whisper.

☼

They left me on Mars. There's a maximum-security prison here, on an island in a luminous Martian sea. It's an ideal place to keep criminals like me far from civilization. I'm allowed visitors once a month, but no aliens of course, and who else would visit me? No one will say whether the Rogovan fleet made it to Earth. No one will talk to me at all.

And so, I spend my days standing at the small window of my cell, gazing at an endless expanse of water shimmering just beyond my reach.

Kaitlin McCloughan *lives and writes in Beijing, where she is employed by a Chinese tech company. In past lives she worked as a scenic carpenter, English teacher, and naturalist. Kaitlin is from Minnesota and is a graduate of Beloit College and Indiana University.*

Before Bastrop

By Michael Collins

Another story that comments on a social issue. By exaggerating an existing problem, Michael Collins encourages us to see in a non-threatening way, the flaws in our thinking toward and about each other. I knew when I read this that I wanted it for the collection. Two fine revisions later, here it is.

Fifteen miles before Bastrop, a five thousand acre reservoir sat in the middle of a sprawling desert wilderness. A razor-wire fence lined the perimeter, and "POACHERS WILL BE SHOT ON SIGHT" signs were posted at regular intervals. A ring of barren land, known as the Inner Rim, surrounded the man-made lake. On the far south side, a guard tower overlooked an arid forest of giant acuna cacti, night-blooming cereus, and organ pipe roots, packed together in a tangled mass. Tractors rumbled in the distance, keeping the buffer zone free of plants and structures, a pristine killing field.

Two men squatted in the forest's Cimmerian shade. They barely resembled men anymore, with shoulders sloped forward, and waist-long beards hanging in tangled folds down their emaciated frames.

"How many shots?" Bradburn asked. Ribs showed through a sagging rip in his shirt.

"Three," Walcott said. "There were three shots,"

"I counted four." Bradburn chewed deliberately on a saguaro bulb, extracting every last ounce of moisture.

Beyond the forest, four charred corpses sprawled on the freshly tilled soil, flash-fried, molded clumps of ash ready to be blown to oblivion by the next gust. Bradburn rubbed a ridge of scar-tissue directly above his navel. He remembered the injury like a petroglyph etched in a dark corner of his mind.

The reminiscence was crystal-clear: a gunshot like a thunderclap, the world crumbling across his shoulders in spike-strips of pain, falling as if from a thousand stories, bleeding out slowly on his back next to God, who was nothing more than an ant-eater crawling from a hole in the ground.

Thirst drove him to run the gauntlet all those years ago. Thirst drove him now, too.

"What do you say we wait for nightfall?" he said. Night had saved him before. Under its cover, he had dragged himself back to the forest, inch by excruciating inch. He remembered floodlights panning the Inner Rim like Sauron's eye, tripped by motion sensors strategically buried in sand drifts. Crawling like a worm, he had finally reached the cover of darkness, leaving a slime-trail of blood in his wake.

"I'm thirsty. Let's do it now," Walcott said, staring ravenously at the glimmering reservoir on the horizon. The tip of his tongue emerged and swung along the cracked terrain of his lip.

"No. We'll wait for nightfall." Dread seeped through Bradburn.

Darkness will save me again.

☼

Floodlamps blasted the Inner Rim.

"We got a runner," Probationary Police Officer Mark McCoy said crisply.

Field Training Officer James Dunn adjusted a thumb screw on his Bushnell Pacifica binoculars until the sight-picture was crystal clear. A poacher made his way across open field, stumbling through furrows, leather water pouches slung over his shoulders.

"Go ahead. Take his ass out."

McCoy pulled the trigger and his M-4 carbine bucked. A steady report echoed across the five-thousand-acre reservoir.

"Again."

McCoy pulled the trigger. An explosion of light and sound marked the .223 round's impact, at three thousand seven hundred feet per second. Dunn lowered the binoculars.

"That was close, Mark. He nearly made it halfway across."

Mark didn't answer immediately. It was his first kill, and he wanted to savor the moment. He lowered the rifle barrel. "If they only knew it's as easy to pick them off at night as during the day..."

Dunn chuckled. "Believe me, they know."

☼

Bradburn sat straight up. For a second, he thought he was back in Bastrop, camping under the stars, counting constellations, marking the time with a warm embrace of his open-ended future. War was only a whisper then. A full, happy life was at his fingertips. The second gunshot echoed, and illusion shattered.

"How many?" he said, recalling Walcott.

"Two," Walcott whispered. "There were two shots..." The whites of his eyes showed briefly. "By the way, you were talking about her in your sleep again. You said, 'Maggie's dying.'"

"Maggie *is* dying."

"They're all dying."

"She needs water."

"They all need water."

"I don't care about the rest of them. I care about *her*."

Walcott hung his head to the side and stared across the Inner Rim, awash in artificial glow. "I wonder if there's anyone left in Bastrop?"

"Everyone's dead in Bastrop," Bradburn said.

"Yeah, but what if somebody's alive? Maybe a whole colony of folks living in the sewers. Like rats."

"Bastrop is a graveyard," Bradburn said. "Rubble and ash and soot."

Bastrop. Only a bullet to the head could make him forget. He had met Maggie there. He could still see her standing in the old library, the smell of her hair wafting down a row of leather-bound books. His first words to her had been awkward, stumbling phrases like a stammering child speaking for the first time.

Later memories came to him: running his hands through her hair, whispering in the dark as the city collapsed in waves of fire.

I'm scared.

I know. Everything's going to be okay, Maggie.

You'll protect me?

I'll kill anyone who touches you. I was told to do this by God.

Bradburn slumped. If only he had known then what he knew now. The blades of his shoulders protruded like arrowheads. In the distance, a tractor rumbled across the Inner Rim, blow-torching ploughed-up remnants, weeds, cactus stems, corpses of bullet-ridden poachers. There had been fewer tractors the first time.

"Now?" Walcott said.

"Yeah." Bradburn stood. "Rock, paper, scissors for decoy?"

"Okay," Walcott said.

Flesh on flesh, fists struck palms.

McCoy leaned against the observation deck sidewall. He exhaled a thick plume of smoke.

Dunn slapped his shoulder. "You did real good for a damn rookie."

Mark took another drag, savoring the rich flavor of burning tobacco. An honest-to-God Cuban. A *Cohiba*, no less. This was a big day.

"How many poachers did you bag and tag your first time out?" he said.

"Dead-eyed two," Dunn said. "Winged a third. Hit him flush in the abdomen, but we never did find the bastard. Must have bled out, though."

"This killing thing is a real cinch," McCoy said. Smoke haloed his head.

"Don't get cocky."

"Why? It's as easy as shooting paper silhouettes at the rifle range."

"Don't underestimate…" Dunn trailed off as his mind drifted through a mist of time and space. Thousands of kill-shots in his fifteen-year career dissolved to distant memories.

"Don't underestimate what?" McCoy said.

"Desperation," Dunn said. He blinked and focused on McCoy. "Don't underestimate the power of desperation."

Bradburn cinched straps. The vest hung, a lead weight against his jutting ribcage. He took a breath. Then another. He tasted traces of water in the air. The star-lit reservoir taunted him like a mirage in open desert. He knew he would never make it. He closed his eyes and let his mind drift on a tide of memory: the texture of Maggie's lips, the silk of her curls. He'd made promises too.

Don't leave me. She was too weak to move from her cot.

You need water.

I need you.

I'll never leave you.

You're leaving me, now. Don't go.

He leaned into the lavender scent of her hair.

We can talk, he said. *You can talk to me, and I'll talk back.*

You'll be gone. You're not coming back.

Maggie, I'll never leave you.

But you are.

"You ready?" Walcott said.

Bradburn looked up. Maggie was a white-faced wraith at the edge of sight. Only the smell of her hair remained.

"You ready?" Walcott repeated.

"Make sure she gets her share," Bradburn said. He snugged two bandoliers across his chest. Bullets made good shrapnel.

"I will," Walcott said. "Maggie'll get her share, I promise."

"Good." Bradburn said. He worked his mouth, but it was too parched to produce saliva. "Good." Then he was flying over the field, wind stinging his eyes. Light blinded him momentarily. He tripped through a trough, caught himself, and ran again.

Walcott counted slowly to ten.

"We got a runner." McCoy swung his carbine to the high-ready position, beaded-up on his target, and pulled the trigger. The figure stumbled, but kept coming, picking up speed.

"You pulled left." Dunn said, binoculars trained on the scene below.

McCoy fired again.

"Pow. Center-mass. Good one, kid."

The poacher dropped to his knees, blood gushing.

"Flush?" McCoy said.

"Yeah, gut-shot, I think."

Slowly, the poacher stood. Dunn noted the pack cinched to his chest.

"Ahh, shit. Son of a bitch is strapped. Go for a head-shot."

"Here comes another," McCoy said. A second figure crawled into view, on hands and knees. Then he was up and running across the Rim.

"Forget the trailer!" Dunn said. "Take out the first guy." McCoy pinched his left eye shut and fired. A plume exploded two feet behind the strapped man, who continued to stagger toward the tower.

"Take him down, goddammit!" Dunn reached for his carbine. One hand on the stock, he swung the barrel up, simultaneously engaging the laser sight. He exhaled slowly, and squeezed the trigger. Red mist exploded from the strapped man's chest. He stumbled and nearly fell.

"Did you hit him?" McCoy said.

"Yeah."

"Jesus Christ, he's still coming."

The pack detonated. With a grinding groan, the guard tower's struts crumpled, and the observation deck came crashing down.

Walcott's eyes watered as he reached the end of the field. He scaled the razor-wire fence, slicing his feet to ribbons. Then he was inside, nothing between him and the reservoir.

Adrenalin gushing, he ran the final yards, fell to his knees, and dipped his hands into cool water. He scooped it to his mouth. Dust and heat and even death flaked from his awareness with each gulp. All that mattered was that he had made it, that his thirst was slaked.

Then he remembered Bradburn's sacrifice. The explosion. *Maggie.* It came upon him, not with a gush of guilt, but a slow welling of hope. Trailing droplets of blood, he filled the leather pouches, one by one, by one, all the while gazing toward the horizon.

Before Bastrop the land was black. But dawn was on its way.

Michael Collins *writes: "I am a sergeant with The Houston Police Department. In my spare time, I love to read, write, and most importantly hang out with my amazing family. I have an M.A. in Creative Writing from Boston University, where I studied under Nobel Prize recipient, Derek Walcott. My stage plays have been performed around the country and have been reviewed favorably by The Boston Herald. My short stories have been published by Dark Moon Books, Angelic Knight Press, and*

Sunbury Press, with upcoming publications by Dark Continents Publishing and Sky Warrior Books."

I would like to thank Stephen Ramey, who offered pointed commentary at every stage of the writing process. Owing to such excellent editorial guidance, I was able to improve all aspects of my story, "Before Bastrop". Thanks, Stephen, for the awesome advice!

To learn more about my writing, please visit my author's website: www.collinsfiction.com

Shuttle Season

By Jen White

Here's a classic SF concept delivered with a decidedly down-under flare by Aussie writer, Jen White. See what happens when you cut budgets? Are you reading this, NASA?

The air was so dry furniture hollowed into brittle skeletons. Willy willies sent folding chairs flying into the bland blue sky and end tables rolling like tumbleweeds over endless expanses of desert, never to be seen again. Nowhere was more desolate than this piece of Australian outback and there were no people more suitable for inhabiting this inhospitable universe than we, all done without the luxury of a spacesuit and often without shoes. This was why the spaceport took so many of us. We would put up with conditions no self respecting urban dweller would stand for.

And then one day the heavens erupted, hawking and coughing overhead. We stopped in our tracks and looked straight up, shielding our eyes against the white light as a shuttle jet cut through the sky, whipping up the icy air.

And then another came. And another.

And the clouds let go their rain.

It was the season of the shuttle.

My brother, Drayer, was a shuttle rider. He had been to the moon many times. "No big deal," he had said with a shrug. "Just another stretch of dusty, dry dirt." And Mars? "Windy, yeah, but nothing a body can't handle."

And here he was, one bright, wet afternoon, strolling down the path to our house, pack slung over his left shoulder, still limping a bit from when he had that accident hooning over the lake bed five years before, but looking strong and tanned and purposeful. Dad was at the door, holding it wide open well before Drayer reached it.

"Well, this is an unexpected pleasure, Dray," Dad said.

"Got a short leave," Drayer said, "so thought I'd drop in."

"And boy are you welcome," Dad told him. "Like always. Come in and rest."

After a hug from Mum, Drayer took his stuff upstairs. We didn't say much, just busied ourselves waiting for Drayer to come back down, wondering why he was here all of a sudden, what had happened? If he had a short leave why didn't he go to the city like he usually did?

"He doesn't seem himself," Mum fretted. "They're working him too hard. He's got to learn to say no."

It was a good ten minutes before Drayer returned and sat on the couch, holding himself as stiff and brittle as the furniture. He waited for us to gather round.

"What is it?" Mum asked.

Drayer took a deep breath and scratched under his eye. "I had to come quick, before the other one."

"What other one?" Dad said. I could hear the worry in his tone.

"Something happened up there," Drayer said. He paused, as if he were still working out what he wanted to say. "Aw, hell." He looked at each of us, *glance, glance, glance*. "We went through an energy shift on the way back. We thought we got through okay, but looks like not completely. I've gone and copied myself. But I'm the real one, and I had to come here straight away to make sure you knew."

"Oh, Drayer," Mum said. "Don't worry, love. We'll just deal with it." She glanced nervously at the front door, as if expecting Drayer's copy to burst through at any moment.

"But that's just it," he said. "They don't know what will happen. To me, to it. It's just wait and see."

"Then you did the right thing," Mum said. "Coming here. Who best to wait with you than family?"

"Where is he?" I asked. "Where's the other one?"

"Ssh," Mum said.

"It," said Dad.

"I don't rightly know," Drayer said, voice firming up with the anger coming in. "I left him scoffing down chicken parmagiana in the canteen."

Drayer's favourite meal.

He shook his head. "If he's an exact copy he'd be here, right? He'd be thinking just like me. But he's not here, so I don't know how much the same or different he is. There's so much I don't know. Hell, it's like a chess game. That's why I thought I better get over here, be with people who really know me, who'd recognise me straight away."

"We didn't doubt, "Mum said. "We knew it was you as soon as you came on down the pathway."

But don't you remember? I thought. *We were all wondering what was wrong. We could all sense the not—quite—rightness of something. Don't tell me you've forgotten already. Don't tell me you're ignoring it.*

"Shouldn't it be in quarantine or something?" Dad said. "How come they didn't lock you both up? I would have."

"The base," Drayer said. "It's all falling apart bit by bit. Business hasn't been that good. Lots of cost cutting, retrenchments. The place is filthy, you should see it. Mice everywhere, and everyone's pissed off and bitching at each other. And no one can make a decision. That's how come. Probably why I'm in this mess now, cutbacks on maintenance. I can tell you, after all this I'm out of there. Jesus, what a mess."

I couldn't sleep that night. Mum and Dad were awake too. I'd found over the years that if I held myself really still so that the sheet didn't move, didn't rustle, and if I turned the air conditioner off for a bit, and the overhead fan, I could hear their whispers.

"I can't believe you aren't one hundred percent sure," Mum said. "Don't you know your own son?"

"We'll, if he's a copy, he's a copy," Dad replied. "Might be an exact copy. How would we know?"

"Maybe we've got two sons now," Mum said. "And there's nothing bad about that is there?"

It's all right to be positive, I thought, *but what if the other one's evil or crazy? What if it's ready to spawn? What if it's a robot? Or what if they're only half Drayer, each of them?* That's how I spent the night, thinking through all the *What Ifs* in this particular situation, mostly bad.

I wonder how Drayer spent the night.

None of us knew what to do with ourselves the next morning. We ate our toast and cereal in silence, and washed the dishes, and then there was nothing left to put our attention to, but Drayer.

"C'mon," I said. "Let's go for a drive. You can drive us over to the lake. It's got water in it."

"Good idea," Drayer said. He looked relieved.

We drove for a couple of hours through the sudden green, the rain sheeting down all around us, beating a steady tattoo on the roof of the car. The world smelled different when it rained, felt different, had a different weight.

"Gotta be careful of potholes," I reminded him. "They're like quicksand now. If we get stuck we'll never get out."

"You don't need to tell me how to drive," Drayer said. "I grew up here. And besides, I drive a shuttle now. That's a bit more complicated than this."

"Remember when we drove over to Ben's place and we got the back stuck?" I said "Took two vans and a ute to pull us out."

Drayer grunted yes, a small smile on his face.

"And remember when we went swimming after the rains two years ago," I said, "and I got caught in a water slip and you had to dive in and haul me out? If you hadn't been there, well, who knows? Never did thank you, so I am now."

"You don't have to keep asking me if I remember this or that," he said. "It's really me."

"It's not a test," I said. "It's conversation."

"Well don't," he said. So I was quieter after that, just listening to the rain and the car noises and my own heartbeat.

"The other one," I asked after a bit. "Is it a copy, or an alien, or what?"

"They don't know." He glanced sideways. "I remember it happening, though, and afterward I felt changed, doomed. I don't know how to explain it. I'm not good with words like you. But I felt... mortal... all of a sudden, precarious. I'm the real thing, I swear, but I don't know what was done to me. That thing, it's stolen something. My essence. My time." He jabbed the steering wheel with the heel of his hand. "What'll I do?" he said, fear in his voice.

"Don't get ahead of yourself," I said. "That's you, always champing at the bit, jumping into things heedless. Slow down. You need to find out exactly what's happened first. Then you can make your plans."

"What if I don't agree with what they find? What if I don't like it?"

I had no answer for that.

When we got back, Dad told us he'd been in contact with the spaceport.

"The message is, 'just sit tight,'" he said. "So far, they know as little as we do."

"I could have told you that," Drayer said. "Besides, who did you even talk to? Most of them wouldn't know what the hell is going on."

"I just hoped they'd learned something new since you arrived," Dad said. "Look, I've got to do something to help. You're my son."

Drayer nodded, though I could tell he wasn't happy. *That's Drayer*, I thought, *his own true, sulky, down in the mouth self.* But maybe the clone was like that too. I couldn't see anything obviously fake about this Drayer, but, just to be sure I took to locking my door of a night.

The rain held off that next day, so Dad insisted on a barbecue for tea. We sat in the backyard by the pool, surrounded by frogs chanting their descant, and the drips of the still wet leaves, and the strong, strong smell of rain. And Drayer tossing down one tinnie after another.

"What's wrong?" I said.

He frowned. "I don't feel all that comfortable being out here, with the sky so large overhead, all them stars and the planets. Who knows what might drift by? If it happened once it could happen again."

"Yeah, but that was up there," I said. "You're down here now, tethered to the earth. Whatever it was can't get you here."

"How would you know? I sure as hell don't." He took a pack of cigarettes out of his top pocket, drew one out and lit it.

"I didn't know you smoked."

"Took it up a few months back," he said. "Everyone on base was doing it. After a time I began to feel left out. Besides, it calms me." He drew deeply and exhaled a cloud of smoke. "What goes on inside a person can be surprising." He puffed again.

I watched him, feeling less certain by the minute.

"God, so I smoke, all right? Get over it. It's like I can never change. If I do anything different it's evidence I'm the wrong one. Humans aren't set in stone, you know. Humans change all the time."

"Come and get it," Dad called over his shoulder. "Chops, snags, onions, the lot."

Drayer sat forward. For the first time since he'd returned, he looked straight at me. "What's your honest opinion?"

I thought about it for a bit. "I've never taken much notice of you," I said. "Never really looked at you that close, and I bet you never looked close at me neither. We don't have to, do we, when we're with each other all the time? It's only with distance, with doubt, that we have to keep checking." I shrugged. "But you seem real enough. Nothing's ringing false." *Or not too false*.

Drayer eased back into his folding chair. "Anyway," he said. "I'm going into trucks. Much safer."

"You never seemed interested in safety before," I said

"Yeah, well after something like this, when every bloody thing you thought you knew and were gets shaken up, you just want a bit of predictability. And trucks it is."

"And you like driving," I agreed.

"And don't you go up either," he said. "I know you want it as bad as I ever did, and now look at me."

"I'll take that one on board, Dray," I told him.

He stood suddenly, knocking his chair down behind him. "Stop bloody staring at me, Mum! I can tell you don't believe me. Oh God, I've lost everything, every bloody thing, even you. Why did I go up there?"

"No, love, it's not that," Mum said. She reached a hand towards him. "It's that I'm remembering all over again how precious you are."

"I can't handle it, Mum," Drayer said, quieter. "Look, I'm going upstairs. I need to have a lie down. Think about things. It's been a big couple of days."

"But Drayer," Mum said, "you've not eaten a thing."

"Let him go, Faye," Dad said. "Let him go."

How must it be, I wondered, *to feel as if you might not be yourself anymore?*

After that, the three of us sat in the darkening yard eating our meat and onions, talking in whispers, not knowing what to think. We left Drayer a plate in the oven, but he didn't come down again.

Drayer didn't come down for breakfast either, so Mum went up to check.

"Keith," she called. "I can't find him. All his stuff is here, but he's nowhere about."

Dad and I ran up, Dad's longer legs beating me to the door. I peered between Mum and Dad at Drayer's bed, the sheet all messed up, the dip in the middle where he'd huddled against the cool of the air conditioning, and I thought to myself that whether it was Drayer or clone Drayer, it can't be very nice in the middle of the night to be suffering so when you've got no one to hold but your own doubtful self.

"What's happened?" Mum wailed. "Why would he go?"

"Hold on, love," Dad said. "We don't know anything yet. Just hold on." He took a last look at the room and went downstairs. I could hear him on the mobile.

Mum bent over the bed as if she were trying through sheer will to make Drayer appear. When he didn't, she began to go through his bags.

"No clues," she said. "How am I ever going to get over this when I can't understand a thing about it?"

Does this mean no more Drayer? I wondered. What would life be like without him?

"Come on down, Mum," I said. I pulled at her arm until she dropped Drayer's things, and came with me.

Dad was standing in the living room, still holding the phone.

"They think we had the copy here," he said. "And he's probably... evaporated. Bloody irresponsible, if you ask me."

"But he felt right," Mum said. "He felt proper. I bonded with him. Maybe the wrong one's disappeared. How on Earth would they know?"

He'd tried to tell me he'd felt changed somehow, but still himself. He hadn't been able to explain it any better. And now he was gone.

"They did tests," Dad said. "The real one's on his way. The real Drayer'll be here soon."

"Maybe they're saying that so we don't sue them," Mum said.

"Now look," Dad said, "we've got to trust them. We've got no choice."

And a few hours later there he was, another Drayer, strolling down the path just like before. And, like before, Dad opened the door wide, and Mum hugged him.

"Just in time," Dad said. "Looks like the sky's ready to open up."

And Drayer smiled his small smile, just as the other one had, and slouched in, and we all watched him as he took his pack up the stairs.

How do we know? I thought. *Is this the Drayer who was born here and grew up here and spent his whole young life dreaming of shuttles? The one who comes back every now and then, and puts up with Mum and Dad and mostly ignores me?* Earth Drayer. Australian Drayer. Desert Drayer. After all, the other Drayer had been so certain he was the real one. How will we ever really know?

Jen White*'s greatest desire growing up was to become an astronaut, eventually owning her own spaceship. However, as she is technologically challenged, she naturally became a writer instead. Jen lived for some time in the Northern Territory of Australia and, although she has now moved to gentler climes, she still finds inspiration in the vibrancy and mystery of Australia's north. Jen's short stories have appeared in magazines such as Andromeda Spaceways Infight Magazine; and in anthologies including Dead Red Heart, Future Lovecraft, and Beware the Night. Jen blogs at jenmwhite@livejournal.com*

A Long-Forgotten Memory

By Elizabeth Spencer

Here, Elizabeth Spencer delivers a memorable tale about forgetting. A thirst for water can drive us to extremes. Is the same true of a thirst for knowledge? (This story also took second place in the annual Parsec Short Story Contest.)

One thousand, five hundred and forty-six years passed before Alucia heard something worthy of remembering.

It was a low, steady rumble, like the growling of a giant cat that echoed from some place high in the heavens. She chased it down the cracked earth that had once been the main thoroughfare of the city, toward the crumbled stones of the eastern gate. The gate once stood so tall that only the towers peeked above the crenellations, but the sands had long since piled up enough to let her reach the top of the battlements.

A giant ship was sailing across the skies, its hull so black that it sucked in the desert sun and left a haze of crackling air behind it. A bubble of leather lashed to its top bobbed in the winds. The whole behemoth moved through the air by the force of dark, spinning *things* that thrummed loudly enough to hurt her ears.

She drank in the strangeness like a man in the desert drank water—deeply, with the desperation of someone who knew they could drown themselves in it and still not be sated. She had never seen anything like this ship. She memorized its speed and the angle it cut across the sky. She noted the time (barely two hours after midday), the wind speed, the wind direction, the heat. She was beginning to count the rivets in its hull when it rushed over her head.

She spun around as the great bulk lowered onto the wide plain that had once sat outside the Grand Palace. She abandoned her count—she could not see the rivets now anyway—and ran as fast as she could toward the ship.

By the time she reached the palace fields, the huge black bulk was steaming and its spinning *things* were sending clouds of sand billowing through the air. A door had been opened in the side, and men were pouring out, hands over eyes as they squinted into the midday light. They were tying the ship down to rocks by the time she reached them.

"Welcome to Shen Aspeth Vio, Jewel of the Desert, Realm of the Acetic Magi and Those Who Followed," she said breathlessly, the words bursting out of her all at once. "I am the Memory of this city."

The men took one good look at her and started to laugh.

"Wouldn't be a magical ruin without magic," one with calloused hands and great broad shoulders said as he finished mooring the ship. "Is that what they used to look like? Creepy eyes."

"Captain won't be pleased," another said.

"May as well tell him."

"Who is your captain?" Alucia asked. The men did not even look at her. They tugged their knots tight, retreated into the ship, and slammed the door shut.

From then on, they did not open their door, and they certainly did not let her in. She could see them sometimes at the windows. Whenever they met her eyes she would stand tall, look eager, and smile. But no one opened the door.

It was cruel of them. This was an *event,* and these were *people,* and they had stories and tales to share. She *needed* them. So she settled herself down in the sands and waited for someone to open the door.

It had been one thousand, five hundred and forty-six years since Shen Aspeth Vio's waters dried up. Alucia remembered. She remembered the wealthy mages who loaded up camels with wealth and water and left before anyone else realized what was happening. She remembered the people who were left behind, who grew angrier and more violent as the water ran low. She remembered the killing, the needing, the dying. She remembered the last people, parched and empty, wheezing for breath through paper-dry throats.

And then there was nearly nothing left to remember. Sand collected against the walls. Towers crumbled. It wasn't *enough.* And so she waited, because she *needed* to wait, even if she wanted to talk to these men so badly it hurt.

Night fell and darkness swallowed the earth before they opened the door. Six men dropped a metal gangplank and shoved something down it, a metal cart as tall as two men, with rattling wheels and a great curved claw at the front.

After that came a scrawny man with messy brown hair and wide glasses, who held a metal box in one hand and a glass wand in the other. He fiddled with the box all the way down, so absorbed that he would have wandered off if not for the sharp, short words from a second man. Alucia eyed this last man curiously. It had been hundreds of years since she had seen a man like this, but he had the bearing of a leader. He had to be the captain the men had mentioned before.

He was an older man, maybe in his forties. He wore a long, leather coat too heavy for the desert and a leather hat with flaps tucked over his ears. His eyes, deep-set into his dark-skinned features, burned with impatience. He saw Alucia, scowled, and stormed toward her.

"You're still here?" he snapped.

The man with the box meandered up behind him. "Perhaps she can't help it, Captain." His voice was so cheerful compared to the captain's that it was almost discordant. "She seems to be some kind of aetheric projection."

"Did I ask you?"

The man shrugged noncommittally, turned something on his box, and waved the wand in front of Alucia. The box let out a keening shriek. "See?" he said, as if it explained anything. "Magic."

"I was brought into this world by a sorcerer," Alucia explained. "Where are you from?"

"Fascinating," the man with the box said. "I don't suppose you'd come back with us?"

He had not answered her question. She tried not to sound impatient. "I cannot leave the city."

"Ah. Bound to the location. Very typical of this era."

"Just what we need," the captain snorted. "Another ruin full of mage-trash." He poked her silvery-white shoulder. "You're alive?"

"No," Alucia corrected. "I'm corporeal."

"Mage details. You have a body. Is there anything else alive in this town?"

"Fifty-five scorpions. Twenty burrowing spiders. A snake that suns on the aviary—"

"People, I mean people."

"Oh." She blinked once, and tallied the years in the time it took her eyes to open. "No one has lived here for one thousand, five hundred and forty-six years."

"One thousand—" the captain sputtered. "What kind of projection lasts a thousand years?"

"By *projection*, you mean me?" she asked pleasantly. "Because that is not my age. That is how long everyone has been dead. I'm three-thousand-and-thirty-two years old." Before he recovered, she said, "Where did you come from?"

"What?"

"Or tell me about your ship. About your people. Your family." She inched closer with each word. "*Anything.*"

The captain's eyes narrowed. He looked over his shoulder at the man with the box, who offered an uncertain shrug. Alucia felt a little like her chest might burst from impatience in the time it took him to respond.

"Why would I do that?" he finally said.

"So I can remember it," Alucia said. Desperation made her voice shake a little. "Tell me your name."

"I don't have time for stories," the captain said. "It's already hotter than the back end of a forge, and we have work to do. Look, Miss…" He paused. "*Miss.* What am I saying? As if you had a name. Who names their puppets?"

"Alucia."

"What?"

"My name is Alucia. And I last saw a person four hundred and thirty-seven years ago. He traveled across the desert on foot. When he reached Shen Aspeth Vio, he was barely able to ask for water. I didn't learn much from him." Her smile widened, "But I could learn much from you."

"Delightful," he mumbled, with a barely visible shudder. "I don't want to have this conversation. So let me clear this up. I am not going to waste my precious time telling you stories. It's been three thousand years since anyone's even thought about this… What was it, a commune for mages?"

"It is called the Realm of the Acetic Magi and Those Who Followed because—"

"I don't care," the captain snapped. "I'm sure there's a historian who might, but it's not me. Look, we don't need magical cities and *ascetic magi*, because we have a damned airship built out of steam and steel, and the only thing it's ever needed a mage for was to forge its engine. I'm an engineer sent here to find magic-soaked alloys for the fleet's next wave of aetheric battleships. And you probably care as much about that as I care about you, because you probably don't even know what battleships are."

Her eyes went wide. "Tell me."

"*No*. Listen. We're here to mine this city. If you're bound here, then the least you can do is keep out of our way."

His words hurt. She must have shown it in her eyes, because he scoffed and looked even angrier.

"What does it mean to mine a city?" she asked tentatively. She did not truly want to know. She only wanted him to keep talking. To say more. To stop telling her to leave.

"I don't have time for this," he snapped. "Leave my men alone and keep away from my ship."

☼

Mining a city was, it turned out, very much like mining anything else. First, the man with the box—Marthiel, his name was—would walk between the old foundations, waving his wand over them until the box responded. Then the metal cart with the claw would dig into the earth, revealing foundations and walls that had not seen light in hundreds of years. This seemed to interest the men from the ship, but was as boring as sunshine to Alucia. She knew every stone, and she would have told them about them if they had asked her. They did not.

Marthiel was the only one she knew by name. At least three times a day his wand would lead him to her and the box would wail until he turned it off. He was always busy, but would, at least, answer her when he could.

“Why do you need stones?” she asked in the early morning of the first day. “Their spells have not worked for centuries.”

“Your mages were very powerful,” he said. “The enchantments on these buildings lasted much longer—and were much stronger—than any our mages can summon now.”

“Why is that?”

“I don’t know.”

That was a curious answer, and also an insufficient one. She puffed out a breath, trying not to be impatient, and asked something else. "What *are* your mages like, then? What do they do? Has magic grown very weak outside Shen Aspeth Vio? ”

“Ah, I would not call it *weak*. And mages, they…” He seemed overwhelmed. “They do quite a lot. They make machines, I suppose?”

"What are machines?”

That did not seem to be easier to answer. He looked bemused and perplexed and fell silent as he tried to come up with an answer. Before he could, someone called out for him, and he excused himself to go wave his wand over the aviary.

Marthiel never had much time. The others were not so kind.

By late afternoon of the second day the men had started to dig up a house that had once belonged to a young mage. Alucia remembered him. He was a handsome young man who died at the age of twenty-three when the wells dried up and he had not the magic to fill them. She remembered every inch of his room—the tapestries, the woven chests—and dutifully amended her memories now that the east wall was lying on his neighbor's house and the western wall was being hauled off by the crew.

She was lying on her stomach along the ruins of his garden wall when one of the men—the man with calloused hands who had laughed when she introduced herself—came by, hauling a stone on his shoulder.

"Tell me about where you came from," Alucia asked. "Is it an empire? Is it run by mages or men?"

"Damn mage-things," he grunted. "Can't you tell I'm busy?"

She could, but she was disappointed.

Later, when the sun had started to slip toward the horizon, she crouched on a statue that had lost everything above its waist more than seven hundred years earlier. Another man was dutifully chiseling away stones that lined the fountain.

"Do mages not enchant stones anymore?" she asked. "Is that why you had to come here?"

The man shot her a dirty look, then yelled over his shoulder. "Does no one know how to un-enchant her?"

It was not enough.

For hours Alucia tried to talk to them, but no matter how she asked, the crew ignored her, mocked her, or turned away. She could not even learn something new from their ship, because the captain yelled whenever she approached. Only Marthiel seemed genuinely interested, and he was busy waving his wand over the town and flagging every piece that had ever borne an enchantment.

It wasn't *nearly* enough. She felt like a cactus in the desert sun, parched and empty and crusted with sand. It was as if she were watching a great, wide pool of rainwater evaporate into the air. There were so many *people*. So many *stories*.

"Why will no one tell me more?" she asked Marthiel on the third day. "Do you fear magic?"

“Oh no,” he said, turning off his box mid-shriek. “Magery is a very respected profession. Mages only use projections like you to talk to each other, and, well...” He shrugged. “Projections aren’t very smart.”

“Does that not make me rare?” she asked. “Do the others realize that I am not like your projections?”

“You can’t blame the men for not making friends. You’re a tool to them. A chatty puppet. But mostly, no one likes mining the desert. They’re probably anxious to be home.”

Home. The word ached. Alucia pulled her knees to her chest and made a muffled noise. Marthiel touched her shoulder in a way that seemed concerned, but one of the others called to him and he excused himself politely, leaving her alone with her want and her need and her fear.

They wanted to go home. They wanted to leave.

Everyone left Shen Aspeth Vio. They left, they fled, they died. The few who had come to the village since the fall of the city had not even lived long enough to talk. And now a crew of men were here, alive and well and vibrant, and they *chose* not to tell her a thing.

It was not fair, and it was not right.

She made her decision on the fourth night.

The men were gathered around a fire they had created in the ruins of the pleasure gardens. They were sitting together, Marthiel and the captain with them, laughing and singing and drinking something that smelled strongly enough that it carried on the wind. Alucia did not conceal herself as she walked past.

“Still begging for stories?” a man said, voice trailing off in laughter. “Come to ask about our childhoods? Our pets’ names?”

“No,” she said. “Not tonight.”

Marthiel looked alarmed, “Are you all right?”

She headed for their ship, black against the dark blue night, a great shadow before the tapestry of stars. The gangplank was propped against the open door. Even outside, she smelled the magic, an acrid and beautifully familiar smell.

The scent led her into the ship's cold metal innards, across hammered iron floors, past walls bearing glass tubes that gave off a puckering light that felt distantly magical—not like the once-glowing stones of Shen Aspeth Vio, but something akin. She heard men cry out far behind her, their boots rattling on the gangplank. The captain's roar split through the night.

"Damn it!" he yelled. "I told you to stay off my ship!"

Alucia descended a walkway to a door heavy enough that she had to dig in her heels to open it. It creaked inward to reveal a giant block of metal, studded with whirling gears and hemorrhaging heat. At least a dozen metal tubes branched into the walls. Their sides were covered with sigils, and they glowed a pale, hazy blue.

The captain's footsteps clanged closer. Alucia stepped inside the room.

Magic. The engine might be foreign, the ship unknowable, but its power, its *magic* sang straight to her heart. She might not know what had become of magic in these thousands of years, or what their mages had meant to create with it, but in that instant she knew how the spells on the engine worked, and what it did. And she knew, most of all, how to kill it.

A hand spun her around. She found herself eye-to-eye with the captain.

"What are you doing?" he roared to her face. "Keep away from that!"

Alucia tore herself from his grasp and walked calmly to the engine. She almost reached it when an ear-shattering blast blew her off her feet. She landed hard on her stomach.

She crawled unsteadily to her knees, trying to understand. Her limbs were intact. Her core was… missing some of itself. She looked back toward the captain. He held a metal tube in his hands. It was smoking.

His were eyes wide and white. "What *are* you?"

Alucia heaved herself up by her arms and placed her hands onto the engine. It was too simple. In a single moment, she gathered all the power that was burning within it into the great, empty expanses of her soul. She had been crafted to hold an eternity of knowledge. There was more than enough room for the engine's spark of magic.

Lights whisked out with a snap.

"Dear lord," the captain whispered. "What have you done?"

Alucia smiled. "I have given us time."

"But the ship…" Something horrible must have dawned, because his voice cracked like glass breaking. "We don't even have more than a week of water…"

That was a story Alucia knew well. Water, and men's need for it, was dull. But she was so relieved, so delighted, so giddy, she did not even tell him that.

"A week is more than enough," she said. "Now you can tell me your stories."

***Elizabeth Spencer** is a fantasy and steampunk author. When she learned the theme of this anthology was parch, she thought of the longing we all get when we're alone and desperately need people—the desert just helped drive it home. She has previously published in Spellbound Magazine. You can find more of her work at elizabeth-spencer.net.*

The Way We Were

By Fruma Klass

We are pleased to end with a story from a master. Fruma Klass' gentle, penetrating, perfectly-pitched tale of werewolves and other werecritters will leave you pondering the big cultural issues of our time. Is anyone truly so different that we should not embrace them?

So we'll go no more a-roving
So late into the night
Though the heart be still as loving
And the moon be still as bright

Yet we'll go no more a-roving
By the light of the moon.
—George Noel Gordon, Lord Byron

Reynaud tilts in the green plastic Adirondack-type rocking chair, just tilts, not rocking. Another sunset throws its thin golden light on his white hair, once dark brown along with his mustache, and Reynaud smiles his thin, bitter smile. Everyone on the porch looks at him.

"Remember?" he says. "Remember how it used to be?"

There is a sigh, a collective sigh across the whitewashed wooden porch. There are just six of us this evening, and we all have things to remember.

"Full moon tonight," says Lupe. "Oh, I do meess it. The weend een my furr and the demp earth and the wanderful smells, even when there wasn't any weend." She shivers deliciously. Lupe is Spanish or, more likely, just Mexican. Or maybe South American—it's not hard to picture her with a Carmen Miranda bunch of bananas and grapes on her head. It just occurred to me maybe old Carmen was one of us? She certainly had a wolfish or maybe vulpine smile. Whatever, Lupe seldom misses a chance for a little drama.

Well, why not? There's little enough drama in any of our lives these days, and it seems a shame to fill up the emptiness with the usual squabbles about who took too much time in the bathroom or who got the biggest lumps of meat in their stew. Or who is thirstiest.

"It wasn't so wonderful all the time for all of us," says little Minna from deep inside her rocker. Her feet are high off the floor.

"Not always, no," Reynaud says. "But at least the hunts were in the daytimes. The hunters in their red jackets, the hounds, the horses—I never got hunted."

"I got hunted all the time," says little Minna.

The porch door swings open with its usual hinge-squeak complaint. Miss Bundy is there, in her starched white uniform and old-fashioned white nurse's cap. "Time for your physical therapy, Mr. Fox," she says. "Time for a little walk. You'll walk for me, won't you, Mr. Fox?"

"For you, certainly," Reynaud says. He winks at her, then struggles to his feet with the aid of his aluminum walker.

His foot, actually. He only has one foot, the right. He says he gnawed off the left when he was caught in a trap one full-moon night, too close to a chicken coop he'd visited before. Be a fine mess if the farmer found a naked man with his foot in the trap when daylight came, now wouldn't it? Those weren't sophisticated city folk; they'd get them a silver bullet and take care of him right away. Those rubes, those rustics, they knew a lot about our kind. And they weren't very politically correct, especially for forty years ago.

Reynaud hops and swings, hops and swings to the door. Miss Bundy holds it open for him, and he hops and swings inside. The door closes, squeaking. I wonder what happened when they found a man's foot in the trap. Well, maybe they never did—maybe something else came along and ate it. A coyote, for instance. Or a bobcat. Could even have been an owl. Something of the night.

"An owl," says little Minna. She's so sharp she can sometimes tell what you're thinking. She shudders for a moment. "Owls can be terrifying."

Lupe laughs. "If I caught wan I'd eat it."

"Did you ever?" I ask.

"I don' theenk I ever got that hongry," Lupe says. "There was always sometheeng better to chase. Sometheeng better would come along, sometheeng that wasn't fast enough. And besides, I always knew I'd be human again een the morning, so I could wait if I had to."

"That's what kept me going," says Minna.

Leonid growls softly from his chair. The chairs are all in a line, so I can't see him unless I lean all the way forward. Or stand up, which I can't do without help. Despite his name, he's a wolf—most of us are. Were. But not me.

"The thrill of the hunt," Leonid says. "Will you catch it? Will it get away? And if you catch it and you—*bite* into it…"

"Oooh," says Minna.

"Aaah," says Lupe.

"…and the sweet hot blood flows out…"

"Oooh," says Minna.

"Aaah," says Lupe.

"…how soon will the pack get there and what will they do? Will they fight you? Will the leader try to fight you, to take the kill away? Or will they just accept you as the new leader, the supplier of fresh flesh?"

Little Minna is trembling now, and her short gray hair trembles along with the rest of her.

"And the mating, the coupling—migod, I could never find a human woman with that kind of passion."

"Think of how different it had to be for women," I say.

Leonid looks interested—now he's leaning forward so I don't have to. "How so?"

"The fear, the terror of getting pregnant."

"You could always take the pill," Leonid says.

"It didn't always work. And suppose you were pregnant at the full moon? Would the baby change too? Or suppose the worst, you went into labor while you were changed."

"The baby would tear you apart," says Minna quietly.

"And then the baby would be eaten by the rest of the pack."

“I can see that,” Leonid says. His tongue slips pinkly out of the corner of his mouth, just a little, and tastes something invisible.

“Well, I nevair got pregnant,” says Lupe. “Or at least, I deedn’t stay pregnant very long.” Firecracker Lupe (she keeps her hair dyed red even though everyone knows she does it, because the roots are so obviously gray) tosses her head back and laughs. “I don’ even know whethair they weere babies or cobs or what.”

None of us women had had children, which means that none of us had anyone to care for us now that we couldn’t care for ourselves. But the men didn’t have anyone either. Reynaud once said that since the lycanthropy gene or genes had not been identified, he wasn’t going to inflict wereness on a helpless infant.

“Weretas,” Zev had said. He had been a professor of Animal Behavior at Penn State, and he liked to show his education sometimes. “*In vino veritas*, spelled with *v*’s, not *w*’s, but pronounced with a *w*, as in *wolves*. Which is why I was a teetotaler. But seriously, though, folks, did you know that the *were* part of the word means ‘man,’ not ‘used to be,’ like the past tense of ‘was’?”

“Then why aren’t mermaids and mermen called werefeesh?” Lupe asked rather petulantly.

“Because they don’t change,” Zev said patiently.

“As we do,” Leonid said. “Or used to.”

And don’t anymore. Not because we stopped being thirsty—we are parched, all of us—but because we got old and our own juices stopped flowing. We didn’t simply decide to stop; you can’t do that. And not just because a newly accepting population, applying its wonderful new devotion to diversity and tolerance for the differently abled, probably wouldn’t do what its grandfathers would have done: kill us on sight. No, if the world at large knew about us we’d be a media sensation. If they weren’t afraid of us (and they might still be) they would probably applaud whenever they saw us. The shopping malls would be filled with imitation wolf suits. Wannabe teenage werewolves would be on every street corner. The air would reverberate with wannabe werewolf songs. I can just imagine them: “*Awoo!*

Awoo! Gonna be a wolf and my sweetie too!" Much, much better to stay in hiding as we have always done.

Besides, we're not all wolves.

So here we are at Mrs. Mengel's Bide-A-Wee Home for the Aged and Wery, which most people think is a spelling mistake for *weary*, those who can spell, anyway. And they don't bother us much when, on special occasions, the staff takes us out in the pink-and-green vans for a Trip. We go with our canes and our walkers and our wheelchairs to firemen's carnivals, to local arts and crafts shows, to movies. Just not to the zoo. And there isn't any Mrs. Mengel.

And just as I'm thinking "the zoo," the strong odor of shit wafts down the porch and hits my nostrils. It's Leonid. His ostomy bag is overflowing again.

"Leoneed, you are steenking op the place," Lupe says.

Leonid shrugs. "I'm really very sorry, everybody," he says. "But I will have to wait until one of the nurses comes out again."

It doesn't matter. As humans, we find the smells of shit and urine disgusting, but our basic animal nature isn't so fastidious. Bodily wastes give us information, sometimes very important, but always interesting. However, Leonid hasn't gone anywhere or encountered anything interesting in a long time. His effluvium says only that he ate a dreary meal some hours ago. As did we all.

"So why can't we have decent food?" says Minna. As usual, she has leaped a synapse ahead. "Why do they give us that sticky macaroni, that awful meatloaf with canned tomato sauce that tastes like sugar, that gluey yellow custard with the lumps?"

"Because they don't like us," Zev says simply. "They're mostly not afraid of us anymore, they just don't like us."

"Or maybe the government has cut the Medicare subsidy again," I say. They're always trying to balance the budget by cutting back on Medicare, so maybe Mrs. Mengel's is getting cut again, and we will go on even worse—cheaper—food, thinner toilet paper. Wouldn't surprise any of us. Mrs. Mengel's is owned and operated by the government, after all.

The sky is beginning to get dark, and a couple of the nurses and aides come out to the porch to bring us in. Some of us can walk with our canes and walkers; some of us can't. Leonid is trundled off to the bathroom to get cleaned up and changed. Minna's legs have cramped from sitting, and she needs help to stand. I haven't left my wheelchair, so I can propel myself indoors without much help. It's dinnertime. Hooray.

So after dinner we are sitting around in the dayroom with the TV, arguing as usual about which DVD to watch. Reynaud is back, looking bitter and tired, but saying nothing. He has been getting very frail lately, *very* dry.

Some of us want a twentieth-century Hollywood musical, some a western, and some an old game show, *So You Want to Be a Millionaire*. The one thing we agree we don't want is *A Werewolf in London*.

We haven't yet decided when Minna starts twisting around in her chair to look at the door behind us. A beat later, the rest of us pick up on first, the distinct menstrual odor, and then the little rustle of a starched uniform.

"Gentlemen and ladies," Miss Crichton begins. Leonid calls her "Miss Crotch"—not where she can hear it—because of her odor. Poor thing, she can't help it. "Gentlemen and ladies, we have a new resident tonight."

The new resident is an enormous African American woman, big shoulders, big hips and belly, big swollen legs, and white hair neatly knotted into a single braid down her back. She can walk, evidently, with two metal canes that have arm rests attached, and she starts toward us. Minna goes rigid.

"Her name is Catherine," says Miss Crichton. "Catherine Katz."

"Kitty," says the woman. "Or Cat." She smiles warmly. Her teeth are perfect, the product of a really good prosthodontist sometime in the past. Her hands don't shake much.

"*Katz?*" says Zev.

"Listen, if Whoopi could be Goldberg, I can be Katz," she says. "And the *Kitty* just followed naturally. Anyway, the Katz was legit. I was married to Marvin Katz before I started singing."

"Was he in show business?" Zev asks.

"He was an accountant. A CPA."

"Would you tell us your birth name?" Leonid asks. He is not usually so interested in someone other than himself.

"I was born in a Jewish neighborhood in Brooklyn, and my mother named me after the holiday I was born on. My birth name was Roshana, Roshana Johnson."

Zev whoops with laughter. When he catches his breath he says, "You're lucky you weren't born on Yom Kippur."

Kitty laughs too. "I have to sit down now," she says. "I can't stand much. May I join you?"

Minna is the only one who doesn't warmly welcome her.

Lupe has been studying Kitty and now snaps her fingers, then winces from the pang of her arthritis. She should know by now that finger-snapping hurts.

"I know who you are!" she says. "You are the great seenger Keetty Katz!"

"Ye-es," says Kitty, encouragingly. "And you are—?"

"Lupe," says Lupe. "I went to see you wance, een Washington. You sang at the Leencoln Memorial. You were wanderful."

"Thank you, Loopy," Kitty says quietly. "I remember that one. It was a commemoration concert. A lot of singers were there—folk, jazz, opera, a grand mélange."

"But I never knew you were wan of us!"

"The last closet," Kitty says. "The last minority."

"As far as we know," says Leonid.

"And some people still hate us," says Zev.

"Well, we can't really blame them," Kitty says. "We did kill people, after all. And drank their blood. At least that's what they believe." She sighs. "Of course I never killed anybody, not any humans."

"Neither did I," Reynaud says.

I didn't either, but I keep silent. So do the wolves. And little Minna is trying not to breathe.

Kitty looks directly at her. "Oh," she says. "Oh, I'm so sorry."

"It's all right," Minna mouths.

"No, it's not. But I don't think I ever chased you. I was in New York most of my life, except when the band was on the road."

"I never left San Jose," says Minna, picking up a strand of strength.

"So you see, I never hunted you," Kitty says. "New York had plenty of mice."

"Ohh," Minna says. She is utterly still.

Reminding Minna that she was a mouse is a major *faux pas*. I mean, we just don't do it. It isn't something to brag about, after all, and as our strengths and abilities slip away, all we have left are our carefully crafted, carefully edited memories. Sometimes even they slip away too. But Minna has probably never felt so secure in her life, as she has here. Except in her childhood, maybe. She won't feel secure any more.

"Look, I was a cat," Kitty says. "What should I chase, cows?"

Lupe changes the subject. "You ever have eeny babies, Keetty?"

Kitty shakes her head. "Got pregnant once while I was a cat. I was some gorgeous pussy, let me tell you."

Leonid giggles.

"But it didn't take. My human body resorbed—or absorbed—the embryos." She turns to Reynaud. Looking at the stump of his foot, she says gently, "Diabetes?" And Reynaud nods *yes*. So much for the story of how he gnawed off his foot in a trap!

"Me too," Kitty says. "*And* high blood pressure. *And* neuropathy. *And* failing kidneys. *And* I'm going blind."

Zev can't resist. "Other than that, Mrs. Lincoln, how did you like the play?"

Kitty rises to the test. "Oy vey, don't ask."

"You really did grow up in a Jewish neighborhood," Zev says.

"One of my favorite quotes," Kitty says: "'No matter how bad things are, you've got to keep living, even if it kills you.' Sholem Aleichem."

"You know, even if you weren't a great singer, a great entertainer, which you are," Zev says, "I'm pleased and proud to have you here."

"I was afraid you'd vote me off the island," Kitty says. Everyone laughs Except Minna. Minna keeps quiet. I do too.

So the days, the weeks, pass. Nothing new happens in Mrs. Mengel's Bide-A-Wee Home for the Aged and Wery. In the outside world, there are always small wars somewhere, a bombing or two, car crashes, weddings, graduations, political campaigns. It pretty much passes us by, like the children on their way to and from the school, across the street.

And we are sitting in the Activities room, thinking about activities, when Ferdie, a kitchen assistant, comes in. Ferdie is African American, brown rather than black like Kitty, thin and somehow delicate-looking, but powerfully muscled nevertheless. He is holding the local *Neighborhood News* and is evidently distressed. "Came out today! Look at this!" he says. "Look at this!"

It's the lead story on the front page.

Werewolves in Town!

It has been reported to this reporter that a gaggle, or should I say a pack, of were-wolves has been living in our town. And they are right across the street from Obama Middle School on S. Main St. Every day our children have to pass them on their way to school and on their way home!

So far the werewolves haven't bothered any of the children, because like vampires, werewolves have no power in the daytime. But what will happen when the school play and other events that take place at night take place? Parents are rightfully worried!

Mrs. Arline Binder, president of the PTA, put it very well. "I'm rightfully worried," she told this reporter. "What's going to happen on the night of the school play and other night-time events?"

The werewolves are not breaking any municipal law by congregating there, and the mayor asks people not to go out there tonight to express their feelings about a pack of werewolves in our midst—and our children's midst.

Zev reads it aloud, then returns the paper to Ferdie. "Fools," he says wearily. "Stupid, stupid fools. It never stops."

"Wereweres," says Leonid. "Well, we have to expect it."

"We always have to expect it," Zev says. "Even when we think we're safe."

"We'll have to hide," says Minna. "We have to find good hiding places."

"How can I hide?" Leonid says. "They'll smell me."

Lupe doesn't say anything, but she looks at Leonid, hard, and he bows his head. Pack discipline—he'll have to hide alone.

And I have a strong desire to get under my wheelchair—as if that would help, or even be possible.

Only Kitty isn't thinking about hiding. "Now dude," she says to Ferdie, "we're gonna need a little help." As she speaks to him, her "ghetto dialect" gets broader, so that she's actually saying, "We goan need a lil hep."

"Oh yes, Miz Kitty," he says. "Whatchoo wan' me t'do?"

She's thinking. "Some flags," she says. "About ten American flags on sticks, small enough to hold in your hand, but big enough to hang on the door."

"Gotcha," he says.

"And a tom-tom. Can you beat a tom-tom?"

"Dunno. I ain't never tried."

"Well, you gonna do it. Get one. A small one."

"Yes, Miz Kitty," he says, rather dubiously.

"Do it right away. I don't know how much time we got."

"Yes, Miz Kitty," he says, and rushes out.

"I'm a grandmother figure," she says. "Nothing in the world beats a black grandmother for inspiring love and absolute obedience. These boys was *raised* by their grandmother. I could ask him to do *anything,* and he'd do it for me."

Minna is staring at her with a kind of adoration. "I think it's who you *are*, Kitty, not what you look like." she says.

"Well, we gonna find out," Kitty says. She stretches, as much as a five-hundred-pound woman in a chair can stretch. "Now we better get something to eat, before dark. Them townspeople gonna come after dark. They think we bite their babies."

She thinks for a while. "Okay, now for backup." Then she says to Minna, "Go into the Walking-Around room and find me the biggest, *the* biggest man in the place. Bring him to me."

"Right," says Minna, and she climbs down from her chair and scurries away.

Kitty goes on. "We get something to eat and we get right out on that porch. We hope that Ferdie gets back here in time.

"How much time we got before dark? What's it now, four o'clock? We got maybe an hour and a half, two hours. We got to be all set up on the porch before they get here."

"Maybe nothing will happen," Leonid says, but he knows something will. We can all smell it. Fear is a very pungent smell, even to dried-up, dried-out husks like us.

Minna comes back with a Physical Therapy attendant named William. He's big enough to lift any of us, except Kitty. Nobody's big enough to lift Kitty alone.

"William," Kitty says, "are you with us? If you're not, if you want to cut out and go home, that's okay. Just tell me."

William is six foot seven or eight, blond and crew-cut. He draws himself up to his full height and says, "Ma'am, I never cut and run from nothin', not in my whole life. And I heard you sing once, when I was a kid. I am gonna stand behind you, whatever."

Kitty laughs. "And that is exactly what I am gonna ask you to do: stand behind me. Keep me from falling down. I'm gonna be standing on that porch and it is very important, very important, that I not fall down. At a given point, my legs won't hold me and my body will try to sit down. Or lie down. Or fall down. It will be your job to keep me upright."

"I'll do that," William says. "I'll do that little thing."

"You stand behind me and when I start to give way, you grab my ass and push, use your whole body, keep me standing up. Can you do that?"

"You better believe it," says William.

Kitty bats her eyes at him. "And oh, would you rather I call you Bill?" She's flirting with him!

William grins. "You call me anything you want, just so's you call me."

"An' you call me Kitty, you hear?" She goes on with the planning: "Any of the staff leaving?"

"Two nurses," William says. "One registered, one an aide. And somebody from Housekeeping."

"That's all?" Zev says. "I would have expected almost all of them to leave. Who would have figured on so many righteous gentiles?"

So everybody eats, cheese sandwiches, and everybody who needs help is taken to the bathroom, and we line up on the porch. Just like any other night, except it's *not* like any other night. "Bite their babies," Leonid mutters. "Who wants to bite babies? It isn't worth it." And after a while we hear them coming.

"Have they got their pitchforks?" says Zev.

Nobody answers. But in fact, they've got better than pitchforks. A good many of the men carry rifles, and some have brought their children to watch what Daddy does. It's like photos I've seen of lynchings a hundred, hundred-fifty years ago.

Ferdie's back, gasping for breath as he bounds up the porch stairs two at a time. He hands out the flags—we clutch them like drowning people clutching straws—and drapes one over the door. Minna tosses him a roll of Scotch tape to stick it in place. Then he squats on the floor behind Kitty and to her left, tom-tom in front of him, leaving room for William.

"When they get here, I'll get up," Kitty says. "You all keep quiet until I signal you."

"What are we gonna do?" Lupe asks. She is flushed with anticipation.

"*Nothing*," says Kitty. "Not until I signal you."

"And then what we gonna do?"

Kitty takes a deep breath. "You're gonna sing."

"I can't sing." A couple of people say it at once.

"I can only sort of squeak," says Minna. "But if Kitty says sing, I'll sing."

"Just don't howl, y'all hear? Now you, Ferdie, you watch my hand. When my hand flaps down, you start beating the drum. Very slow—watch my hand. When I need you to speed up, I'll show you like this." She flaps her hand faster.

The townspeople are getting close, and they look determined. Kitty heaves a sigh. "Showtime," she says, and stands up. Both hands on the railing in front of her, she leans toward the crowd across the street.

"Hello, neighbors!" she calls out, looking delighted to see them. And then she starts to sing the opening song from *Mr. Rogers' Neighborhood* about beautiful days and neighborliness. Who doesn't know that one?

The crowd stares at her. Whatever they expected, this wasn't it.

"But it's too hard for me to put my sneakers on these days," Kitty says, "so I'll sing something else. You want to sing along with me, you just go right ahead.

"When I was a kid I used to go to something called hootenannies. That's where I first heard the great American songs from people like..."

Ferdie's tapping the tom-tom, following her elbow rather than her hand, because she can't let go of the railing.

"...Woody Guthrie. Songs everybody knows..."

And she swings into:

> *This land is your land, this land is my land,*
> *from Callyfornya to the New York eye-land,*
> *this land is your land, this land is my land,*
> *this land was made for you and me...*

At her signal, we all join in, and Minna's "squeak" turns out to be a very pretty, though very soft, soprano. Here and there in the crowd some of the townspeople start singing along.

"Because this is our land, you know," Kitty says in her deep, rich contralto. "Our ancestors way back when came here for the same reasons yours did, to work and build a better life. Well, to tell the truth, my ancestors didn't come here on their own. They were dragged here kicking and screaming, but today we're proud to be Americans. All of us, Americans together."

Many of the people in the street are nodding. They're an ethnic mix, white, black, Hispanic, a few Asians. And a few gay couples. That's important.

"And we *are* Americans," Kitty continues. "We've fought in every war, we've been wounded, we've *died* for this country. This man"—she gestures at Reynaud—"lost a leg for America, and he's proud of it. You should be proud of him too, and grateful."

Unexpectedly, she swings into Gilbert and Sullivan, a little changed:

For he might have been a Rooshian,
A Frenchman, Turk or Prooshian,
Or an Austriyli-an
But in spite of all temptations
To belong to other nations,
He is an American,
He i-i-i-is an American.

She points to Lupe. "This woman was a Navy nurse. She spent years in service, and believe me, you don't want to know what-all she's been through. To serve America, to protect her, to protect you and your family. And now that they're old and feeble, are they any more likely to hurt those they served than they were then?"

A quick, joyous change. "Hey, who's having a birthday today? *Some*body is."

After a while, an embarrassed-sounding voice calls out, "I am."

"What's your name, fella?"

"Jack," the man says. He's one of those with a rifle.

"Happy birthday, Jack," Kitty says. She motions to us and we start singing together:

Happy birthday to you
Happy birthday to you
Happy birthday, dear Ja-ack
Happy birthday to you!

Many people in the crowd are singing too, but not yet all of them. Kitty shifts gears, back to patriotism. "People have milestones in their lives," she says. "Our country has milestones too, and we don't want ever to forget them. Here's one for America." And she begins:

God bless America
Land that I love
Stand beside her
And guide her
Through the night
With a light
From above...

She's channeling Kate Smith, I think, but it isn't just Kate Smith. The America is Kate Smith's, yes, but the God is Mahalia Jackson's. And there's Ferdie, tapping the tom-tom as if we had rehearsed. At a signal from Kitty, we raise our little flags and wave them slowly. Kitty sings the song all the way through, twice, and Kitty's voice rises, deepens, carries the crowd up with her.

They're all singing by the time Kitty ends with, "My home sweet home." One girl, about eleven, breaks away from her family and comes to the bottom of the porch steps. "I wanna sing with you!" she says breathlessly. She looks back at her parents. "I wanna sing with them!"

"Sure, honey, you can sing with us," Kitty says. "You can sing with us any time you want. If it's okay with your parents." She looks at them, across the street. She's taking a chance, but this whole thing has been one big chance.

The mother nods.

The girl runs up onto the porch, parks herself next to Reynaud, and stares with fascination and sympathy at his truncated leg.

Kitty is starting to slide downward, and William closes in behind her. He is supporting her with his all his strength, and she maintains her footing.

"I don't know how many of you remember a speech made way back in 1974 by a wonderful black woman," Kitty says. "A U.S. senator." Her voice is clear and resonant without any microphones. They can hear her all the way in the rear of the crowd.

"Her name was Barbara Jordan," Kitty says, "and she was talking about the beginning of the Preamble to the Constitution of the United States: *We, the people.* 'It's a very eloquent beginning,' she said. 'But when that document was completed on the seventeenth of September in 1787, I was not included in that *We, the people.* I felt somehow for many years that George Washington and Alexander Hamilton just left me out by mistake.'" Kitty pauses. "I know that feeling," she says. "I'm a black woman like her, but when she finally got included in *We, the people*, I didn't. None of us did. Because we're *different.* Some of you were different too, but now you're just all Americans. And now I have to ask you, am I included in that *We, the people?* Are my friends?"

How could anyone step up and say, "But you're werewolves. You'll bite our children"?

Kitty smiles down at the girl. "And you, dear. What's your name?"

"Mallory," the girl says. "And I want to be your neighbor."

Kitty glows. "You are all our neighbors," she says to the crowd. William, behind her, clutching her hips and pushing them forward to keep her standing up, is straining.

"Any time you kids are on your way home from school," Kitty says, "remember you're welcome to drop in and visit. You can sing with us, have a cookie, play a little checkers—you might even let us win once in a while."

Some people laugh out loud, and even a few holding rifles grin.

"If your parents don't mind," Kitty adds, "and they know where you are."

It's wonderful. I have not felt so alive in years. Lupe, promoted to Navy nurse, sits tall and straight as if she really had been a Navy nurse. Reynaud holds his leg out in front of him. It's clear that he's working on a new—and better—reality about how he lost his foot.

Minna whispers to me, "Do you think we'll actually get cookies?"

"One last song," Kitty says, "before we break up. Old people have to go to bed early."

"So do kids!" a child shouts.

Kitty starts, in that big, rich voice that had captivated hundreds, maybe thousands of audiences. In this moment, she is all the great black woman singers rolled into one—Bessie Smith, Marian Anderson, Leontyne Price, Billie Holiday, even Ella Fitzgerald—as if they all dropped in to lend her strength. I don't know how she manages to meld them all into a single glorious voice, especially with the song she selects, but she does.

My country, 'tis of thee
Sweet land of liberty,
Of thee I sing...

And they sing along with her, with us, and we wave our flags and Ferdie slaps the tom-tom as they drift home.

Land of the Pilgrims' pride
Land where my fathers died
From every mountainside
Let freedom ring!

Our lives have changed, a lot. The food is still awful, but at least there's enough of it, and there really are cookies and even milk for the children who drop in. Sometimes they need help with their homework and sometimes they just want to be companionable. I think the school is supplying the milk. Even without drinking it ourselves, we don't feel quite so parched these days.

Although Reynaud had seemed the most frail, it appears to be Leonid who's drifting into weakness and witlessness, what the staff calls "senile dementia." And Kitty, who played her last performance so magnificently, is just another whining, complaining old woman most of the time, except that she has some sort of special friendship with Zev.

"It's over," she says. "The fat woman sang."

But she won't let go of her insistence that I tell her what werebeast I was. And I can't tell her. I can't even tell Minna. How would they treat me if they found out that I was just a stinking dried-up old werecockroach?

Afterward

And there you have it, our seventh annual "open" Triangulation anthology. Please remember that publications such as ours survive on word of mouth. If you enjoy the series, if you find a particular story that resonates, please share that information with your friends, drop a review on Amazon.com and goodreads. Tweet it, blog it, tumble it, reddit, nominate us for awards. It's not enough to read the anthology because you want to be published here someday ("here" won't exist if we don't get more folks reading). There are stories in this collection that deserve wide attention. We work with authors to make that so. It's no accident that Triangulation: Morning After received NINE recommendations from Tangent Online's annual recommended reading list. That's nearly half the collection singled out for praise.

David Hartwell describes the small press as the "minor leagues" where authors hone their craft in preparation for major publications. Collections such as ours are useful in working the kinks out of a swing, learning to drive with power, or field your position. We are a stepping stone because we work with authors to improve their craft.

Do you value that? It's really up to you whether we continue. If sales of *Parch* and donations accumulate enough money to pay authors, we'll publish again next year. If not, we won't.

The good news is that we do have resources remaining to publish the long-delayed *Steel Cities* anthology later this year. Stay tuned for that.

And if you really want to help, please consider donating to our **2015 Fund Drive**, which will be posted at **www.parsecink.com** shortly. A donor has pledged to match the first $500 we collect. It's a chance to double the clout of your own donation. Please take advantage.

Steve Ramey, New Castle PA, 2014

www.parsecink.com
www.facebook.com/ParsecInk

Triangulation: Morning After

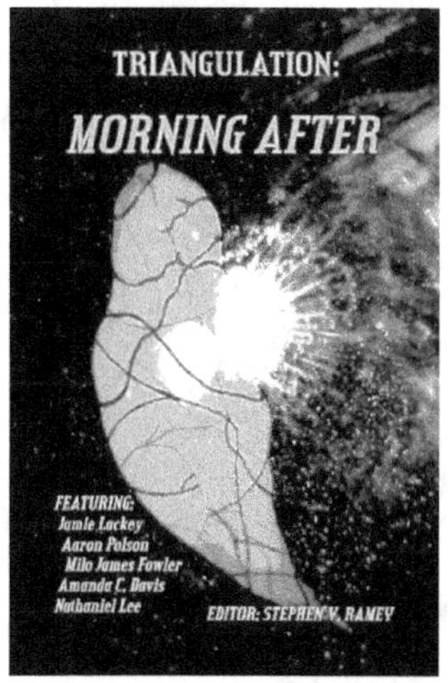

24 stories from established veterans to first time published authors. This year's contributors include: Kylie A. Bullivant, Nathaniel M. Lee, Milo James Fowler, Bruce Memblatt, Marshall Payne, Camille Alexa, Aaron Polson, Jamie Lackey, Hollis M. McMasters, Amanda Davis, Erich W. Mulhall, Kenneth Chiacchia, Christine Lucas, Susan H. Gray, Madhvi Ramani, Kalisa A. Lessnau, Susan Urbanek Linville, Tami M. Harris, Alex Gorman, Henry Tjernlund, Michael D. Shreve, Gordon A. Graves, Gary W. Cuba, DeAnna J. Knippling

What will your Morning After bring?

Metamorphosis? A daunting moonwalk? Un-death? An end to eternal night? A squirrel in your shower, Jesus in the lobby, a meeting with Mr. Higgs? Green grass, child of prophecy, Cthulu in your backyard, a menagerie of beasts, a sacred drum? It's all here, and more, in this thoughtful, touching, entertaining collection.

NINE in Tangent Online Recommended Reading List 2012

"All Unlooked For" by Nathaniel Lee (Triangulation: Morning After) F***
"That Goldurned Hole" by Gary Cuba, (Triangulation: Morning After) SF**
"Lilith" by Madhvi Ramini, (Triangulation: Morning After) F**
"What Now, Callisthenes" by Christine Lucas (Triangulation: Morning After) F**
"After the Pipers" by Camille Alexa (Triangulation: Morning After) SF*
"Nocte Finem" by Henry Tjernlund (Triangulation: Morning After) F*
"Nyabinghi's Sacred Drum" by Susan Urbanek Linville (Triangulation: Morning After) F*
"Course Correction" by Kenneth B. Chiacchia (Triangulation: Morning After) SF*
"Protection from the Darkness" by Jamie Lackey (Triangulation: Morning After, 2012) F

Available at Amazon.com, Barnes and Noble, and other fine booksellers.

Triangulation: Last Contact

28 stories from established veterans to first time published authors. This year's contributors include: Gwendolyn Clare, Aaron Polson, Shanna Germain, Amanda C. Davis, Eric Schaller, Nathaniel Lee, John Walters, Desmond Warzel, Jaime Lee Moyer, Deborah Walker, J. M. Odell, Sandra M. Odell, Sarah Frost, Cynthia Ward, T. F. Davenport, Madhvi Ramani, H. L. Fullerton, James Beamon, Dawn Lloyd, Christopher Nadeau, H. M. Tanzen, M. Yang, David Sklar, Stephen Gaskell, Charles Patrick Brownson, Eric Zivovic, Amy Treadwell and Hugo and Nebula award winner **Robert J. Sawyer**.

What Will Be Your Last Contact?

A leprous knight? A helpful robot? A caged phoenix? A generous dragon? Within these pages, you'll discover the dust of Martian civilization, Rumpelstiltskin's true face, Roanoke's fate, and much more. From marmots with computer problems to boll weevils on steroids, from mermaids to cyborgs. You want an endless party? No problem. How about a perfect dewdrop or a Saudi superhero? Has your love interest eaten a pharaoh? You'll find it all in this impressive collection of short fiction.

SEVEN in Tangent Online Recommended Reading List 2011

"God in the Machine" by Charles Patrick Brownson SF ***
"In Ruins" by J M Odell (*Triangulation: Last Contact*, 7/11) F***
"Eziekiel" by Desmond Warzel, (*Triangulation: Last Contact*, 7/11) SF**
"Norms" by Cynthia Ward (*Triangulation: Last Contact*, 7/11) SF**
"The Charnel Pit" by Stephen Gaskell (*Triangulation: Last Contact*, 7/11) F**
"The Good Daughter" by Aaron Polson (*Triangulation: Last Contact*, 7/11) SF*
"Ocean Daughters" by Jaime Lee Moyer (*Triangulation: Last Contact*, 7/11) F*

Available at Amazon.com, Barnes and Noble, and other fine booksellers.

Triangulation: End of the Rainbow

19 short stories by David Sklar, Mark Onspaugh, Kylie Bullivant, Brenta Blevins, Amanda C. Davis, Peter S. Beagle, M.Z. Hoosen, Amy Treadwell, Tinatsu Wallace, Cate Gardner, Matthew Johnson, Ron Sering, Eugie Foster, D.K. Thompson, Aaron Polson, Jaime Lee Moyer, Marshall Payne, Erin Hoffman, and Cat Rambo.

What will you find at the rainbow's end?

A Hawaiian princess? A French widow in a magical house? An imaginary friend? Transcendence? Hell? Within these pages, you'll find all this, and more.

TWO in *Tangent Online* Recommended Reading List 2010

"Commander Perry's Mystic Wonders Show" by Jamie Lee Moyer (Triangulation: End of the Rainbow F*

"A Womb of My Own" by Tinatsu Wallace (Triangulation: End of the Rainbow SF**

"PARSEC Ink's annual sci-fi/fantasy anthology uses what initially appears to be a cheerful theme to unite a number of varied and unlikely short stories. I'm at a loss as to how I haven't heard about the yearly series until now... Literary magazines have never made very much money. I understand it's a hard business with few rewards. But I just can't stand to think anyone who's participated in the creation of this book would believe they've failed when they've obviously succeeded so very well." —Eat Your Books

"After reading such an impressive collection of stories, Editor Bill Moran's afterword comes off as particularly bittersweet. Each Triangulation is clearly a labor of love, and heavy labor at that. One can only appreciate the care expressed not only for the anthology, but quality fiction as a whole, when too much of today's audience seems to have forgotten how to appreciate it." —Patrick Rutigliano, Shroud Magazine

Triangulation: End of Time

What happens when you ask writers to come up with stories based on the theme "End of Time?" Well, you get stories that are apocalyptic, stories that are whimsical, and stories that are whimsically apocalyptic. You get continents running amok, zombie stampedes, and cryogenic mishaps. You get hurricanes, killer comets, and all-consuming deserts. You get frivolous time travel, alien invasions, and trickster gods. In short, you get this anthology.

Featuring Ian Creasey, Dario Ciriello, Tim Pratt, Jeff Parish, Idan Cohen, Jetse de Vries, Michael Stone, Kurt Kirchmeier, D.K. Latta, Ashley Arnold, Matthew Johnson, Rebecca W. Day, Trent Walters, Scott Almes, Jessica E. Kaiser, Terry Hayman, Katherine Shaw, Jared Axelrod, Sue Burke, and Geoffrey Thorne.

Triangulation: Taking Flight

Rockets funded by bake sales! Zeppelins filled with Nazis! Were-crows! Magic carpets trying to take flight! Ghostly jetliners trying to land! The 2008 edition of PARSEC Ink's Triangulation anthology takes to the sky with twenty short stories from established pros and new writers alike. Read about balloon animals in existential crisis, postmen uninhibited by space or time, and the joy of seeing stars with a little help from a friend.

Featuring Reesa Brown, Amy Treadwell, Elizabeth Barrette, Katy Darby, Rachel Swirsky, Paul Stefko, Gail Sosinsky Wickman, Shanna Germain, Matthew Johnson, Jacob Edwards, Gerri Leen, David Seigler, Ian Creasey, Marc Vun Kannon, Matt Betts, Stephen V. Ramey, Lavie Tidhar, Shweta Narayan, and Eugie Foster.

Triangulation: Dark Glass

What if the only way to save your soul was to betray your God? How can a race of xenophobes exact vengeance a thousand years after their own extinction? If ugliness had a voice, what would it say? Triangulation: Dark Glass includes sixteen short stories, a tour of the afterlife, a dancing dead man, Darwinian ghost orgies, soul-shattering street hockey, a genie's wish, evil that lurks under the sidewalk, and Miltons. Lots and lots of Miltons.

Featuring Mark Onspaugh, D.K. Thompson, Kenneth B. Chiacchia, Rachel Swirsky, Aaron Polson, Lon Prater, D.J. Cockburn, Gerri Leen, Jason K. Chapman, Kelly A. Harmon, Kathryn Board, Amy Treadwell, David Seigler, Kurt Kirchmeier, Loretta Sylvestre, and Craig Wolf.

www.ingramcontent.com/pod-product-compliance
Lightning Source LLC
LaVergne TN
LVHW050631100826
845148LV00011B/1826